Tomahawk'd

By Diane S Bauden

TOMAHAWK'D
© 2008 BY DIANE S. BAUDEN

ISBN 10: 1-933113-90-1
ISBN 13: 978-1-933113-90-6

First Printing: 2008

This trade paperback is published by
Intaglio Publications
Walker, LA USA
www.intagliopub.com

CREDITS
Editor: Ruth Stanley
Cover design by Sheri
(Graphicartist2020@hotmail.com)

DEDICATION

For Amy
Perhaps this is the me you see ☺

ACKNOWLEDGMENTS

A very big thank you to Intaglio for giving my girls a good home. I think we're going to be very happy here. To Day and Ruth, thanks for cleaning up my messes. To Ann, thanks for being my sounding board. To all of my loyal readers who waited patiently for my muse to return, you guys rock!

To my mom and dad, if it weren't for our summer vacations together, I'd never have this place in my heart. I'm so grateful and miss you terribly. — #7.

Chapter One

1985 – The Northwoods Island City

The crunch of tires on the pebbled drive alerted the cabin's young occupant of an arrival. Her two excited eyes, one blue and one greenish-brown, appeared in the cabin window and watched a small blue Toyota pull into a parking space. The cabin's young occupant, a skinny, dark-haired girl, observed as a family emerged slowly from the vehicle.

Turning from the window, Jackson Thomas shouted to her aunt, "Jackie, they're here! They're here!"

Arriving quickly in response to the call, Jackie Thomas patted her niece's shoulders as they both looked out the window at her latest guests.

Hands resting on the windowsill, Jackson looked on restlessly as a man and woman stepped out of the car and walked back to the now open trunk. She was about to look away when the rear door opened and revealed a girl, about her age, who got out of the backseat. Sighing unknowingly, she watched closely as the girl's parents handed her a teddy bear suitcase and a pillow.

Chuckling at her niece's emotion Jackie said, "Looks like you'll have someone to play with after all, Jack."

The girl nodded enthusiastically, looking up and smiling at the older version of herself, then turning her attention back to her potential playmate.

1

The little blond girl was smiling at something her father said then started to look around the property. Apparently mystified by all the tall trees, young Erin Hawkins' feet moved slowly in a circle as her head tilted back as far as humanly possible.

"Erin, honey, be careful. Watch where you're going," her mother warned.

"Yeah, Peanut, you look like a Pez dispenser gone wrong."

"Daddy!" Erin cried, swinging her head around toward her father then following that with a long, drawn out "Mom" as she looked to her mother for assistance.

Stifling a laugh, Katie Hawkin's swatted her husband's arm. "Joe, be nice. We just got here. God knows after six hours in the car, the last thing she needs is more ribbing from you."

"Sorry, Peanut." He tweaked her nose. Looking to his wife, he continued, "Let's check in and find our cabin."

The family grabbed the lightest of their bags and headed toward the main cabin. Only their footsteps were heard as they followed the wooded path that led to the main office of The Northwoods Island City, not far from the parking lot. As they walked, the Hawkins took in the scenery reverently, not wanting to disturb any denizen of the gorgeous landscape and the nature surrounding them. Everywhere wildflowers were in full bloom of purples and oranges. The fragrance in the air was nearly overwhelming. The sound of waves hitting the shore could be heard from not too far off as they reached the cabin that housed the office. Not seeing a doorbell, Joe knocked on the screen door.

Jackie opened the door with a welcoming smile on her face. "Mr. and Mrs. Hawkins?"

Joe and Katie smiled back at their hostess and nodded. "I'm Katie Hawkins and this is my husband, Joe, and our..." She looked back to find that Erin was transfixed by a bird's nest in one of the trees close to the cabin. Smiling, she finished, "That's Erin, our daughter."

"Nice to meet you all. Welcome to the Island City." Jackie extended her hand. "I'm Jacqueline Thomas, but please call me Jackie. I hope you enjoy your stay. You picked a great time to visit."

Joe's eyes sparkled with curiosity. "Why's that?"

"It's still too early to be considered fall, but late enough that the seasonal tourists aren't hanging around. There are a number of water shows still happening this week, but you'll have a lot of the lake to yourselves most of the time," she explained as Jackson inched her way to the door.

Joe looked down to see mismatched eyes looking back at him. He was amused at her cutoff jean shorts and dirty knees. "And who are you, little lady?"

Standing up proudly, Jackson stretched out her hand in imitation of her aunt. "I'm Jackson Thomas, sir. It's nice to meet you."

Her broad smile made Joe grin. When she repeated her actions with Katie, the woman's expression mirrored her husband's.

"Well, Jackson, it's nice to meet you, as well." Joe looked to Jackie. "Your daughter?"

"No, thank God!" she said in a kidding tone. Receiving an outraged look, she patted the girl's head. "Jack's my niece."

Two sets of eyebrows raised in tandem. Katie said, "You look so much alike, I would've thought you were her mother."

The look of sadness that flitted over Jackie's face was quickly masked. "I get that a lot. Her mom and I were identical twins." She watched as Jackson eyed the smaller girl in pink overall shorts who was still enthralled with the bird's nest.

Catching the past tense, Katie said softly, "Oh, I'm sorry."

"Thank you."

Silence settled in like an unwanted guest and both parties felt the comfort level drop. Before it became protracted, Jackie smiled and said, "Why don't I show you to your cabin?"

Grateful for the change of subject, the pair grabbed their bags and moved out of the way as Jackie and Jackson stepped outside.

"You'll be in cabin six. It's one of the only cabins with air conditioning. With the scorchers we've been having, I'm sure it'll be welcome. Even this close to the lake, the days have been awful and the nights not much better."

Joe nodded his appreciation. Turning to his daughter, he called out, "Hey, Erin, come on! We're gonna find our cabin."

Jackson turned to him with a charming smile. "I'll show her where it is, sir."

Grinning at her niece, Jackie said, "She's a regular eleven-year-old Welcome Wagon. She knows this place better than I do."

"Okay, Erin, listen to Jackson, okay?" Joe picked up her discarded suitcase and pillow. Chuckling to themselves, Erin's parents turned to follow as Jackie led the way to their home for the next month.

From her spot near the nest Erin shouted out, "Okay, Dad." She turned to look at Jackson for the first time and immediately noticed her eyes. "Wow!"

Looking around her for the cause of Erin's excitement but finding none, Jackson was confused. "What? What is it?"

Erin hesitantly reached for the taller girl's hands. "Your eyes! How did you do that?" Her voice was awe-filled as she stared shamelessly into the objects of her attention.

Jackson grinned and rolled her eyes. "Oh, them. Well," she began the story her aunt had told her, "I was lying down one day on the grass over there..." She stopped and pointed in the direction of the land in front of the lake. "I fell asleep on my side. While I was sleeping, this eye turned into the color of the sky above it," she said, pointing to her right eye, "and this one turned into the color of the ground below it." Jackson laughed at the girl's amazed expression.

A look of wonder on her face, Erin studied the different colored orbs. "Like magic!"

"Yeah, something like that." She grinned at the younger girl. "So, you're Erin?"

Erin realized she hadn't introduced herself to her new friend. Letting go of Jackson's hands, she said, "Yep, my name is Erin. What's yours again?"

"Jackson."

"What kinda name is that for a girl?"

Jack sighed and put her arm around Erin's shoulders. "Let's go find your cabin. I'll tell you some other time."

"Come on, tell me," Erin prodded. "I can keep a secret if it's a special story." She looked up at Jackson with sincerity.

Charmed beyond measure, Jackson found herself agreeing. "Okay, I'll tell you. I was named after my grandpa, Jackson Thomas. My Aunt Jackie was supposed to be a boy and wasn't, so they named her Jacqueline. Then, my mom thought I was gonna be a boy so she named me after him, too. When I popped out, it was pretty obvious I was a girl, but they didn't change my name. I'm kinda like Jackson the second! It's a family thing." She shrugged her shoulders. "I know it's not a regular girl's name, but it's still pretty neat." She smiled.

"That is *really* neat!"

"So can we go and find your cabin now, shrimp?" she teased.

"Hey!" Erin ducked away from the taller girl's arm. "I'm not a shrimp! You're just a…a big tree!" A pout forming on her lips, Erin crossed her arms over her chest.

Hiding her amusement at the flummoxed young girl, Jack replied, "Okay, so what should I call you then, if you aren't a shrimp?"

Confused, Erin replied, "Call me Erin."

Stroking her chin in thought, Jackson shook her head. "You don't look like an Erin. What's your last name?"

"Haw…Hawkins," she stuttered, not understanding how she didn't look like an Erin. She *was* Erin.

"How about I call you Hawk? We've got some hawks that fly around here sometimes. I think they're really cool."

Standing taller, Erin decided that she liked the name her new friend was suggesting. "I like Hawk." She bit her lip in thought. "Can I call you Jackie?"

"Um, no, that's my aunt's name. How about—"

"How about Jack?"

"Sure, shri…Hawk," she quickly amended, seeing the hurt look on Erin's face. Having corrected the moniker, she was graced with a beautiful smile from her younger companion. Seeing Erin's face light up convinced Jackson she would spend the whole month making Erin smile as much as possible. "Let's go find your folks." She put her arm around Erin's shoulders, only to have Erin grab her hand, pull it to her side and entwine their fingers as they skipped along toward cabin six.

"So, where do you live?" Jack asked

"I live at two-five-two Forest Way, Paldeer, Illinois." Erin smiled with pride at being able to recite her address so quickly.

"I live here," Jack offered, gesturing around with her free hand.

"Wow, do you still have to go to school?" Erin looked at the lake. "This is vacation!"

Snorting a laugh, Jackson replied, "Of course, Hawk. I gotta learn stuff other than how to catch fish."

Eyes wide, the blond-haired girl asked, "Can you teach me how to catch fish?"

"Nothin' to it."

Jackson's confidence reassured Erin that she would indeed, much to her excitement, learn how to fish this summer. Erin squeezed Jackson's hand, anticipating a fun-filled vacation with her new friend.

Joe and Katie Hawkins enjoyed the brief jaunt to cabin six with their hostess. They briefly walked along the waterfront before they reached their destination, with Jackie showing them the boathouse, fish house, and sandpit area.

Jackie Thomas was very proud of her resort and liked to talk about it to her guests. "My grandfather opened this resort over fifty years ago. I can't remember a time when I didn't love this place."

Katie smiled. "It's quite obvious that you love it very much. It's so serene and just…breathtaking. I can't believe it took us this long to come out here."

"If the fishing is half as good as I've heard, I'll never want go back to work," Joe said with a nod.

Jackie looked sympathetically at Katie. "I'll just apologize now then if he quits his job."

"Oh, dear Lord, he can't quit. He's the boss!" Katie exclaimed, laughing.

Chuckling along with Katie, Jackie said, "Well then, I hope you've got good people taking care of things for you while you're here."

"Actually, we close the shop for a month at this time of year. It gives everyone a nice breather. Our clients know our schedule, so any pressing needs are taken care of before we shut down. It really works for everyone." Joe closed his eyes and inhaled the fresh air. His lungs seemed grateful of the reprieve from the pollution of the city. "Everyone comes back refreshed and ready to work hard. Our employee turnover is low because of it as well. It's a system my dad instituted when he opened our doors. It just works."

Jackie regarded her new guests thoughtfully. Of average height, Joe had wonderfully warm green eyes, brown hair that had begun to thin, and a tiny bulge in his midsection. He seemed to be very kind. His wife had strawberry-blond hair and pale blue eyes, and was very thin. She also seemed kind. They were charming and witty, and Jackie thought they were very likeable indeed. "If everyone had policies like that, I think people would be much happier—kinda like that kindergarten nap rule, or three months off for summer vacation. Some things should just carry over into adulthood."

"Right on," Katie chimed, laughing along with her husband.

Jackie led them to the front door and ushered them inside. The couple smiled at the classic charm of the cottage. Avocado green and mustard yellow tones were prevalent in the small square kitchen. An old yellow range and oven stood proudly in the center of the small counter with a window above it. The green refrigerator and the kitchen sink completed the L-shaped counter. Carpet of a red, black, and green plaid was laid throughout the cabin. Curtains that matched the green in the carpet hung on rods over every window. Joe sat on the gold couch and bounced a little to check for bad springs, while Katie was shown the bathroom, which had a shower, toilet, and sink with exposed pipes that led into the wall and floor.

Finally, Jackie led Katie into the main bedroom. Katie threw her bag onto the bed and called for Joe to bring in the others. "This is charming, Jackie. We're going to have a great time here."

Joe joined the two women and handed all but Erin's things

to his wife. "Yeah, this place is great. I think the TV even has cable."

Katie rolled her eyes at Jackie, who smiled knowingly at her. Turning to Joe, she confirmed, "Yes, it's a recent upgrade here at the resort. There aren't that many channels available through our provider yet, but they've said they'll have over a hundred channels by the end of the year. Next year, we should have a huge lineup for you." She grinned at his wide-eyed expression.

"I'm sure I can guess your schedule this month, honey. Fishing all day, and crashing on the couch in front of the television set at night." She smirked as she put her hands on her tiny waist. "Am I close?"

Joe blushed at his wife's ability to read him. "Uh… uh…"

Katie cut off his stammering. "Mmhmm…that's what I thought."

Laughing at their comfortable banter, Jackie said, "Well, folks, if you need anything, pick up the phone and push pound, or just come on over to the office. Please enjoy your stay." As Jackie turned to leave, she remembered a detail she'd not mentioned, "Oh, and Joe? Your boat is docked in slip number four. It's the white and blue nineteen-foot Harbercraft. It's got a one hundred and fifty horsepower engine, so you'll be able to fish *and* ski if you want. Lake Tomahawk offers many activities for you to enjoy. Oh, and we've also got a giant tube if you want to take Erin out on it. Jack can't get enough of tubing." Hearing her niece's footfalls, she opened the door to greet the girls. "Speak of the devil."

Jackson grinned at her aunt. "Never speak of the devil, Jackie. He'll getcha when you're not lookin'."

Disregarding her niece's jibe, she noted the girls' entwined fingers. Raising an eyebrow, she asked, "So what do you think so far, Erin? Has Jack scared you with her mice and bear stories?"

Erin's eyes shot wide open. "Wha…what mice and bear stories?" She looked to Jackson then her parents for confirmation of this awful possibility. Inside the cabin, her parents shook their heads, looking as if they were going to say something.

"Jackie!" the dark-haired girl chided. She looked at Erin. "She's pulling your leg. We don't have those things here." She narrowed her eyes at her aunt. "*Do* we, Aunt Jackie?"

Sensing what Jackson was trying to tell her, she relented. "Ah, no, Erin, we don't have them here. Jack sometimes makes up those stories to entertain herself. I just wanted to make sure she wasn't telling tales."

Jackson squeezed Erin's shoulder reassuringly. "If I'm not scared of this place, living here all the time, you can be here for a month and not be scared, right, Hawk?"

Erin looked at Jackson and puffed out her chest with a confidence she didn't feel. "Nnn...no, I won't be scared." Her saucer-sized eyes gave as much credibility to her statement as if she had said water wasn't wet.

"Come on, Hawk, let's go find your room." Jackson brushed past her aunt and smiled at Erin's parents. She waited as Erin collected her bag and pillow from her father.

Erin's parents looked at each other, both mouthing, "*Hawk?*"

"First bedroom on the right, Peanut," Joe said. Jackie waved as she left to tend to some things at the main office.

Jackson led Erin to her new bedroom and Erin looked around in awe at the large double bed in the center of the room, large dresser, and closet. "My room at home isn't this big!" she gushed.

Giggling at her companion, Jackson added, "Usually more than one person stays in here, but not now. It's all yours."

Erin threw her pillow on the bed, sat down and opened up the teddy bear suitcase to begin sorting through her belongings.

"So what grade are you in, Hawk?" Jackson asked, sitting on the bed next to Erin.

"I'm going into fourth. What about you?"

"Sixth. Next year is junior high. It's gonna be rad."

Erin smiled as she pulled some things out of her suitcase. First thing Jackson noticed was a large pad of paper and colored pencils. "So what's that stuff for?"

"I like to doodle. My mom thought I'd have lots to draw up here," Erin explained. Recalling the bird's nest she'd seen earlier, she knew her mom was right.

Jackson considered Erin's statement and knew the perfect

place for the girl to sit and draw. "Do you want me to show you around, or do your folks need you?"

"Let me go ask. I wanna see more birds!" Erin grabbed her art supplies and looked expectantly at Jackson.

Jackson grinned at her enthusiasm. "Well, let's go!"

The girls went into the living room to ask permission to go exploring.

"Mom, can I go on an adventure with Jack?"

"I'm just going to show her around, ma'am," Jackson added.

Katie and Joe looked at each other and smiled.

"All right, Erin, but I'd like to take a walk on the trails. I thought you might find that fun, too."

Erin's head bobbed up and down. "I'd love to do that, Mom. Can we do it after?"

Katie saw such pleading and excitement in her eyes that she didn't have the heart to quash her little girl's plans. "We'll do the trails tomorrow. I bet you could find lots of things to draw."

"That trail will take you into town, as well. My Aunt Jackie likes doing that instead of driving." Jackson smiled.

Katie was taken by the gregarious young girl. "Thank you, Jackson, I may do that." She turned back to Erin. "Okay, sweetie, listen to Jackson and be back by dinner."

"Thanks, Mom!" Erin threw her arms around her mother.

"You're welcome." She chuckled. "I love you, honey. Have fun."

"We will. I love you, back." Erin took Jackson's hand and pulled her toward the door.

"Hey, what about me? Don't I get a hug?" Joe asked.

"Oh, sorry." Erin released Jackson's hand and dashed into her father's outstretched arms.

"I love you, Peanut. Be careful out there, okay?"

"Love you, too, Daddy." Erin grabbed Jackson's hand again as they ran out the door and toward the waterfront.

"Come on, let's go sit on the pier. You can see the fish swimming really close." Jackson tugged on Erin's overall strap and the two raced to sit on the chairs that were on the large T-shaped dock. Erin held her pad of paper tightly and kept her pencils in her pocket.

Boats went by on Lake Tomahawk and Jackson waved to a few people she knew. A big smile graced her face when one of the boats swept toward the shore then swung back out into the lake, creating a large wake of water. The waves that came at them were high and when they met the pier, the spray that flew into the air hit the screeching girls as they tried to run away. Droplets of water raced down their faces as they ran off of the dock. Erin pushed her hair out of her eyes as she tried to get the water off of her face. The bubbling laughter filled Jackson with warmth as she listened. A large toothy smile lit Erin's face because she knew that Jackson would make a great playmate while she was there.

"I got soaked!" Erin cried out. "I'm glad my paper didn't get too wet." She started to leaf through her pages to make sure.

"Oh, I'm sorry, Hawk. I forgot about that." She watched Erin turn each page and noted the drawings. "Hey, those are cool. Is that your tree house?" she asked, pointing to one of the drawings.

"Yeah, my dad built it for me. He said I would be closer to God in it."

Jackson rolled her eyes and folded her arms across her chest. "You can't get closer to God unless you die."

Looking into the mismatched eyes of her new friend, Erin nodded fiercely. "Yes, you can! The higher you are, the closer you are to heaven and the closer you are to God. My daddy said so!"

Erin was close to tears so Jackson sighed and backed off some. "Hawk, you can believe what you want, okay, but remember what I said about being named after my grandpa?"

Erin nodded.

"Well, my mom wanted to name me Jackson. That's when she thought I'd be a boy, But God took her before she saw me, so then no one changed the name, out of respect. Almost my whole life, I've climbed every hill, every tree, every *thing* to get closer to her and it doesn't work." She took a deep breath and looked up into the sky, willing her own tears away. "I stopped trying," she finished quietly.

Erin looked at her for a long time letting what she'd said sink in. *Her mommy died.*

A small hand on her forearm drew her attention. Erin whispered, "I'm sorry God took your mom, Jack."

A small smile found its way to Jackson's mouth. "Thanks, Hawk. Jackie says Mom watches over me now." Erin kept her hand on Jackson's arm as they shared a warm connection. After brief contemplation, Jackson asked, "Wanna see my favorite place in this whole resort?"

Intrigued, Erin replied, "Sure!"

"Come on, then, let's go."

Jackson led Erin around the resort, showing off the grounds and everything around them. She was very proud to be a part of the Island City.

"See all these big pine trees? Jackie said they were that tall when she was a little girl. They must be hundreds of years old." They walked past the fish house. "Don't go in there, Hawk. It really stinks.""Why?" Erin was paying close attention.

"That's where the fishermen gut and clean all the fish they catch so they can eat them."

"Ew. I won't be going in there."

Jackson laughed and led her around the wooden cabins. "We have a couple cabins with fireplaces so people can stay here in the winter. It gets pretty cold up here, though." She pointed to a family playing volleyball. "We've got two volleyball nets, shuffleboard, and sandpits for horseshoes, too. And, if people want to have cookouts, we have barbeques and benches for everyone." Jackson's proud smile was radiant. "You can even roast marshmallows over there if there's a fire in the fire pit."

"Cool!" Erin had much to look at as her tour guide pointed out new things.

Passing by the main cabin, the girls saw Jackie in the front talking with another guest. Jackie waved to them and smiled.

"Hi, girls!"

"Hi!" they called back, waving.

Past all of the cabins, they headed into thicker woods and onto a path leading toward the boathouse. The green needles of the spruce stood out starkly against the white papery bark of the birch trees. Lifting her sneaker-covered feet so the branches on the ground wouldn't trip her, Erin tried to keep pace with Jackson.

The boathouse came into view. It was a large wooden building painted brown with a flat rooftop. It resembled a large four-door garage with a wooden pier on either side of it. The side door was open and Erin saw a glimpse of the four boats that were housed inside. When the two walked in, the first thing Erin smelled was fish.

"Ew, it's stinky in here."

Smiling, Jackson replied, "Yeah, but you get used to it and it's not nearly as bad as the fish house. Besides, we're not gonna stay in here. Come on," she instructed, "but watch your step. I don't wanna have to tell your folks I let you fall in the lake." They exchanged smiles as they walked across the wood plank floor.

Jackson carefully led them to a ladder that went up to the loft of the boathouse. Erin looked at her sketchbook and realized she'd have to leave it below to hold on to the rungs of the ladder. Looking down at Erin from the third rung, Jackson saw her friend putting her pad down.

"You can bring it; just stuff it in your shorts."

Erin looked doubtful, but undid one of her straps to accommodate the pad and, to her disbelief, the sketchbook fit inside her overall shorts. "Thanks!" She secured her strap, grabbed on to the ladder, and followed Jackson up to the loft.

Looking around, Erin said, "Wow, it's cool up here." She looked out the window at the clear blue sky above the calm lake. She saw birds flying around a bridge off in the distance. She started to unclasp her strap to remove her sketchpad only to have warm fingers touch her arm.

"Not yet. We're still going up."

Eyebrows raised, Erin questioned, "We're going higher?" She swallowed. "How high up are we going?"

"Look over here." Jackson walked over to the wall, traversed a small set of steps, and opened a large, latched shutter. Once the shutter was open, another ladder appeared on the outside of the boathouse. "Now watch me."

Jackson reached up to grab hold of a wooden grip above the

opening, stepped forward, and swung around onto the ladder.

Erin's eyes went wide for the umpteenth time since she'd met Jackson and watched as her friend maneuvered her body onto the ladder. "Jack, I can't do that! I'm gonna fall."

Jackson swung easily back into the loft. "No, you're not, Hawk. It's easy. I'll let you go first and I'll be right behind you to make sure you don't fall. Okay?"

When Erin looked uncertain, Jackson asked, "Do you trust me?"

Looking into the clashing eyes, Erin saw confidence and certainty. She nodded her blond head.

"Okay, first thing you're gonna do is come up these steps and hold on to the grip up here." Erin followed her instruction and held on to the grip with one hand. Jackson held her other hand and guided it to the outer rail of the ladder. Once Erin realized she had a firm grip, she lifted her front leg to wrap around the wood of the ladder and landed a foot solidly on the bottom rung. Smiling confidently, she swung her small frame around to fully face the ladder. She brought her other foot and hand to the ladder and held on tightly.

Jackson kept some of her personal belongings inside the loft for these types of adventures. She pulled out a blanket and draped it over her shoulder, picked up a wooden box, which went inside her pocket, then grabbed onto the grip.

Looking up, Erin saw the boathouse roof. She looked down into Jackson's patient eyes. "Are we going onto the roof?" she asked before climbing.

"Yep. Just keep going until you reach the top. It's flat so you won't fall off."

"'Kay."

The two climbed up the ladder and reached the top without trouble. The roof was blacktopped and smooth. The heat coming off the roof was visible in waves in the air. Jackson stretched out the blanket so they could sit without being burned.

"I did it, Jack! I climbed all the way." Erin was extremely proud of herself.

"Yep. I knew you could. Good job." Taking Erin's shoulders,

Jackson turned the girl to face the water. "Look at that. Isn't Lake Tomahawk beautiful?"

Looking around her, Erin saw they had a canopy of trees around them. The sun was beating off the water creating a portrait in her mind that she'd only seen in books and movies. The air left her lungs in a long, slow, reverent breath. "Wow, this...this is so pretty up here." She looked at her companion. "I can see why this is your favorite place."

Unclasping her strap, she removed her sketchpad and put it on the outspread blanket. She reached into her pocket and pulled out the box of colored pencils, then sat down and continued to look around, in awe of the magical place.

Jackson removed the wooden box from her pocket and sat next to her. Placing the box away from Erin, she closed her eyes and took in a long deep breath.

"I always feel so much better when I'm up here. Doesn't matter if I'm happy or sad, I always just feel better." She shrugged and smiled at Erin's grinning, freckled face. "Just don't come up here when it rains. When it's wet, that ladder is slipperier than grease." She blushed at the memory of having to explain why she was "swimming" fully clothed in the lake during a rainstorm to her aunt. "I found that out the hard way."

"Did you fall?"

"Yep. Big ol' splash." She smirked. "I'm lucky I didn't hit anything on the way down."

Giggling, Erin opened up her sketchbook to a blank page. "I wish I coulda seen that. I bet it was funny." Looking at her friend's disgruntled expression, she amended, "Only because you didn't get hurt."

"Right," Jackson said, her tone a bit sarcastic. "Well, don't expect me to save your sorry butt if you fall off now."

Selecting a gray pencil, Erin began to draw the scene in front of her. Jackson watched as her hand moved around the page. Considering Erin was only nine years old, the talent was evident in the girl's strokes. The shape of the bridge was well constructed, followed by the rippling water around it. Birds soon joined the composition. Slowly, shorelines and branches were drawn. As she drew, Erin's eyes scoped all around, trying to see every little thing possible.

Jackson was so intent about watching Erin delve into her work that she almost forgot about her own special gift. Reaching next to her she opened the wooden box to reveal a black recorder. After putting the small pieces together, Jackson inhaled, put the mouthpiece to her lips and gently exhaled.

The music suddenly coming from her right startled Erin. Turning, she saw Jackson playing and smiled broadly at her. Jackson winked and continued to play. The tune was wistful and instantly crept inside Erin. She found herself closing her eyes to listen more intently. Jackson's eyes closed as well as she let the music wash through her.

When the song came to an end, Erin opened her eyes and looked at Jackson. "That was really pretty."

Jackson blushed softly at the welcome praise. "Thanks. I sit up here a lot and just play." She held the recorder out for Erin to see. "This was my mom's. My aunt said she used to sit up here and play all the time. Once I learned how to use it properly, Jackie gave it to me. I play it almost every day."

"You're really good at it. I've never played any instrument."

"Have you ever tried?"

Shaking her head, Erin responded, "Nah. I like to draw." She shrugged. "I like to listen to music, but I don't want to play it."

"Just like I like to look at pictures, I just don't want to draw them."

"Exactly! You're smart, Jack."

"Nah. I'm just good at faking it."

The girls talked, played, and continued to practice their respective talents over the next few days. Erin drew her pictures while Jackson played her recorder and watched the talented hands form their masterpieces.

The two had felt an instant bond between them. Small glances and touches made that bond grow every day they spent together. They weren't sure exactly what the feeling was between them, they just knew they couldn't wait to see the other and feel it again.

Erin's parents were thrilled she found such a good friend in Jackson. With Erin out playing most of the day, they were able to spend many hours reconnecting with each other. Joe took the boat out many times with Katie along for the ride. He tried to teach her how to cast with a fishing rod, only to find himself frequently untying knots in his line. Realizing she wasn't going to win any fishing awards, Katie resigned herself to using the bamboo pole they had purchased for Erin.

No muss, no fuss, Joe thought, relieved he wouldn't have to worry about his gear anymore.

Instead of fishing, today they were going to hook the big inner tube to the boat for Erin and Jackson to ride. They told the girls after breakfast that they were going to get it ready. Erin was very excited. She'd never done anything like that before. Jackson assured her it would be "totally awesome." With Erin believing anything and everything Jackson told her, she knew, without question, it would be.

Chapter Two

1986 – Paldeer, IL – Letter to Erin from Jackson

January 7, 1986

Dear Hawk,

Happy New Year! Can you believe it's 1986? I totally can't! Thanks for your last letter. Sorry it's taken me such a long time to write back. Christmas was very cool, how was yours? I wish it didn't cost so much money to talk on the phone. I'd much rather talk to you than ~~right~~ write these stupid letters. Well, they're not stupid, but you know what I mean. ☺ Aunt Jackie said to tell you hi. I think she really likes you.

Thanks for the birthday card! It made my birthday extra special, Hawk. You even got me Snoopy! That was totally cool.

I can't wait till the end of the summer when we can hang out again. I miss you, buddy. I'm glad your folks are bringing you back up north!

You know, I never taught you how to fish last time. I promise to make it up to you this year, okay? I think it was because we couldn't get you off that tube! Ha, Ha. You really cooked across the water. Probably because you weigh like next to nothing. I'm saying "like" a lot. My friends at school say it like all the time. It's driving my aunt crazy. Sometimes I say it on purpose. ☺ Shh! Don't tell her I said that!

Hey, guess what? We had an end-of-term show. All the band members played something. I played a solo on my recorder in front of the whole school before Christmas break. I was so scared I almost peed my pants! One of my classmates plays the ~~paino~~ piano really well. She was my ~~accompanymint~~ accompanist for the song. Sorry for all the scratches, Hawk. I try to spell words right so you don't think I'm an idiot. After I wrote them, I looked in the dictionary and saw they were wrong. OOOPS! ☺

We got a new girl in class. Her name is Jennifer. I like hanging out with her. She's from California. Her hair is so blond it's like white. She's really cool. I think you'd like her. She likes to play sports and she's tall, too, so I guess we'll get a new girl on the basketball team!

We've got so much snow I can't believe it. The trees are pretty, though. I think you could draw them perfectly. It's weird that you've never seen this place in winter. But it's kinda boring since you can't really go anywhere since it's so cold out.

Anyway, tell me how your art project went in the fair. You sounded really excited about it when you wrote. I hope you won first place! You're really talented, Hawk. Never stop drawing or your biggest fan will be really sad.

I'll write better next time, I promise.

Friends 4 Ever,
Jack

1986 – Island City – Letter to Jackson from Erin

February 9, 1986

Dear Jack,
Thanks for the letter. Do you know I keep all of your letters in a shoebox? My mom says I shouldn't keep so much cludder, but I keep it hidden in my closet so she won't see. Happy New Year to you too. My Christmas was a-okay. I got some cool art supplies. My dad said he found the best ones since I take such good care of them. I got a big art pail to keep the pencils and pastels separate.

I got so much paper too. It's totally awesome. ☺

I'm glad you liked your birthday card. You said Joe Cool was rad, so I sent him. Wow, twelve years old. You're almost a teenager. I'll be eleven in September, that will be rad, too.

I won first place in my art fair, Jack! I used that first picture I drew from the roof. Everyone said I capjured the water perfectly. You were right! I don't think I could stop drawing ever. I love it too much. ☺ *So, don't worry, okay? I have so many pictures from last summer. Remember how mad you got when you saw that I drew you? You shouldn't be mad. It just shows you are special.* ☺ *I don't draw everyone. I bet I can draw you better by the summer.*

You're not an idiot, Jack. You're one of the smartest people I know. You are talented too. You play your recorder so good. I can't believe you had to play in front of everybody! I would have peed for sure. ☺

We have some snow here too. I bet you have more. Yeah, I probably won't see your home in the winter. That kinda makes me sad. But you haven't seen my house either. I can't wait to see you too. I'm glad my dad found your place. We wouldn't be friends if he didn't. Do you think we'll be friends 4 ever? I hope so. I like using the 4 instead of spelling it out. That's really cool. See, you're smart. Ha, Ha!

You can teach me to fish this summer. Maybe my dad will let us go on the boat with him. He said I would have more fun doing the tube anyway. I did like that a lot. You cooked on the water too! I still remember how hard it was to hang on with the turns. I'll be stronger this summer so I don't fall off so much.

Okay, my mom is calling me to eat dinner. Yuck, pot roast and brockly.

Write again soon.

Friends 4 ever,
Hawk
PS. Tell your Aunt Jackie I said hi.
PPS I like her too! ☺
PPSS I won't tell her you say "like" on purpose!

1986 – Island City – Letter to Jackson from Erin

July 24, 1986

Dear Jack,
I'm coming in a week to see you! I am so excited. I like that my dad's shop closes in August. We get a whole month to play. He says he needs the break as much as his workers do. The car ride is going to be so long. That's the only part I don't like. I hate having to wait to stop to pee. When you gotta go, you gotta go! ☺

My mom said I could bring my art supplies again since I drew so many pictures last time. My art teacher said that my strokes are improving and that I have a great style! She said she couldn't wait to see my pictures from this summer when we start school. It was so awesome she said that in front of the whole class on the last day of school.

My summer has been okay, but I'm really ~~exciting~~ *excited to come to Wisconsin again. Paldeer is cool and everything, but I miss my best friend, Jack.* ☐

I told my neighbor Ricky that I was going there for vacation again and he called you a cheesehead. What does that mean? He's just a big jerk anyway, I only play with him because my mom told me to. I don't like him at all. I'm glad we don't go to the same school.

I gotta clean my room to pay for all the stamps I'm using. My mom said you should earn things you want. I guess that makes sense.

Okay, Jack. I'll see you really soon. You don't have to write back if you don't want to.

Friends 4 ever,
Hawk
PS My dad got me a super cool fishing pole!
PPS So you better show me how to fish this year.

1986 – Paldeer, IL – Letter to Erin from Jackson

July 28, 1986

Dear Hawk,
You might not even get this letter before you get here. But if you do, I'm really excited to see you in a couple days.
If you don't get this letter and read it after you get back home. It was totally awesome to see you and I miss you already! SSS (sorry so short) I got a lot to do before you get here!

Friends 4 Ever,
Jack

PS Tell Ricky to come to Wisconsin and say that! I'll squash him.

Chapter Three

2002 – Chicago

Erin Hughes strode back and forth, the telephone glued to her ear, eyes scanning the ceiling, hand pulling her hair as she paced. She couldn't believe what she was hearing. She held the phone away from her head, flipped it off with her middle finger, then squeezed and shook it with both hands. Her face scrunched up while she silently screamed toward the phone. Bringing the receiver back to her ear, the annoying voice continued.

"Jeremy, just stop it! If we have to go over this one more time, I'm going to do something I won't be responsible for," she threatened. "I've been through enough, don't you think?"

The voice on the other end of the line chimed in, "Look, Erin, I want this more than you do. Just settle, damn it."

Grinding her teeth, Erin answered sharply, "Of course you want it more! If you and that…that woman want your freedom, I have a solution. I. Want. My. House. It's just that simple. I picked it out, I paid for most of it and I furnished it. It's not my fault you knocked her up. You should've kept your pecker in your pants!" she screamed.

His silence was his response. After a few moments, he spoke softly. "Er…please. We can't do this anymore. Our marriage wasn't perfect. You know that. We both made mistakes. I just…"

"You just went to another woman instead of coming to me."

Though exasperated with the conversation, she continued, "Had you come to me first and told me you weren't happy, I'd have so much more respect for you right now. But no, you had to cheat first and wait to get caught. If you aren't willing to give me the *one* thing I've asked for, you can have your lawyer contact mine, and *then* you'll have to pay up the ass." Erin took a deep breath. "I don't want you calling me anymore unless you can be reasonable, Jeremy."

Erin's husband seemed to be considering her words, as he took a long time in answering. When she thought he'd hung up, she heard, "Fine. Let's just do this."

"Fine. I'll call my lawyer. I'll have mine contact yours so this can be over." She sighed, running her fingers through her hair, pulling a few strands behind her ear. "I don't want to fight anymore."

"Sweetheart, I don't either."

"Don't call me that! You don't get to be a nice guy anymore. Just promise me that when you get the papers, you'll sign them. Please, Jeremy?" She was almost pleading.

"I promise."

Wanting to add, *just like our vows, you son of a bitch?* but not wanting to continue the conversation, Erin just said, "Thank you, I appreciate it."

"Take care of yourself, Erin."

"I always do." With that, she hung up the phone. Sitting on her couch, Erin put her face in her hands and cried at her situation. She was more upset she didn't even see the affair coming than at the actual dissolution of her marriage.

I know I didn't love him like I should have. I should have been the one to leave. I was comfortable and it made my folks happy to see me with him, especially Mother. This is my own damn fault. The niggling truths were always in the back of her mind.

Jeremy was a nice man, goodlooking, generous, but there had always been something lacking in their relationship. The passion, the flip-flops in her belly, the ache that was supposed to come when she was away from him—she just didn't feel that way. About him.

Now, at twenty-six-years-old, she would be divorced and, once again, single. Rubbing her eyes with her fists, she sighed and looked around her home. "At least I get to keep you."

"Mrrrrow." A soft mew came from the study doorway. Erin's eyes brightened as the small orange tabby walked toward her. She scooped up the cat and held her as she began to purr. "I get to keep you, too, little Grace." The rumbling against her chest brought a watery smile to her face. "You've always been here for me, haven't you?" The cat continued to purr and rub noses with her owner.

Walking out of her study, Erin traversed the hallway, up the stairs and into her studio. There, on the walls, she studied the landscapes and seascapes she had created—some from memory, others from within her mind—absently petting the animal in her arms. They spanned the time from when she was a small girl to her adult self. She was proud of what she'd accomplished in such a short time.

When she was twenty, a friend of hers who knew Kimberly Parks, the owner of an art gallery in town, got her a job there. On a whim, Erin had asked if she could put up some of her own artwork when they were having a slow period. Much to her surprise and delight, her boss agreed, and gave her a small corner of the gallery to display her work. The drawings and paintings sold quickly, with requests for more. One admirer of her work said that Erin "brought a childlike spirit to her outdoor visions that Thomas Kinkade could only dream of doing."

Erin clung to those words like a lifeline. It gave her the inspiration to keep going, since her true muse was no longer in her life.

"Jack."

It was the merest whisper as she looked at the memories that hung on the walls. Because of Jackson, Erin had kept working on her craft until she had found her niche. One aspect of her work was never made public, nor shared with Jeremy or anyone other than her subject. *The Serenity Collection*, as she called it, was her private and most heartfelt work. They were black-and-white pencil or charcoal drawings, but they captured more colorful memories than any of her other works.

Maybe one day she'd offer that grouping of collected works for sale, but for now, she had them in her closet, stored in several boxes, away from eyes that weren't worthy. It had been a few years since she'd even looked at them.

Sometimes curiosity overwhelmed her to the point of picking up the phone. Then words from her memory would come back to haunt her and she'd put the receiver down. *"Please don't call or write to me anymore, Jack. It'll be too hard."*

Jackson had respected her request for almost seven years and hadn't called her. They hadn't corresponded at all, either. Not even a birthday card. The emptiness she felt without Jackson in her life had led her to Jeremy. He had been at one of her shows and couldn't stop gushing about her talent. One meeting turned into several, then six months down the road, with her mother's enthusiastic approval, they were married. At twenty-one, Erin had a husband, a successful career, a beautiful home, and every amenity she could want. The only thing lacking was the joy she used to feel. The smile on her face was for show only; rarely did it reach her eyes. She'd learned to play a part so well that no one ever realized it was just an act.

She slowly slid open the closet door that enclosed her treasures. Putting the little cat down, Erin pushed aside rows of hanging clothes and reached toward the storage cubbyhole that held her boxes. The first one she grabbed contained her most favorite drawings.

As she opened the box, her heart began to hammer in her chest. Wisps of dark-shaded, windblown hair appeared as she slowly pulled out the first drawing. The profile appeared and Erin's eyes filled with new tears as it was removed completely from the box.

"Oh, Jack."

The picture was a profile of Jackson with her eyes closed as she played her recorder. Erin remembered that day so vividly: the blue sky, the calm waters, and the serenity she felt when she was with her best friend. She trailed her fingertip over the image on the canvas, her heart breaking all over again. Putting the drawing down, she slumped against the wall, reached inside her button-down shirt, and rubbed the pigmented skin above her left breast. "I'm so sorry."

Erin stayed in that position for almost an hour. Grace crawled into her lap and contentedly fell asleep. Erin's memories plagued her already tortured soul as she idly stroked the cat's fur. With Jeremy soon to be out of her life, she would have no one. *Well, no one but Kim. ... Uggh, the gallery!*

"Come on, Gracie. I've gotta get this stuff together or Kim will have my hide."

Erin got up and started to collect some of her works for an upcoming show. Since Kim had opened the door to opportunity when she'd needed it, Erin continued to use her gallery as her hub. Kim was very grateful to her young protégé.

In a mutually beneficial relationship, Erin knew that The Parks Gallery had done well with her works; people called from all over asking where they could find more of her paintings. Hence, her upcoming show. Commissions also came all the time and Erin fulfilled what she could. Sometimes the images came clearly and other times she had to turn down requests. If her heart couldn't see it, the creativity just wouldn't come.

2002 – The Island City

Jackson Thomas reviewed her lesson plans for the next week and tucked the paperwork inside her brown leather briefcase. Relaxing in her recliner, she closed her eyes and smiled in the knowledge that summer vacation would begin in a few weeks. She could then use that time to catch up on things at the resort that had been niggling her.

It had been five years since she'd gotten her teaching certification. Once she'd figured out what she wanted to do when she grew up, it had been easy. She taught music to gifted middle school children during the school year and helped her Aunt Jackie run the Island City Resort. There was always something to do there. Cabins needed upgrading, boats needed winterizing, the landscape needed tending, but all in all it was a wonderful place to be. *All too soon it'll just be me.*

Hearing the small bell ring, Jackson blinked her eyes and hurried to her aunt's bedroom to see what she needed. The ailing woman was in bed, covers tucked tightly around her and an oxygen mask over her mouth. Jackson put on her happy face.

"Hey, Jackie. What can I get you?" she asked, running her fingers through the thinning hair of her aunt. "Do you need something to drink?"

With a small nod, Jackie rasped through the mask, "Yes, please. My throat is dry."

Jackson removed the mask, grabbed the glass from the bedside table, and held the straw to parched lips to allow her aunt a few good gulps of water before putting the mask back in place. It broke Jackson's heart to see her aunt hooked up to so many devices. Machines directed medicine into the frail body through intravenous tubes. Jackie's hands were bruised from the needles being inserted and removed.

"Thank you," Jackie whispered.

As Jackson sat on the bed, there was a light knock on the door. Jackie's night nurse, Cindy, had arrived for her shift.

"How's my girl doing today?" she asked brightly, bringing a smile to the faces of both women.

Jackie gave Cindy an "okay" sign with her bruised hand. A string of harsh coughs erupted from her body. Jackson jumped off the bed so Cindy could raise it to try and ease her patient's coughing. After a few unbearable moments, the coughing subsided and Jackie was breathing more comfortably.

Cindy and Jackson exchanged a worried look, then returned their gazes to the woman in bed. Jackson gently held Jackie's hand and started humming to her. The familiar tunes were a comfort to both women. Songs Jackie had taught her niece were ones she and her sister had known when they were kids. Jackson's fingers idly combed through the hair on her aunt's head until she drifted off to sleep. Feeling the grip on her hand relax, Jackson knew she'd finally fallen into a deep sleep.

Caring for the woman who'd raised her had been an easy decision for Jackson. She wanted Jackie at home instead of in a hospital, knowing quite well her aunt would not want to make her final departure from this world from any other place. The Island City had been her home almost her entire life. When her parents left the resort to her in their will, Jackie had been more than willing to keep the place going. Jackie had raised her to love and respect nature, and in doing so, she'd learned to love the resort just as much. No one but her would be running the Island City until she found someone to run it with her. Or perhaps, like Willy Wonka, she could find a child, so she too could raise them to respect and love this place as much as she did. *Unfortunately, I don't think osmosis can produce a child for my future. And I certainly don't wanna start casing my own school.*

With Jackie asleep, Cindy ushered Jackson out of the bedroom and closed the door. A worry line etched her face. "The pneumonia has gotten worse really quickly, Jack. I want to be honest with you and not sugarcoat it."

Jackson nodded. Knowing where Cindy was headed, she braced herself. "How much time do we have?"

"Unless a miracle happens, I don't think she has more than a couple of weeks." She hesitated. "If that."

The news, as dire as it was, wasn't surprising to Jackson. Until six months ago, she'd thought her aunt was the picture of health. Then she'd seen Jackie's physical condition plummet after the chemotherapy treatments. The colorectal cancer she was fighting wasn't even going to be the disease that killed her. As a side effect of her treatments, Jackie's immune system had shut down and she developed pneumonia. Now she was as weak as a newborn kitten and Jackson was unable to fix her. Both Cindy and Janet, the day nurse, loved Jackie from day one. They would have done anything for her, but all they could do was pray that the medicines would cure the pneumonia so the rest of her body would have the chance to rebuild its strength.

"So what do we do next?" Jackson asked.

"Just keep her as comfortable as possible. Janet and I will do our part, as will her doctor. It's up to her and God now."

Jackson didn't want to debate with Cindy about God. She hadn't known Him to play fair with the people in her life, but didn't want to upset anyone else. "I'm heading outside for a bit to make sure our guests have everything they need. When she wakes up, let me know, okay?"

"Okay, Jack." Cindy put a hand on her shoulder. "You're doing the best you can for her. Never doubt that."

"Thanks, Cindy."

Jackson left the main cabin with one destination in mind. She climbed the ladder leading to the roof of the boathouse. When she reached the top, she let the tears come. She couldn't begin to count the number of times she had cried up there. Anytime she was riddled with sadness, she would go up there and unleash it into the wind. She sat with her denim-clad legs hanging over the side. Far below, she could see schools of fish swimming in the water. Closing her eyes, the tears came in earnest.

"I think this is it. I don't think she can beat this anymore." Her tears fell into the water below. "I hate doing this alone!" she cried.

Jackson had had a few girlfriends through the years, but none held her heart the way Erin had. She had even considered settling on one girl, Marcie, but knew it wouldn't be fair to herself, or to Marcie. It was the closest Jackson had come to wanting more than just a physical relationship with someone. But when her eyes opened in the mornings and met the brown eyes of her lover, her heart just couldn't do it. She bade Marcie farewell and had been alone since. That was over a year ago. Once Jackie became ill, she had no time to give to a girlfriend anyway.

She lay back on her side and rested her head in her hand. Unconsciously, her free hand found its way under her V-neck sweater to caress the pigmented skin above her right breast. "Hawk, I miss you so much." The thought of Erin brought on a new wave of tears from the broken heart that had never healed. Jackson knew things would be better if Erin were with her.

She remained on the roof of the boathouse for more than an hour. The sun began to set on the water and it always took her breath away to watch. When the last of the color dipped into the horizon, she made her way down the ladder to check on her guests. After making sure everyone had enough linens and shooing the kids out of the fish house, she went back to the main cabin.

Cindy was sitting in a rocking chair in the family room. She smiled when she heard Jackson return. "Hey, did you have a nice walk?"

"As good as can be expected." They shared a sad smile. "Did she wake up?"

Nodding, Cindy said, "Only for a few minutes then she fell back asleep. She should wake up soon, though."

Jackson nodded at the update and sat on the couch. Releasing a long breath, she raked her fingers through her hair. She leaned back on the couch and closed her eyes.

"Jack?"

Opening them slowly, Jackson looked at Cindy. "Hmm?"

"Who's Erin?" Watching the color drain from Jackson's face startled her into a near panic. "Jack! Are you okay? You look like you've seen a ghost."

Mustering some saliva into her dry mouth, she swallowed before speaking. "How do you know about Erin?" Barely managing to get the words out, Jackson's eyes closed again, this time in pain.

"Jackie mentioned her when she woke up. Something about needing you to call her," she explained, not understanding what was going on.

Jackson opened her eyes and shot up off the couch. "I can't!" Her eyes were wide, like a scared child's. "Why would Jackie need me to call her?" She began to pace like a caged animal.

Cindy watched in surprise as the normally stoic woman came apart at the seams.

"She told me not to call her, Jackie knows that!" She crumbled onto the couch and put her head in her hands, grasping her hair tightly. "I can't." The words were strangled.

The tiny ring of a bell caused both women to hurry to Jackie's room.

Jackson gave her aunt some water and put the glass on the side table. Jackie, seeing her niece's red eyes, knew she'd been crying and reached up to touch her hand. The younger woman looked down at beseeching eyes and knelt on the floor.

"What is it, Jackie? Are you in pain?"

Swallowing excess saliva in her mouth, Jackie looked to Cindy. "Could you leave us for a little?" She breathed a few times. "I want to talk to Jack."

Understanding their need for privacy, Cindy nodded and closed the door as she left.

"Jackson...what's on your mind?" She paused. "And don't tell me nothing or I'll get out of this bed and knock some sense into you."

Chuckling at her aunt's "threat", Jackson knew they needed to talk about the Erin situation. "You know I can't call Erin, Jackie. Why did you tell Cindy to tell me that?"

Rolling her eyes at the stubbornness of her niece, Jackie said, "I...I'd like to see her."

Jackson wasn't sure what to say to that. "Jackie...I...I don't know if I can after all this time. It's been seven years..."

"Seven years you'll never get back."

Understanding reached the mismatched eyes. "I know."

"Honey, I've watched you live your life since Erin left." She paused to catch her breath. "I've seen you go through the motions, but not once have I seen the happiness in your eyes that I used to. I know what her mother did to you guys was wrong, but sometimes you have to fight to get the girl."

"But..."

"Don't make the same mistake I did."

Jackson didn't understand her aunt at first, but when she reached into the recesses of her memory, a tall woman with red hair came into view. A woman she had known for only a short time. Realization hit her like a ton of bricks. "Sandra?"

Jackie nodded slowly. "Don't let the love of your life walk away from you. If I could go back...and change that error in my judgment...I would do it in a second. I should've fought harder."

"I always wondered why you broke up. You never told me." Jackson's voice was rough with emotion.

"You were... what, sixteen, and going through so much that summer dealing with your own sexuality. I didn't think it was right to dump all of that on you. But it was really hard for me."

"But…you've always seemed so happy." She had never realized her aunt was missing someone so precious to her.

Jackie reached up and cupped her niece's cheek. "My little Jack… Sometimes you're so naïve. I was happy because I had you." A tear ran down her cheek, but Jackson stopped it before it went into her ear. "I couldn't have loved you any more…even if I were your real mother."

Tears flowed freely down the young woman's face at the declaration. "You are my real mother. I love you."

"I love you too, baby."

The two women embraced, as far as the technology around them would allow. Jackson couldn't remember a time she'd felt so great a loss. She'd not known her grandparents enough to mourn them. Jackie told her stories, though, and a slew of photographs were always at the ready, just in case she needed a refresher course.

Jackie was quite worn out from their exchange. "Honey, I need to rest, I'm beat."

"Okay." Jackson got up to leave.

"Promise me that you'll make that call."

Jackson contemplated the ramifications of making such a promise.

"Please? Do it for me."

For seven heartwrenching years, she hadn't done it for herself, but Jackie was asking it of her. And Jackie would get anything and everything she wanted, no matter what. "I promise."

After letting Cindy know Jackie was asleep, Jackson went into her room and closed the door. Flopping wordlessly onto her bed, she reached into the top drawer of her night table and grabbed her address book. She flipped the pages over until she landed on the tab with the letter "H" on it. Just seeing the name brought on a flurry of emotions she had no earthly idea what to do with. She just hoped, for Jackie's sake, Erin's family still lived in the same place.

With shaking hands, she picked up the phone and began to dial. When it started to ring, her heart raced.

"Hello?" the long-remembered voice answered.

"Mrs. Hawkins?"

"Yes?"

She swallowed. "This is Jackson Thomas."

"Jackson, how are you, dear?" *Dear? You condescending little...* "It's been a long, long time."

Not long enough, lady. "Yes, it has." *Here goes...* "Um...I'm calling to see if you can give me Erin's contact information."

"I see."

Jackson didn't miss the change of tone in Erin's mother's voice. "My Aunt Jackie is terminally ill and would really like to see her," she explained, trying to stop the narrow-minded and bigoted woman's thought process.

"Oh." Jackson heard the change in Katie's voice. "I'm so sorry. What's wrong with her?"

"She has cancer. The chemo knocked out her immune system and she developed pneumonia. Unfortunately, the doctor doesn't think she has much time left."

"Oh no, that's terrible. I really liked her."

Jackson snarled, knowing exactly how the woman felt about her aunt Jackie. *God, you haven't changed a bit.*

"I know Joe, God rest his soul, really enjoyed her company when we vacationed up there."

"Oh." Jackson's voice dropped in sympathy. She'd always thought the world of Erin's dad. "I'm sorry. I didn't realize Mr. Hawkins had passed away." She felt a true sadness at his loss. Erin probably could've used an ear or a shoulder to cry on. She knew their relationship had been very important to Erin. *Poor Hawk, I wish she had called me.*

"Yes, back in ninety-seven. He had cancer, too. We didn't know how bad cigarettes were for us when we were younger. They made them sound so good for you. Even though he'd quit a long time before, the damage was still inside him," she explained. "The Lord will take good care of him, though. Don't you worry."

"Well, again, I'm very sorry." She tried not to sound like she wanted off the call as much as she did. "Would you have Erin's phone number or address that I could contact her...for Jackie?" she added for good measure.

"Of course. She and her husband, Jeremy, are still in the city. They're so happy and doing so well that they're trying for a grandbaby for me. Let me get my book. I always get her number confused."

Her husband? ...A grandbaby? Could this get any worse? I'm gonna throw up. Knowing she had missed something Katie had said, Jackson asked, "I'm sorry?"

"I said, do you have a pen ready?"

"Yes, go ahead." She clicked her pen and wrote the information in her address book.

After some uncomfortable small talk, Jackson thanked Katie for her help and wished her well. Hanging up the phone, Jackson's head hit her pillow. She closed her eyes, quickly trying to quash the nausea threatening to overwhelm her.

"She's married and making babies?" she whispered to herself. As much as it didn't surprise her, considering what had happened, it still didn't sit well.

"Aw, crap, if I don't do this now, I'm never gonna do it." She blew out a huge breath, wiped her sweaty palms on her jeans, and picked up the phone. Heart racing, she dialed the Illinois number and waited to hear that sweet voice again.

Chapter Four

1990 – The Northwoods Island City

Erin jumped out of the car as soon as it stopped. The car ride had been unbearable. Six long hours with her mother was enough to give her a headache, especially with her ragging. Katie wanted Erin to spend more time drawing than doing most of the things she usually did with Jackson. She didn't think that Erin playing in boathouses at almost fifteen was very ladylike. Erin frequently didn't agree with her mom's ideas, but this was one thing she wouldn't compromise on. If Jackson wanted her to play in a puddle of slime, she was gonna do it. *We're best friends!*

A tall, lean girl with a big smile lighting her face met the Hawkins' car. Eyes shaded by sunglasses, Jackson waved at Erin's parents as they exited the car. Running toward Jackson, Erin collided with her taller, equally excited best friend. The embrace they shared was warm and regenerating for both girls.

"Hey!" they both said in unison, pulling back to look at one another.

"Look at you! You've gotten so tall!" Erin said, admiring the five-foot, eight-inch frame of her friend. Pinching her side, she added, "You need to eat a Snickers bar or something, though. You're so thin!"

"Yow!" Jackson shrieked at the pinch. "It's not my fault you got hit with the short branch. Besides, I don't see you being too fat either." Jackson looked her up and down, Erin was blossoming into a beautiful young woman and she very much liked what she saw.

Erin blushed hotly at the open appraisal. "I started training for the high school track team, so I've been running this summer. If you'd bothered to read my letters—"

"Hey! I read every one of them." She paused and looked guilty. "I'm just not a good pen pal these days. I'm sorry, Hawk."

Erin locked their hands together, just as she had during their first meeting. She hated knowing her mother would lecture her again about keeping her friendship with Jackson in perspective and acting like a girl supposedly should. Katie had wanted to send Erin to cheerleading camp instead of bringing her to the Island City this summer, only to be told by Erin that it was not an option for them go anywhere else. With every letter that arrived from Jackson, Katie would plead with her daughter to spend more time with her classmates and pay less attention to her tomboyish friend.

Not caring about anything now that they were together, Erin assuaged Jackson's guilt. "I know you're busy helping Jackie; it's all right."

Erin put a hand on her forearm and Jackson nodded, relief flooding her. Unwilling to tell her the truth about the lack of letters, Jackson just grinned.

Joe and Katie Hawkins walked up to the girls. Katie scowled as Erin intertwined their fingers. Putting on a polite face, she gave Jackson a brief embrace, as did Joe.

"It's good to see you again, Jackson," he said. "You're almost all grown up."

"Good to see you too, sir. Yeah, I'm working on it. I'm so happy you all like it here enough to keep coming back."

"Like Erin would let us vacation anywhere else now," Katie said, only half joking.

"No way!" Erin chimed in. "That's *not* an option."

Jackson looked from Erin to her mother, feeling extreme tension.

"Well, it's a good thing your aunt charges us cheap rates or we'd have to go someplace else," Joe kidded.

"Dad! You know you said the fishing here is better than anywhere else." She looked at Jackson's smiling face. "He just likes to push my buttons."

"It appears he's gotten good at it." She smiled at Joe, who laughed. Erin lightly backhanded Jackson in the belly, giving her a fake scowl. "Okay, okay I take it back!"

The girls shared a smile and felt the warmth radiate between them. It felt good to be back together.

Erin's mother watched the exchange with a growing unease, but was pulled away by Joe asking for assistance with unloading the car.

After the car was emptied and pleasantries were exchanged, Jackson told them they'd be in their regular cottage, cabin six. "I'll let Jackie know you're here. Go on ahead to the cottage, the door's open." As they started down the path, Jackson's voice stopped them. "And let me know what you think. We renovated the kitchen this year." A beautiful smile illuminated her face.

"Oh, how exciting. I can't wait to see what you've done to it." Katie's feigned enthusiasm was evident only to Joe but as soon as she looked away, her skeptical demeanor returned.

"See you girls, later." Joe waved. "Oh, and Erin, same rules apply, like home."

"I know, I know, home before dinner," she groused.

"You got it." He waved again then led Katie through the grounds to their cottage.

Alone at last, Jackson asked, "Wanna come and say hi to Jackie? I know she'd love to see you."

Erin nodded quickly. "Absolutely! I'm sure she's sick to death of you. I bet she could use another face to look at." Erin laughed and turned to go.

"Oh, um." Jackson put her hand on Erin's shoulder as she started to walk away. "I wanted to tell you something."

Stopping to face her fully, Erin replied, "So tell me."

"There's someone else staying in our house."

Erin's stomach jumped. "Who?"

"My, um…well, I know you probably won't care, but um…

well, Jackie is a lesbian and her…"

"She is?" Erin blurted, eyes big at the unveiling of such huge information. "I've never met one before!"

"It's not a big deal, really. You don't even realize she is until someone tells you," she said. "Her girlfriend, Sandra, is staying with us."

"How long is she staying with you?"

Shrugging, Jackson answered, "I'm not sure. I just know that I've never seen Jackie so happy. So, she can stay forever as far as I'm concerned."

Seeing a darkness cloud Erin's eyes, Jackson squeezed her shoulder. "What's wrong?"

Erin took a deep breath, feeling the need to make a confession. "Jack, you can't tell my mom about Jackie. She would really flip out." Her blue eyes penetrated Jackson's. "I've heard her talk about gays in a really bad way. I don't want her talking like that about your aunt."

Jackson looked into the concerned eyes of her friend. "Thanks for telling me that, Erin. I appreciate it."

"Erin? Since when do you call me that?" she asked, a red eyebrow shooting up her forehead.

"Well, we were talking about something serious, so I thought I should use your real name."

"Well, don't. You are the only friend I have who doesn't call me that and I really like that fact. So, please, call me Hawk, okay?" she asked with a small smile.

"You got it." She drew Erin in for another hug. "It's so good to see you, Hawk. I really missed you."

Burying her face into the fresh clean smell of her companion, Erin reveled at the incredible feeling of being with Jackson again. "I missed you too, Jack."

Jackson pulled away and made an observation. "Your hair has gotten really dark, Hawk, almost red."

"I know. I used to be a total towhead, but it's changing. I kinda like it, though, so it's cool."

"Let's go say hi to Jackie." She picked up Erin's bags and the two walked over to the main cabin.

Jackson grabbed hold of the screen door and shouted, "You better be decent; we got a VIP guest coming in!"

Hair slightly tousled, Jackie flew from her bedroom and looked at her niece as if she were going to say something nasty. With one look at the guest, her face lit up. "Erin! It's so great to see you!" She rushed to the teenager and threw her arms around her.

"Hi, Jackie. It's great to see you too," Erin said, pulling out of the embrace. "My dad and mom have already gone to settle in. I wanted to say hi before this one takes me all over the place." She smiled warmly at Jackson, who returned one in kind.

From the hallway, an attractive, tall redhead watched the interaction between the girls. She announced herself with a clearing of her throat.

Jackie turned around quickly and let the smile she felt blossom on her lips. "Erin, I want you to meet my um, my fri…"

"It's okay…I told her, Jackie." Jackson and her aunt studied each other for a few seconds.

When Jackie realized that Erin would be okay with her introduction, she continued, "This is my girlfriend, Sandra. Sandra, this is one of my favorites, and definitely Jack's favorite guest."

Erin didn't fail to notice the red that scorched Jackson's face and neck following that admission.

Sandra walked over and offered her hand. "Hi, Erin. It's nice to meet you. I've heard so much about you from this one." She pointed to a still blushing Jackson. "I feel like I already know you."

"It's really nice to meet you, Sandra. I hope we see more of each other this summer."

Sandra smiled, feeling as if Erin was older than Jackson had let on. "Such a nice, polite girl you are. What are you doing hanging with the likes of her?" She pointed again to a gape-mouthed Jackson.

"Close your mouth, Jack. You look like a wide-mouthed bass my dad might catch," Erin said, earning a laugh from Jackie and Sandra.

"Oh, I like this one. Let's keep her and toss the other one back." Sandra continued to laugh.

"All right, that's enough! Is it Pick On Jack Day or something?" she said, arms crossed over her black Guns N' Roses shirt.

"No, we all love you, Jack. We can't help it if you're easy to tease." Her aunt tried to placate Jackson while burying her tongue in her cheek.

"That's it. Hawk, we're outta here." Jackson leaned over and kissed her aunt on the cheek. "I *might* be home later, *if* anyone cares."

"Hey, before I forget, your friend Molly called while you were out." Sandra handed her the message she'd taken.

A strange look passed over Jackson's face. Erin caught it immediately. "Do you want to call her back before we head out?"

"Uh, no. That's okay. I'll call her back later. Thanks." She crumpled the note and put it in her jean shorts pocket. "Come on, Hawk. Let's go say hello to the lake. It missed you." Jackson put her arm around Erin's shoulder and the girl responded with an arm around the slim waist. With a slight pull, they separated and headed out the door.

Sandra and Jackie shared a knowing glance at their retreating figures. "Oh, boy. Do you think they have any idea?" Sandra asked her partner.

"I think so. Jack came out to me right before her sixteenth birthday, but I'm not supposed to tell you that. I don't know about Erin, but I do know about Molly and Jackson. I'm not supposed to tell you that, either."

"Yeah, I was gonna ask you about them next."

"Ooo boy, I have a feeling this summer is not gonna be pretty. I think my little Jackson has bitten off much more than even she can chew." Jackie laced her fingers with Sandra's.

"She does have a big appetite, though."

"Mmmm, must run in the family," Jackie said saucily, arms wrapping around the tall redhead's neck.

Leaning in for a small kiss, Sandra whispered, "Lucky me." She ran her fingers up and down the slightly smaller woman's back.

"Lucky us," the dark-haired woman said, correcting her partner. They leaned in once more and shared a much deeper kiss, filled with every ounce of love they felt for each other.

Pulling apart, Sandra rested her forehead against Jackie's shoulder. "I wish I could take you to bed." She kissed the side of Jackie's head.

Heart beating wildly with arousal, Jackie managed to say, "God, I want you, too. I'll show you how much later."

"Uggh." Sandra buried her face in Jackie's sweet smelling hair. They swayed in each other's arms for a long while, each relishing the feel of the other. "Come on, let's find something *nonsexual* to do around here. I need to breathe some fresh air."

"Let's go play shuffleboard. That's the least sexual thing we can do without actually working."

Sandra giggled at her partner. "You're on. I get to be black this time, though."

Releasing her grasp on Sandra's hand, Jackie opened the door. "You can have black if you can beat me to the court."

"Okay, you're on. On the count of three."

Together they started to count, "One, two, th…"

Jackie dashed out of the house before three was counted. Sandra chased after her cheating girlfriend and easily beat her to the board, much to Jackie's surprise and dismay.

Grabbing the black slide, Sandra smiled in triumph. She handed the red slide to a grumbling Jackie then walked to her side of the court. "Shuffleboard, anyone?"

Putting on her competitive hat, Jackie sneered and growled, "Puck you."

"Oh, that was bad, even for you." Jackie grinned then watched as Sandra's black disc slid effortlessly into the tip of the scoring triangle. Grin fading, she mumbled, "I should've gone down to the lake with the girls."

Erin kept her eyes closed as she breathed in the fresh air coming off the lake. The girls had stopped at the cottage to drop off Erin's bags then went down to the waterfront. Jackson had kept a hand on her shoulder as they walked down the pier. Erin thought it felt like the most natural thing in the world. Reaching for Jackson's hand, she gave it a squeeze before releasing it.

"It's so good to be back here." The smile never left her face. "I feel so different when I'm here. It's like this place calls to me." She blushed. "I guess that sounds pretty dumb, huh?"

Eyes twinkling under her sunglasses, Jackson shook her head. "No, it's not dumb at all. Some people don't understand the beauty of this place. But for some, you know—people like us, the love and respect for the nature around here is a gift. Whether you accept that gift is another thing. The fact that you have, says a lot about you, Hawk."

"My gosh, Jack, you speak so worldly now."

Laughing softly, she replied, "No, I'm just so happy you feel that way about this place. I don't have many friends who love it like you do," she explained. "Oh, sure, they love coming down here to water ski and that sort of thing, but the rest of it is so foreign to them."

"Well, I'm not just any friend, you know." Erin grabbed Jackson's hand to give it a light squeeze.

Don't I know it. Jackson looked into the warm eyes that reflected the sky and wished she could open her heart fully to Erin. "No, you're my *best* friend." She looked out over the water, keeping Erin's hand in hers, idly caressing it with her thumb. "I could live here, err, I *hope* to live here, the rest of my life. I want to find someone to run the resort with me when my aunt can't any longer. I don't think it'll be as easy as it sounds."

"Sure it will, Jack. Who wouldn't want to spend their life here with you?" *If it wouldn't make my mom go into a tizzy fit, I'd do it in a heartbeat.*

"You never know, Hawk. You never know." They shared a warm smile then Jackson offered a suggestion, "You wanna go down to the boathouse? You can grab some of your art supplies and I can play you a soothing tune on my recorder while you draw. Actually, I'm playing the oboe now, too, so I could let you hear that. It has a totally different sound. Whaddya say?" Jackson was so hopeful about spending more time alone with Erin she could hardly deal with the emotions coursing through her.

Erin was so filled by Jackson that any time spent away from her felt like a lifetime. Excited by Jackson's new talent, she agreed enthusiastically. "Let me go get my supplies and I'll meet you up there." Erin knew her mother was going to be annoyed and didn't want Jackson to have to deal with that.

Not really understanding why she shouldn't go with Erin, she just nodded. "All right, I'll see you in a little while." She felt the wad of paper in her pocket and knew she had to call Molly soon anyway. "I'll give my friend a call back and meet you up there. Cool?"

Grateful for not having to explain her solo route, Erin gave Jackson her most winning smile. "Cool. Let's say fifteen minutes?"

"Done."

The girls parted ways. Jackson passed Jackie and Sandra on the shuffleboard court. They were yelling fake obscenities at each other and drawing quite a crowd of onlookers with their comedic banter. She loved the way they played and egged each other on. The love she felt coming from them was palpable and for that she was grateful. Jackie had been alone for a while before Sandra, and now her aunt seemed very happy. Jackson wished she had that to look forward to in her own future.

Inside the main cabin, Jackson picked up the phone and dialed Molly's number.

"Hey, you," Jackson said when Molly answered.

"Hey, I thought you forgot about me," Molly said with theatric sadness.

"Never. My best friend from Chicago is here." Not hearing a response, she continued, "You know...Erin? I know I told you about her. We've been best friends since we were kids."

Blowing out a breath, Molly said, "Yeah. I just forgot she was coming today. I thought we could spend some time together. Maybe go swimming or um," her voice dropped lower, "go up to the boathouse loft?"

The insinuation went right to the southern regions of Jackson's body. Her face sporting a rosy tinge, she said, "Uh, no, I don't think that would be a good idea. Erin doesn't know about me and I really don't want to tell her yet, okay?"

Feigning hurt, Molly said, "What kind of best friend is that? If she is your best friend, she'd accept you any way you are. So am I not supposed to see you for the next month? Is that it?" Her voice was starting to rise.

"No!" Her voice matched Molly's then softened, "No, it's not that. Just don't expect me to, you know, do stuff while she's here. I wouldn't feel right."

"You'll just have to come over to my house, then. I know I won't be able to not touch you for an entire month."

"That's fine. I'm sure Jackie will let me take my car when I have to go to your house."

"Have to?" she questioned.

"Need to," Jackson amended, dropping her voice to soothe any possible waves Molly might want to make.

"Mmm, that's better. I need you now."

"Sorry, I can't right now. I promised Erin that we'd sit on the roof so she could do some drawing. You should see her art, Mol, she's so talented."

"Really?" Molly's voice dripped with sarcasm.

Not taking the bait, Jackson continued, "Yeah, she is, and I promised, so we'll get together another day, okay? How's tomorrow? I'd like you two to meet."

Oh, goody. "Sure Jack, I'll come by in the afternoon."

Jackson's face lit up. "Great! We'll have a lot of fun, I swear."

Erin's decision to go alone had been a good one. When her mother saw her leaving with her backpack, she immediately questioned her.

"Are you going to that filthy boathouse again?"

Rolling her eyes, Erin answered, "Yes, Mother, I'm going to do some drawing. That's the best place to draw here." She tried to keep the daggers from her eyes. In the months leading up to their vacation, her relationship with her mother had become strained. "You said you wanted me to draw, so I'm drawing. But I get to draw on my own terms or it won't come out right."

"Fine, just don't get yourself dirty. I think your father wants to take us out to Bosaki's for dinner tonight."

"Cool, can Jack come, too?" Erin asked, hopeful despite knowing what the answer would be.

"Can't you be away from her for two seconds and just be with us for one night?" her mother asked incredulously.

"I spend eleven months a year with you, Mother. I haven't seen Jack *in* a year. Can't I be happy to spend time with my best friend?"

"You know, I was *never* that happy to see *my* best friends. I just don't understand it."

"Well, Mother, then maybe you never had a friend as good as Jack because I miss her *all* the time when we're apart."

Her mother looked at her as if she'd sprouted two heads and repeated, "I just don't understand you."

"Well, that goes both ways." Erin slung her backpack over her shoulder. "Can I go now? I'll be back before dinner." Her eyes took on a rebellious stare. "I won't get *dirty*, either."

Walking in from the bedroom, Joe felt the tension in the air between his wife and daughter. "Who's getting dirty, Peanut?"

"No one, as I have told Mom. She thinks I'm eight years old and am gonna get all dirty in the boathouse."

Rolling his eyes at his wife, Joe tried to placate her. "Honey, she hasn't come back dirty from that place since our first time here. Just let her have some fun this summer before she starts high school, okay?"

"Fine, just go," she groused and stalked into the kitchen.

"Have fun, Peanut, okay?"

"I don't get it, Daddy. We get along fine until Jack or vacationing in Wisconsin comes up. I can't breathe one word about Jack without her ragging on me. I would think she'd want me to have someone to hang with while we're here. What did Jack ever do to her?" she asked, tears forming in her eyes.

Joe opened his arms and Erin fell instantly into his warmth. He embraced his daughter and patted the sack on her back. "Don't you worry about your mom, just have some fun. Paint me a sunset, okay? You know they're my favorite." His chin rested on her head.

Nodding into the clean smell of her father's shirt, Erin gave him one last cuddle. "Okay, Daddy. I'm getting pretty good with the pastels now. I'll try one for you."

"That's my girl." He brushed her cheek with a callused thumb. "Go have fun."

"Is it true you're taking us to Bosaki's for dinner?"

"Yep, so don't be late."

"You got it."

Erin climbed up to the boathouse roof, following the sweet new sounds coming from Jackson's oboe. Reaching the top rung of the ladder, she watched as Jackson played, unaware of her arrival. Her eyes were still covered by sunglasses, but Erin knew without question they were closed and she was lost in the melody she was playing. When the last note ended, Jackson rested the oboe across her lap.

"You can come up now, sneaky pants."

Jackson's words startled Erin. "I didn't think you'd heard me. I could've sworn you were someplace else while you were playing," she managed to get out while swinging her body over the ladder.

"I always know when you're near." She shrugged. "I always have." Erin's smile was contagious and Jackson found herself smiling back.

Pulling her pad of paper from the waistband of her shorts, Erin realized something aloud, "You know, ever since that first time up here, I always tuck my sketchbook into my pants if I need both hands for something. I can't help it."

Jackson laughed at the admission. "Well, I'm glad my advice has stuck with you for so long. I don't know many people who've listened to me and remembered what they heard."

"Like I told you before, I'm not just anybody."

Erin took a seat next to Jackson on the blanket spread out on the rooftop. Looking out over the water, awe washed over her anew. "It never fails. Every time I look out there, I'm just speechless. It's so…breathtaking."

Looking at the new instrument in Jackson's lap, she was instantly curious. "So, when did you start playing this? I know you were fiddling around with the flute and piccolo, but isn't this like a clarinet?"

"Excellent question, Ms. Hawkins. It just so happens that the flute, piccolo, clarinet, saxophone, recorder *and* oboe are all in the same family."

Erin marveled again at how much Jackson had grown up. Even though she was only sixteen, she knew a great deal about music. "You should teach music, Jack. You know so much about it."

Scrunching up her face, Jackson replied, "Yeah, but I don't know if I could do the teaching thing. Knowing what I know about kids, they're assholes, and I don't think I could handle not being able to smack them if they got out of line in my class."

Laughing at her friend, who was normally a pacifist, Erin replied, "You would be fine and you know it. Once you get into something, you get everyone around you so hyped on it." Erin remembered an example. "Do you remember how crazy you were over that stupid potato salad from that convenience store across the lake? Soon after your outburst, my parents, your aunt and everyone else at the resort were cruising on their boats to get some. You could've written a prizewinning essay about it."

Laughing at the memory, Jackson agreed. "You're right. I can get pretty nuts over something I love." She turned to look at Erin and the air seemed to stop moving altogether.

Erin felt the shift and swallowed hard. Neither of them heard the footfalls on the ladder.

"Well, isn't this cozy?" Molly's jealous voice broke the connection.

Jackson's head whirled around and met the cocky smirk of her girlfriend. "Molly! What are you doing here?" Jackson blurted, her face flaming with surprise and instant nausea.

"You sounded like you really wanted me to meet the infamous Erin, so here I am." Reaching the top, she turned to look at the visitor. Coolly assessing the pretty, reddish-blond girl with the sky blue eyes, she extended her hand. "It's nice to finally meet you."

Erin, feeling the tension radiating from Jackson's body, extended her hand carefully. She regarded the small, attractive blonde and felt that she was in unfamiliar territory. A little jealousy seeped into her heart. "It's nice to meet you, too, Molly."

The air crackled with Jackson's anxiety. She didn't know how to calm her racing heart. Trying to act as if she was under control, Jackson pointed to the blanket beside her. "Have a seat. Erin was just going to do some drawing and I was going to...um..." she lifted her oboe, "practice for a while."

Erin's eyes went wide as she listened to Jackson stumble over her words. *She called me Erin? What is going on with her?*

"You know, Erin, the way Jackson talks about you, I would've thought you were much older. You're just a kid." She was hoping to wipe the smile off of Jackson's face, and it worked...but not to her advantage.

"Hey! She's starting high school in the fall. She's not that much younger than I am. Or is being a senior this year making you forget that you have freshmen walking down the same hallways with you every day?"

"Jack, it's okay," Erin's small voice stopped her rant. "She doesn't know me yet. Perhaps by the end of the summer she'll change her mind." Erin smiled sweetly at Molly.

"Yes, Jack, maybe I'll change my mind," she repeated, ice dripping from her smile. "So, what are you playing? Are you working on that little thing you wrote? What was it called, 'Hawks in Flight' or something?" Jackson's cheeks flamed at Molly's words.

Erin's face lit up like a Christmas tree. "You wrote a song?" She cleared her throat for emphasis. "About a *hawk* in flight?"

Jackson wanted to jump off the roof of the boathouse right then and there.

"It's really good, she should play it for you sometime," Molly added, touching Jackson's bare knee. Jackson jumped up and pretended to stretch. Molly looked at her angrily and stood as well. "What's wrong, Jack? Don't you want to play it for her?"

Erin watched the strange interaction and wondered why Jackson would bother being friends with someone like Molly. *She's really bossy.* Feeling like she was in the way, she stood with the other girls and started to make an excuse to leave when Molly opened her mouth again.

"Jack, look at me." Molly reached up and took off her sunglasses, smiling when she saw two blue eyes looking at her. "Ahh, there are the blue eyes I love."

Erin's brow furrowed, her posture stiffening. Eyes wide, she cried, "What happened to your eyes?"

Before Jackson could answer, Molly piped up, "Colored contact lens. Doesn't she look so much better? Those different colored eyes really freaked me out."

Erin's anger at the girl almost overwhelmed her. Her voice was calm despite the maelstrom burning in her belly. "Actually, no, I don't think she does. Sorry, Jack, but I really loved your eyes before. They were unique and special." The "loved" slipped out before she could stop it.

Jackson was tired of being talked about like she wasn't in the vicinity. She grabbed her sunglasses and put them back on, trying not to drop her oboe. "Look, Molly please don't talk about me like I'm not even here. I can speak for myself." Turning to Erin she said, "It was supposed to be a surprise. I didn't tell you so I could show you myself. I wanted to see what it was like to have two of the same colored eyes. Like everyone else."

But you're not everyone else. You're unique and special! "Well, if you like them then that's good. I do like your eyes the way they were without the contact lens, though." Feigning tardiness, Erin looked at her watch. "I gotta get going anyway. My mom has some stuff for me to do before dinner." Turning back to Molly, she spoke politely. "It was nice to meet you, Molly. I hope we see each other before I leave."

"I'm sure we will."

Jackson watched as Molly waved and smiled a saccharine smile that made her stomach roil. "I'll see you after dinner?" Jackson asked hopefully.

"Sure." Erin tried hard to smile as she picked up her pack and slung it over her shoulder, then carefully made her way down the ladder. As she walked down to the loft window, she heard Molly's whisper. "They're so unique and special," she said mockingly. "I told you she was a kid." And Jackson's, "Knock it off, Molly. The show's over."

Trying to keep her emotions in check, she swung into the loft and down to the main boathouse. She was confused by Jackson's behavior and angry at how she was treated by Molly. Realizing she'd left her pad of paper on the roof, she debated whether to go back and get it. "Screw that," she said, knowing Jackson would take care of it, and she followed the small path that would lead her back to the cabin grounds.

Up on the roof, Molly and Jackson were still debating what had transpired.

"You owe her an apology, Molly. She didn't do anything to you and you attacked her like a jungle cat. What the hell is wrong with you?"

Eyes softening, Molly realized she'd hit a nerve and tried a peace offering. "I'm sorry, Jack. When I saw you two up here I got really jealous and my mouth kind of took over."

"You have nothing to be jealous of," Jackson lied. "We've been friends since we were like knee high. Every summer she and her folks come to stay with us. I love her like a sister and would really appreciate it if you were nicer to her next time."

"Okay, Jack. I really am sorry." She tried to give Jackson a kiss only to have the taller girl back away.

"Don't! I told you I didn't want to do that stuff while she was here."

"I don't see her anywhere, Jack, do you?" Blowing out a breath, she continued to rant. "Me coming over was just a bad idea. I'm going home. I'll see you tomorrow." She turned to step onto the ladder and stopped. "Unless that's no good for you either."

"It's fine, Mol. Just come tomorrow. We'll go skiing or something. Erin's never skied before, I'm sure she'd like to try something other than the tube."

"Great!" she snapped. "I can't wait to do everything Erin

wants to do. See you later, Jack."

Molly flew down the ladder, leaving Jackson to ungracefully plop down on the roof, oboe in hand. She noticed Erin's sketchbook at the edge of the blanket. Shaking her head, she looked out over the water.

Oh, this isn't gonna be good, at all.

Chapter Five

1990 – The Northwoods Island City

A few hours later Erin was sitting on the dock. Her stomach was upset after the afternoon she shared with Jack, and eating greasy fried fish for dinner hadn't helped her situation at all. With the sun starting to set, her fingers began to work in earnest. The colors coming off the water were incredible. Purples and pinks with a hard line of red on the horizon. It was just beautiful. Her pastel sticks were bringing out the colors as well as her matching mood.

What happened up on the roof was strange, if not a little unsettling. Molly and Jackson definitely had a history of which she knew nothing about. Jackson hadn't ever mentioned Molly, and when she'd found out that Molly knew of her, her thoughts were troubling.

Why would she hide that from me? It's obvious Molly doesn't like me for some reason. I just hope Jack will tell me what's going on. I don't like this one bit.

Hearing footsteps on the dock, her heart sped up. *Speak of the devil.* She didn't need to turn around to know who was approaching. Jackson sat down in the chair next to her and didn't say a word. Erin used her peripheral vision to watch her while she pretended to draw. Jackson sat quietly watching the sunset.

"So, what's up with Molly? Any idea why she hates me so

much?" Erin asked flat out. *And why didn't you tell me about her?*

Jackson didn't answer right away. She was battling with so many emotions that she wasn't sure which ones she wanted to face. "Molly is a spoiled brat sometimes, Hawk. She can be the nicest person, but like today, she showed fangs I'm not too fond of."

"What's up with you not calling me Hawk around her? I feel like there is so much you haven't told me. I think you stopped writing to me because of her." Erin worked on, finishing her drawing before the sun disappeared below the horizon.

If you only knew how much I haven't told you. "You're right. I was hanging out with Molly this summer and before I knew it," she snapped her fingers, "August was here and then so were you. I'm really sorry about that. You know how much I love your letters," Jackson said. "I'm so sorry about today. I really hated the whole thing." She ventured a hand on Erin's shoulder.

Erin's eyes met hers for the first time and she noticed the contact lens had been removed. Trying to hide her smile, she replied, "I didn't hate all of it. It was really nice before she showed up." She reached up and squeezed the hand on her shoulder, then resumed working her magic on the page. "Although, I don't think you should hang out with a person who wants you to change yourself." She pointed to her eyes. "Your eyes *are* unique and are a part of the awesome person you are. Don't let her take that from you. *No one* should be allowed to do that."

Jackson started to dispute the assertion, but Erin put her fingers on her mouth. "You know I'm right." Jackson smiled, and the fight was over before it began.

Jackson moved closer to look over Erin's shoulder. From the edge of the shore, Katie stood and watched the girls together, unable to suppress the discontent she felt. The closer Erin and Jackson got, the uneasier she felt. She knew there was more than friendship growing between them. It was a sinking feeling, and she would not allow it to happen if she could help it. *No daughter of mine will act that way.* "Erin, make sure you come in at dark!"

Erin, nearly jumping off her chair, turned around to face her mother on the waterfront. "Can I stay out until at least ten, Mom? I'm working on a great picture for Dad."

Trying not to be completely unreasonable, she compromised. "Ten o'clock, but no later."

Smiling with a brief wave, Erin called, "Thanks."

"Good night, Mrs. Hawkins."

"Good night, Jackson," she returned coolly, and then went back to her cottage.

"Hawk, what's up with you and your mom? She never used to give you a curfew while you were here."

Taking a deep breath, she stilled her fingers. "Jack, I wish I knew. She has been such a… God I don't even want to say it! Do you know she tried to get me to go to cheerleading camp instead of coming here this summer? I couldn't believe it. Like there was *any* way I'd choose not to come and see you if I could."

Jackson was at a loss. "I don't know, Hawk. What does your dad say about it?"

"He says not to mind her, but I *do* mind. It's like she doesn't want me to be friends with you or something. What the heck made her feel that way? You're my best friend in the world; how can she not want me to be around you?"

Jackson's arm went fully around Erin's shoulders and drew their bodies close. "I don't know, Hawk. I'll just try to be extra charming so she isn't so hard on you." Without thought, she kissed the top of Erin's head. Eyes closing, Erin let her head fall against the broad shoulder beside her.

"I love you, you know," Erin whispered.

Pressing her lips against her head again, Jackson replied, "I love you, too, Hawk."

"Promise me something?" Erin kept her voice low.

"Anything."

"Tell me about Molly when you're ready, okay?"

Not really wanting to think about her at the moment, Jackson agreed. "I will. I am sorry I didn't tell you about her. It might have been much more evenly matched this afternoon. She came out swinging, man. I didn't think she'd be so jealous of our friendship."

Feeling her face redden a little, Erin confessed, "I was a little jealous of her, too. She was acting like you were her possession. I did *not* like that one bit."

Jackson bit off her smile at Erin's admission, grateful Erin was so different from Molly. There was no comparison. If there ever was any reason she had to choose between the two, Erin would win hands down. For right now, she would relish the idea of having her girlfriend and her best friend in the same place. She felt extremely lucky indeed.

"Do you want to try water skiing tomorrow?"

A sudden fear washed over Erin. "I…I don't know. I'm kinda scared about it, really. Maybe I should just stick to tubing."

"Well, you can if you want. I think we're gonna take the boat out tomorrow and go skiing. You're always welcome to try, but we'll hitch up the tube to the boat if you'd rather do that."

"You wouldn't care?" Erin was feeling like the kid Molly said she was. "I feel stupid."

"There is no reason for you to feel stupid because something scares you. If you don't want to do it, just go tubing and have a good time."

Jackson's calm voice burred in her ear making Erin feel more loved and content than she'd ever felt. Erin breathed a small, relaxed sigh.

Breaking the warmth of their contact, Jackson asked, "So how's that picture coming? It's gonna be dark soon."

"Oh! I almost forgot about it." Her face blushed hotly. She held the picture up to view. The sunset was captured almost perfectly.

"Wow, Hawk, that's really beautiful. You've gotten so good with your work, people are gonna be paying oodles of dollars just to own your pieces. Mark my words."

Erin blushed a deeper red under the praise.

"Thanks, Jack. You've always been in my corner when it came to my artwork. I can't tell you how much I appreciate that."

Smiling softly, Jack said, "You're welcome. I'll always be your biggest fan."

"Speaking of fans, will you play me the song you wrote? I'd

really love to hear it."

Jackson nodded. "Of course I will. I named it after you because of your love of this place...and, well, our friendship. It means a lot to me." Jackson hoped the look in her eyes didn't show too much of her heart. The last thing she wanted was for Erin to be unnerved by the depth of the love she had for her. "I never told Molly I called you that and, well, it's none of her business. I don't think she would like it very much since I know she'd put the two things together. The less ammunition she has, the better for all of us."

Erin couldn't understand why Jackson wanted to be friends with someone like that. It wasn't her place to say who Jackson could be friends with, so she shook her head and said nothing.

"Come on, let's put this away and go hang out at my house. Jackie and Sandra are gonna watch *Ghost* tonight. I've never seen it, so if you'd like to come over, we could watch it with them. Sandra makes a mean cheese popcorn with Velveeta. Really messy, but *really* good."

Erin nodded, happy to be on more solid ground with her friend again. "Sure, I wanted to see that too. Let's go."

The girls walked to Jackson's house where they were greeted by the sight of a very friendly kiss being shared by Jackie and Sandra. Jackson heard Erin's small gasp and immediately cleared her throat. "Get a room, you two," Jackson said, though not fazed in the slightest at their normal behavior.

The women pulled apart quickly, clearly embarrassed at having exposed Erin to their affection.

Jackie saw the deer-in-the-headlights expression and wanted to make sure Erin wouldn't run out of the house. "Are you okay? I'm sorry if that freaked you out."

The red on her cheeks spoke volumes about the swirling tides in her stomach. "Nn...no, no. I'm fine, really. It's just um...wow." She laughed nervously. "I, ah, don't see a lot of that from regular people... Well...not to say you aren't regular..." She started stammering. "I'm just gonna sit over here and not say a word." She went and sat on the sofa.

"Awww, Hawk, I'm sorry you had to see that." Jackson's

lips thinned and she stared narrowly at her aunt. Sandra had the sense to leave the room. Jackson sat down next to Erin. "You want something to drink? It might bring down the color in your face."

Erin's hands immediately went to her cheeks, warm and red from the images of the heated kiss flowing through her brain. *Incredible.* "Yeah, maybe some water would be good," she managed to squeak out.

"I'll get it." Jackson jumped up and went into the kitchen, silently flagging her aunt to follow her.

In the kitchen, a heated round of whispers took place. "Jackie, how can you do that in the front room? Anyone could've seen you!"

Jackie became defensive. "Excuse me, but this is *my* house and if I want to kiss my girlfriend, I'm damn well going to!"

Feeling hurt, Jackson countered, "You *knew* I was going to bring her back here. I told you I was going to the dock to get her."

Nodding, Jackie began to apologize. "You're right, Jack. And I'm sorry Erin had to see that. But hell, the more people see it, the more natural it'll become. God, I can't even touch Sandra when we're with her family. I just can't stand to do that in my own house. I'll go in there and apologize."

"I'm sorry I overreacted. You know *I* don't care if you kiss her, I see it all the time. This is just very new to Erin and I don't want her to be freaked every time she comes to the door."

"Have you told her about you and Molly yet?" Jackie asked.

Jackson's eyes went wide and she stealthily looked around the corner to see what Erin was doing. Seeing that she hadn't moved, Jackson went back to her aunt and shook her head. "No, and I don't think I'm ready to. I think she'd be okay with me being a lesbo, but I don't think she'd be fond of me being one with Molly. They kinda met today and it wasn't pretty."

"Ooh, I want to hear that story after she leaves."

"Only if Sandra makes cheese corn."

The deal in place, the two women returned to the family room, Jackson carrying a glass of water for Erin. Jackie went to tell Sandra that she needed to make the best damn cheese corn to make it up to Jackson and her friend.

"How you doin'?" Jackson asked, handing Erin the glass of water.

"You know, I'm fine," Erin said truthfully. "After the initial shock of it being, you know, two girls, well it was pretty okay. You can tell they really care for each other." She whispered the last part, making Jackson smile.

"Yeah, they do."

Sandra and Jackie came back into the family room and Sandra announced she would be popping corn for the film. "Go ahead and start the movie, I've seen it a few times already. I'll have this corn made in about ten minutes. And Erin, it'll be the best damn popcorn you've ever had." She winked, causing the teenager's cheeks to flush.

"Thanks, I'm looking forward to it. Jack says it's really, really good."

"You'd better believe it's good," Jackie chimed in.

The three sat on the couch and Jackie started the film. Sandra brought the popcorn in and then inched her way to the floor by Jackie's feet.

Erin's eyes closed in extreme pleasure at the taste of the first kernel.

Jackson's mouth watered as she watched Erin lick the cheese from her fingers. She knew at that point with the way her hormones were acting, she needed to pay close attention to the movie.

The following afternoon was, in a word, perfect. The scorching heat had cooled down to a very pleasant eighty-two degrees. It was an ideal day to spend on the water.

At one o'clock sharp, Molly arrived wearing next to nothing of a bikini. Jackson gave Molly a hug that lasted longer than Jackson wanted it to, but she didn't want Molly's jealous tirade to start any sooner than necessary. The feel of Molly's body was so good against her own that Jackson closed her eyes and sighed. "So, are you ready to ski?" Jackson asked her girlfriend.

"Sure, or I can just lay on the pier and make Erin drive while I watch you do your magic on the water." Jackson blushed at the compliment then noticed Erin's approach to the gravel drive.

Erin had seen Jackson hug Molly. She noticed Jackson's eyes had closed and wondered what Molly could've said to garner that response.

"Hi, there," Erin greeted, putting the thoughts aside. "Nice to see you." Molly barely acknowledged her.

Shorts covered Erin's bikini bottoms but she was wearing a revealing top, which outlined a strong but feminine torso. She kept her tank top tucked into the waistband of her shorts. Jackson's eyes were glued to the outline of Erin's shoulders and the swell of her breasts. Her unfocused gaze was cut short by a light pinch to her side.

With a shake of her head toward Molly, she tried to change the subject. "Are you guys ready? The water is so perfect today, I can't wait to pound the waves."

Both girls latched onto Jackson's incredible energy and silently agreed, for the moment, to be civil. Molly added, "My brother got us some beer, if you want to bring it on the boat."

Erin's eyes were wide, but Jackson answered with a shake of her head. "You know I won't drive the boat if I drink. If you want to drink, that's fine, but Jackie's only been letting me drive it this summer and last. I don't want to crash it."

"That's fine. It's in a cooler, so we can drink it later." She looked back and forth between Jackson and Erin. "Is that cool?"

Both girls nodded, although Erin had never had more than a couple of beers before, so she was less than comfortable. She didn't want to seem as childish as Molly said she was.

Jackson could tell she was having second thoughts and reassured her, "It's okay if you don't want to drink, buddy. You can just hang out."

Jackson had a way of making Erin feel so good. Even if a situation was making her feel less than comfortable, Jackson was always there to say just the right thing. Molly discreetly rolled her eyes and started walking toward the lake.

They made their way to the boat slips and took out the Formula Bowrider ski boat. With almost three hundred horsepower, the floating fiberglass could pull anyone through the water behind it.

"This, my friends, is the boat of all boats, my dream boat. After she bought this, Jackie nearly fell to the ground when I leapt into her arms."

Erin laughed. "I bet."

Molly jumped easily into the boat, making herself at home. Because she was a year older than Jackson, and because Jackie would not have to get in the boat every time Jackson wanted to ski, Jackie was agreeable to letting Molly drive the watercraft.

Jackson was bringing the life jackets out of the boathouse with Erin in tow carrying the water tube. Erin cheerfully waved to her dad as he and a few cabin friends were pulling out to go fishing.

"Have fun, Peanut," he called. "Don't forget to hold on."

"Ha, Ha. Don't forget to bait your hook," she shot back, to the amusement of his friends.

Jackson looked back at Erin. "I'm so glad he's regularly catching some fish. Otherwise, he might not come all the way back here each summer."

"I know. I almost want to put some big fish in his cooler to make sure he keeps *wanting* to come back."

"Ah, I think the trap was set a long time ago, Hawk. I can tell he has a lot of fun while he's here." She paused. "Your mom, on the other hand…"

"Don't go there, I'm just waiting for her to suggest a trip to Disneyland next year," Erin said, only half joking.

"Hey, come on you two! The sun is calling me!" Molly yelled from the boat.

"I wonder what the sun called her," Erin quipped, earning a small chuckle from her friend.

Jackson ran back to the boathouse to get the skis and towrope. Molly and Erin put on their life vests and waited for her to return. In minutes, Jackson had checked the gas levels, attached the towrope, and put the skis on. She was more than a little excited to wedge through the water.

Molly was at the helm with Erin next to her on lookout. When the rope was just taut enough, she gunned the engine, pulling Jackson up easily. The smile on Jackson's face grew exponentially as the number of turns and wave jumping increased. Molly easily steered the boat through the lake while Erin watched Jackson fly effortlessly through the water. When they got close to shore, Jackson dropped her left ski and tucked her left foot into the rear binding of the right ski.

Side to side, Jackson rushed through the water with Erin looking on. Molly added a little more gas, making Jackson's adrenaline soar. She watched Erin wave every once in a while, and could tell she was having a great time. The smile never left her face. After her last trip around the lake, she motioned to Erin to tell Molly to go to shore. With Erin doing just that, they slowly made their way to the pier.

As the boat slowed, Jackson dropped the towrope and skied until she sank to the bottom of the shallow lakeshore waters. She pulled her feet from the bindings and walked up onto the waterfront. Ski in hand, she walked around to the other side of the pier to pick up the other ski that was floating toward the shore.

"That was so friggin' awesome!" she shouted, feeling like she could walk on this very lake.

"You were incredible, Jack! You've gotten so good!" Erin gushed, much to the ire of Molly.

Putting on her happy face for Jack, she jumped onto the admiration bus, and added her twist. "Sweetie, you were fantastic out there. Nothing was gonna touch you." She smiled sweetly and Jackson smiled back, raising an eyebrow.

She slicked the hair back from her face and shook her head. "Man, what a rush!" She laughed happily. "Mol, you wanna go next?"

"Sure. Will you help me with the skis? Your feet are bigger than mine."

"Yep. Let's just secure the boat real quick so it doesn't go anywhere."

Sweetie? Erin didn't understand Molly's possessive thing, but she wanted it to stop. She wasn't a threat to Jackson and Molly's relationship, especially living four hundred miles away. *Molly needs to get over it.*

Molly and Jackson resized the skis to fit her smaller feet.

When they were ready, Jackson jumped into the boat. She untied the dock lines from the cleats and once the boat reached water that was deep enough, started the engine.

Erin smiled at the carefree expression on Jackson's face. It melted her heart completely. This was her home, her calling, and outside of her mother not being with her, she looked to Erin like the happiest person alive.

Erin watched as Molly set herself up in the water. Balancing behind her skis, she positioned the rope between them. Jackson looked back and waited for the line to be taut. When she was ready, Molly gave her a thumbs-up and off they went. Jackson gunned the boat as Erin again took the lookout position.

About halfway around the lake, they encountered some choppy water. When Molly tried to compensate for the fresh waves, she fell into the water.

"She's down!" Erin yelled.

Jackson steered the boat in a slow circle toward Molly so they could get her the rope. When they reached her, Molly was less than happy. "God damn waves." She spat water as she bobbed in the lake. "The tip of my ski dropped under one of the swells and I bit it, hard."

"Are you okay to keep going?" Jackson asked, idling the engine.

"Yeah, just need to straighten out."

Erin looked at her with a smile. "You were doing great until you went down," she said sincerely.

Molly took it completely opposite. "It's not as easy as it looks, but you wouldn't know that, would you?"

Her fear replaced by anger, Erin replied, "Not yet, but when you're done, I'm gonna try."

Jackson turned and put a hand on her shoulder. "Are you sure? You don't have to do that. You know she's just baiting you."

Staring back into the shaded eyes of her best friend, she said, "I'm doing it."

Shaking her head with a laugh, Jackson said, "You're the boss."

Looking back, Erin saw that Molly was just about ready.

Molly gave Erin a thumbs-up, or it could've been her middle finger, Erin wasn't sure from that distance. "I think she wants to go!" she yelled to Jackson.

Turning back to make sure, Jackson got a, "Go already!" from a wet, pissed off Molly.

Jackson gunned the engine and Molly stood right up, a smile back on her face. Erin looked over to Jackson, who was steering with an enormous smile on her face. She had pushed her sunglasses onto her head to keep her hair out of her eyes. Jackson noticed she was staring and looked over and winked.

Molly made it around the lake a couple of times then signaled to come in.

When the boat reached the shore, Erin jumped onto the pier and went down to where Molly was removing the skis. Showing Erin how to adjust the skis, Molly helped her get the equipment on.

"Now just make sure you keep your knees bent and your arms straight. Lean back, but in a crouched position, so you aren't dragging your butt in the water," Jackson said from the boat. "I'm gonna pull away slowly until the rope is tight. When I start to pull you a little, give Molly a thumbs-up when you're ready, and we'll punch it." Erin gave a nervous nod and Jackson asked one last time, "Are you sure you're ready?"

Looking at Molly's cocky stance with her arms crossed, Erin's chin lifted and she met Jackson's eyes. "Yeah. Let's do this!"

"That's my girl!" Jackson cheered, earning her a hateful glare from Molly. Jackson threw her arms wide in disbelief of her girlfriend's jealous nature. "I'm just encouraging her, Jesus!" Not wanting Molly to drive and drag Erin too fast, Jackson sat behind the wheel. "Tell me when she's ready." Molly moved right next to Jackson on the bench, facing the rear of the boat.

Erin was settling back in the water, trying to get a feel for the skis, keeping the tips up. "You can do this, Erin. You can do this," she coached herself. "If that scrawny wench can do it, so can I." Her words surprised her, but looking at Molly's smirk as she sat close to Jackson hardened Erin's resolve. Raising a shaky hand, she gave a thumbs-up and hung onto the towrope with all her might.

Getting the go-ahead from Molly, Jackson gunned the engine. After a few seconds of battling for balance, Erin stood on the skis and adrenaline shot through her. The smile on her face felt the size of Lake Tomahawk. *Who needs tubing when you can do this!* Her heart was racing but she was still standing, and having a ball. As the boat turned left, Erin moved over to the right side, picking up speed. She bent her knees, using her legs as shock absorbers to ride the waves.

"How's she doing?" Jackson yelled at Molly.

"She's doing great. She's bouncing off the waves like a pro." Molly was not pleased. *Another point for the great Erin.*

"Fantastic!" Jackson briefly looked back to see Erin's smiling face as she battled the water around her.

When the boat slowed on its next turn, the slack on the rope increased and Erin found herself slipping backward, very close to the water. As Jackson gunned the engine and the rope tightened again, Erin was jolted forward. The handle flew from her hands, wrapped around her right leg, and got caught on her binding. She fell onto her back. "Oh, shit!" With the rope caught on her ski, the boat continued to pull her, dragging her under the water.

Molly smiled. She figured she could let Erin bob around out there for a while. She leaned over and kissed Jackson's cheek and stuck her tongue in her ear. Jackson playfully batted her hand away, completely unaware of Erin's situation.

Erin held her breath as she was dragged below the surface. *Help me! Stop the boat!* Panic had set in a few long seconds ago. Erin's chest started to burn, and then everything went black.

When Molly looked back, waiting to see Erin bobbing far from the boat, she noticed that the rope was not bouncing off the water, but held a ski with a body still attached to it. Realizing she'd made a fatal mistake, she screamed, "Oh, shit, Jack, she's down! She's caught! Stop!"

Jackson immediately killed the engine and looked back at Erin's motionless body, still being pulled by the boat. The lack of speed and the buoyancy of her vest brought Erin above the water.

In total shock, she screamed, "Hawk!" Looking at Molly, she yelled, "Take the wheel but don't turn on the engines."

She threw off her sunglasses, stepped one foot on the back end of the boat, and launched herself toward Erin. Jackson swam as fast as she could to her best friend. When she reached her, Erin's face was pale. She grabbed the ski and pulled it off her foot and then tugged on her vest.

"Hawk? Hawk, honey, can you hear me?" She felt for her mouth as she floated, not feeling any air coming out. "She's not breathing!" she screamed to Molly. She grabbed Erin by the vest and, keeping her head above water, dragged her back to the boat. "Hold her!" she yelled to the blonde as she climbed small ladder rungs to get aboard. "On three, we lift her in and lay her down. We need to do CPR on her now! One...two...three!" Both girls held on to Erin and pulled with all their might to get her over the side of the boat. Erin flopped gracelessly to the floor and Jackson immediately undid her vest and began CPR.

She tilted Erin's head back, pinched her nose, and leaned down to breathe twice into her mouth while watching her chest rise. She put her palm down in the middle of her chest between her breasts, covered it with her other hand, and began to pump. "Come on, Hawk, breathe! Breathe, God damn it!" She breathed again into her mouth twice and began to pump.

Molly looked on with frightened eyes, knowing that her jealousy and stupidity might have cost this girl her life.

On the fourth attempt with Jackson pumping on her chest, Erin's mouth filled with water and she coughed and spat it out. As another water-filled cough erupted, she finally took in a lungful of air, much to the relief of the other two. Jackson gently rolled Erin to her side.

"Hawk?" Jackson whispered through her tears, not knowing when she'd begun to cry. Erin's eyes opened, then shut when another round of coughing violently burst from her body. A little more water was released from her lungs and she took another few uneasy breaths.

Erin opened her eyes, not knowing where she was right away.

Jackson leaned on her side to face her. "Hawk, can you hear me?" She pushed the wet hair out of Erin's eyes.

Blinking and staring glassily into the mismatched eyes she loved so much, Erin finally answered, "Jack, is that really you?"

Her eyes filled with tears and she began to cry. Jackson immediately grabbed and held her as they both wept from their fear and facing their mortality for the first time in their young lives. Jackson and Erin clung to each other for several moments while Molly sat and watched.

"It's me, honey, it's me. I gotcha, you're going to be okay," Jackson choked out between sobs. She began to rock Erin back and forth as their hearts slowed to a normal cadence. "I'm right here, Hawk, I'm right here."

In disbelief of all that had just happened in such a short period of time, Molly digested her careless behavior, the accident, and after hearing Jack call to her, put Erin and Hawk together. Not used to being slow on the uptake, she decided to save that bit of information until a later time.

The boat ride back to shore was uneventful. As they pulled into the slip, Jackson saw her aunt and Erin's mother on the pier waiting. Cursing silently, she knew they must have seen at least some of what had happened. She docked the boat, killed the engine, and tied off the cleats.

Katie immediately ran to Erin as she unsteadily exited the boat. "Honey! Are you okay?" She held Erin out at arm's length to look her over. Outside of red-rimmed eyes, her daughter seemed fine, physically.

Erin nodded solemnly and briefly leaned against her mother before walking slowly down the pier. She sat heavily on one of the chairs and stared out into the water.

Katie walked over to Jackson as she was getting the last of the equipment out of the boat. "This is *your* fault! My daughter could have died out there! How reckless and stupid are you?" she shouted, inches from Jackson's astonished face.

"Mrs. Hawkins, I wasn't—"

"Don't you dare tell me what you were and were not doing. I

saw her go down and I saw you dragging her without stopping!"

"Katie, please. I'm sure it didn't happen that way. Jack is very responsible." Jackie tried to defuse the situation, hoping she was right about her niece.

"Oh, really? And just how did it look to you?" She shot daggers at Jackie. "Clearly she *isn't* responsible or this wouldn't have happened. Do you always let her go boating unsupervised like this?"

Molly's soft voice interrupted from behind Jackson's shaking body. "Ma'am, it was my fault."

Katie's eyes shifted from Jackson to Molly. "Who are you?"

"Mm…Molly. I was on lookout and I didn't see her fall right away," she lied. "I told Jackson as soon as I realized she'd gone down. Jack stopped the boat immediately. I'm terribly sorry." She looked into unreadable eyes. "Jack saved her life, please believe that." Molly wasn't sure why she was saying all of this. Perhaps her guilt was winning out, or maybe she just wanted Jackson to hear her defending her.

Katie looked between the two girls then across the pier to Erin, who watched with wide, horrified eyes as her mother made an ass out of herself. "Is that what happened, Erin?"

Erin looked at Jackson and knew without question she had saved her life. "Yes, Mother, Jack saved my life. If she hadn't given me mouth-to-mouth, I wouldn't be here right now." She started to get angry. "Please stop shouting at her like she did something wrong. I don't know what your problem is with her, but she's done…nothing! Leave her alone!" she shouted and ran off the pier to her cottage.

Face red with embarrassment, Katie glanced at everyone around her. "I'm sorry." Looking to Jackson, she said a quick "thank you" and very briskly left the pier.

When she was out of earshot, Molly said, "What a bitch!"

Jackie whirled around to face her. "She saw her daughter almost drown. How do you think a mother would react?" Jackie put her hand out to Jackson. "I want the keys for a while."

Jackson nodded sadly and handed the boat keys to her aunt. She didn't want to touch them anytime soon anyway.

Jackie took the keys and stormed off to the main house, thanking everything holy that Erin hadn't been hurt or killed.

Not able to say much, Jackson turned to Molly. "Look, um, I don't think I'm gonna be very good company right now. You can go if you want."

Molly was not about to let Jackson get rid of her that easily. "No way, Jack. You need me right now. You've had a huge scare. Let me be the one you lean on now." The insinuation of her not being Erin wasn't lost on Jackson. She looked doubtfully at Molly, but her need won out and she nodded.

"I think I need to just relax and sit for a while, if that's okay." Jackson adjusted the skiing equipment in her arms. "Let's put this stuff away and we can go sit up on the roof. Okay?"

"Sounds good. I want to be here for you." Molly put her arm around Jackson's shoulder as they walked down the pier toward the boathouse.

Jackson noticed the unused inner tube and a wave of emotion flowed through her. Desperately aware of how close she was to losing it, she clenched her teeth and motioned to Molly. "Will you roll that in for me?"

Clueless of Jackson's distress, she squeezed her shoulder and smiled. "Of course."

When Joe arrived back from fishing with his friends, he rested his poles on the side of cabin six and walked inside. The first thing he saw was Erin, wrapped in a blanket, sitting on one end of the couch, crying; his wife sat on the other end looking very angry.

"What did I miss?"

His voice penetrated Erin's funk, making her look up. "Oh, Dad!" She flew off the couch and against his body. He immediately wrapped his arms around her and looked to Katie. She glared at her daughter and his eyebrows rose in question.

"We're not coming back next year, Joe. Erin almost died out on the water today," she said tersely.

Joe looked astonished, but waited for more information. "Okay, slow down." He pulled Erin away from him so he could look at her. "What happened, Peanut?"

"She got in—"

"Katie, please; I'd like to hear it from Erin. She's the one who seems upset here."

"Oh, and I'm not upset? You know, maybe if you spent a little more time with her, this could have been prevented," Katie lashed out, needing to release her anger. "I'll be in the kitchen fixing dinner." She got up off the couch and stomped into the other room.

"Come on, Peanut, let's sit down and you can tell me all about it."

The two moved as one as they made their way to the couch to sit. Erin leaned against her father's strong shoulder as his arm wrapped around her. "We went water skiing and there was an accident." When he didn't comment, she continued. "I was doing really great. I got up and everything, Dad," she said proudly.

When she finished telling him what she remembered of the accident, he wrapped his arms tightly around her and kissed the top of her head. "So, your friend Jack is a hero, then."

"Not to Mom. She thinks she's the devil herself," she spat looking toward the kitchen. "Daddy, I just don't get her. Jack is my best friend. Yeah, we had something bad happen today, but she saved my life and still Mom was mean to her."

His jaw muscles worked as Joe warred with conflicting emotions. Katie had become unreasonable when it came to Erin's friendship with Jackson. Anytime her name came up, Katie bristled and either said something rude or changed the subject. He was going to get to the bottom of it before the night was over. Her little tirades were getting very old.

"How are you feeling now? Are you having any trouble breathing? Should we have you looked at?"

"No, Daddy; I'm fine. I'm just wiped out. I think I'm gonna go to my room and take a nap."

He kissed her head again and nodded. "That's a good idea. You'll feel better after a little shut-eye." Erin stood. "I love you, Peanut. I'm glad you're okay."

"Love you, too, Daddy," she said, walking to her room and quietly closing the door.

Joe got up and stood outside of the kitchen giving himself a pep talk. *No good will come of this if I just lay into her.* From the doorway, he saw Katie chopping vegetables for dinner with a butcher knife. *On second thought, maybe now isn't such a good time.* Taking a deep breath, he entered the kitchen.

Katie heard his footsteps and turned, hand on hip. "I want to leave," she said firmly.

"No."

"No?" she asked, incredulous.

"No. Damn it, Katie, we're paid through the month, we're already here, and quite frankly, you're overreacting as usual."

"Overreact—"

"Yes! Okay, so there was an accident. Yes, but that's what it was, an accident. From what Erin told me, Jackson saved her life." When her body clearly stiffened at the mention of Jackson's name, Joe lowered his voice. "What is your problem with her? She's done absolutely nothing but befriend our little girl. Hell, they've been friends since they were kids. Tell me, what is your damn problem?"

"She's not normal, Joe, okay? I've seen the way she is with Erin. It's not right!"

His face took on a look of disbelief. "What in God's name are you talking about?"

"She's a queer, I know it," she hissed. "The way she touches Erin's arm or some part of her when she talks to her. Last night, she had her arm around her on the pier. Oh, but silly me, Erin said she was simply drawing *you* a sunset."

"She did, Katie. It's on the table over there. That was the truth."

"That's not the point!"

Backing up and crossing his arms, he leaned against the counter. "Then tell me—what is the point of this?"

"Didn't you hear me? I think she's a lesbian." The last word came out as a whisper.

"So what, Katie? So what if she is. How does *Jackson* being a lesbian hurt our daughter? Did you see her *force* Erin to kiss her? Did you see her force Erin to do *anything?* She has done nothing to Erin but be her best friend. Nothing, Katie!"

Katie knew she was not going to win the argument, but she'd be damned if she wasn't going to protect her daughter. "Not yet, Joe, but it's coming. You mark my words."

"You're crazy, you know that? Sometimes you just push too damned far!" He pushed off of the counter. "You and Erin have been at each other's throats regarding Jackson for the last year and I'm really growing tired of it." He started out of the kitchen, but stopped and turned to his wife. "And if you think I'm leaving here because you have your head screwed on wrong, you are even more deluded. I came up here for some peace and relaxation, and I'll be damned if your ridiculous imagination will take that from me. If you don't want to stay, then I suggest you rent a car, because we're not leaving."

"We?"

"Yes. You don't think I'm gonna let you take Erin home, do you? She loves it here. The only time she doesn't talk about this place is when we're actually here. Jesus, would you lighten up?"

"No, Joe, I won't lighten up. If you want to see your little girl become the victim of a predator, that's not okay with me. It's not right or natural, what they do. It's not."

"But verbally abusing your daughter *is* right? Don't you see that you are alienating yourself from your daughter? I swear to you, Katie," he took a deep breath, "you need to change the way you treat her or we're going to be making a much bigger decision than where to vacation in the summer."

"Is that a threat?" Her voice was low with menace.

"No, Katie, it's a fact. I will not be able to live with a woman who purposely tries to demean her daughter on a daily basis, especially because of some ridiculous notion she has stuck in her brain!" Deciding to throw fuel on the fire, Joe added, "Let me ask you this, Katie. What if Erin *did* come out one day and say she was a lesbian? What would you do? Would you continue to crucify her? Would you throw her to the wolves? Or would you be supportive and comfort her while she was going through a horribly confusing time in her life? Ask yourself that and you let me know if my 'threat' is out of line."

He stomped into the living room, leaving a slack-jawed Katie to digest her husband's surprising words.

Chapter Six

1990 – The Northwoods Island City

Jackson and Molly were tucked on the roof, sitting on a blanket. Jackson had been extremely quiet since they had climbed up there. A couple of hours had passed, with Molly trying to make small chitchat just so she would talk to her. They had gone to get some dinner earlier when Molly got hungry. Jackson brooded in the car the entire trip and only spoke to say what she wanted in the drive-through lane. Other than that, Molly had done all the talking, much to Jackson's aggravation.

Molly had tried to get Jackson to play her recorder or something to take her mind off of what had happened. Jackson didn't want anything to do with anything at that moment.

"What are you feeling? Talk to me, sweetie." Molly stroked Jackson's back with her fingertips.

Jackson sighed for the millionth time, not wanting to talk to Molly. She was dying to talk to Erin about the accident, wanted to know how she was. Something. She felt numb and wanted the hurt she was feeling to go away. Her fear of Katie Hawkins had kept her away from cabin six.

"Look, I told you hours ago that I wasn't going to be good company. I really don't feel like talking." *To you.*

"I know, Jack, but you'll feel better."

Sighing with annoyance, Jackson said, "Hey, you've got that cooler in your trunk. What I'd really like is a cold beer. That just *might* make me feel better."

Finally having something to make her girlfriend happy, Molly jumped up to retrieve the small cooler from her car. Jackson watched her climb down the ladder as she looked out over the water. The sun had set and she just wanted the peace that she knew would come from sitting up there. Jackson's thoughts were filled with the memories of seeing Erin's lifeless body in the boat—images that would stay with her forever. It was the worst experience she'd ever had in her short life and one she didn't want to encounter ever again. The only thing setting her mind at ease was that it was she who had saved Erin's life. All of the lifeguard and CPR training her aunt made her go through had paid off. After many lectures about the liability of the resort, Jackson finally acquiesced to the training and now was so glad she had. Erin was alive. The alternative was something she couldn't even imagine. Nor did she want to.

Hearing Molly's footsteps on the ladder brought Jackson back to the present. *A cold beer, that is definitely going to hit the spot.* When Molly brought up the twelve-pack out of the cooler, Jackson's eyes lit up.

Molly plopped the wet cardboard box down between them. "The ice had melted and got this all soaked. I just grabbed this to make the climb easier. She pulled out a bottle and gave it to Jackson, who immediately twisted the cap off and downed a significant amount in one swallow.

"Ahh, that's the stuff right there," she said, then belched loudly, to her own amusement.

"Oh gross, Jack. You sound like my dad."

Jackson downed her beer in a matter of minutes then reached for another. She opened a second bottle, planning to drink it more slowly than the first. Molly was only halfway done with her first. Jackson took a deep calming breath, feeling better than she had in hours. She took a long look over the water. "It is so beautiful here."

Molly scooted closer to her and draped an arm around her. "Yes, it is."

"Thanks for bringing the beer. I didn't think I was gonna want it, but now I'm really glad it's here." She leaned over and lightly kissed Molly's lips. "I'm sorry for being so moody."

Molly's insides swirled at the tone of Jackson's voice. She knew the alcohol was mellowing her out and she'd soon be pliable. Molly had never met anyone, especially not a girl, who could kiss like Jackson. She couldn't wait to taste those lips again.

Erin had been lying in bed for several minutes after waking from her nap. Her eyes adjusted slowly, realizing that night had fallen. Her father had come in a couple hours prior asking if she wanted dinner. Shaking her head, she opted to sleep more instead. The boating accident had really scared her, and as much as she wanted to see Jackson to talk about it, she knew it would just create more problems with her mother.

Flashes of her accident stormed her dreams. She had woken with a start after the last one and decided to stay awake. She watched the movement of the shadows on her bedroom wall. There was a slight breeze moving the tree branches outside of her room. A full moon was shining brightly through the open window. The temperature, like the day, was perfect—not too hot and not too cool. Her bladder dictated her next move and she got up to use the bathroom. When she opened the door, she saw her dad asleep on the couch in front of the television. Thinking that her mother had gone to bed, she continued to the bathroom.

As she approached the door, her mother came out of the bedroom. "Hi, honey. How are you feeling?"

"A little draggy, but much better. Sleep did wonders for me."

Katie touched her hair, gently tucking it behind an ear. "I'm so glad you weren't hurt today."

A small smile made its way to Erin's mouth. She was waiting for the snakes to appear in her mother's hair. They never came. "Thanks, Mom."

Katie pulled her daughter into a heartfelt hug. "I thought I heard you out here, so I wanted to say goodnight. I love you, honey. I was really scared today; I didn't mean to embarrass you."

A genuine smile reached Erin's lips. "I love you too, Mom. I think everyone was a little on edge after what happened." She closed her eyes and took a deep breath, soaking in the comfort her mother was giving. "I think I'm gonna walk out on the pier. The moon is full tonight and I really want to sketch it." The two pulled out of their hug. Seeing the disapproval on her mother's face, she said, "I'm not going to see Jack, Mom; I promise. I just want to sketch and take some of the awful imagery out of my head."

Feeling badly, Katie nodded. "I'm sorry. Just be careful, and don't stay out too late, all right?"

"Sure, Mom. Wake Dad, though. He's starting to snore out there. He's gonna scare the wildlife." They shared a smile and Erin bade her mother goodnight.

After using the facilities, Erin brushed her teeth and her hair to rid herself of sleep. She wanted to sketch the moonlight on the water and didn't want to miss a thing due to tiredness.

She walked into her room and grabbed her pack of supplies and her sketchbook. She watched as her mom ushered her dad off the couch. "G'night, Dad."

"Where you off to, Peanut?" he asked in a sleep-garbled voice.

"Just to the pier to do some drawing. I won't be out late." She walked over and gave him a kiss on his cheek. "See you in the morning."

"Night, Peanut."

Erin left the cabin and walked to the pier. Grabbing one of the chairs, she positioned herself directly in front of the full moon, marveling at its glory. It was huge, larger than she could remember seeing a moon. She grabbed her sketchbook and a pencil and began to draw.

Jackson was already on her fifth beer when Molly finished her second beer. She was feeling a little wasted and knew Jackson was way beyond that. Since she'd consumed the fourth bottle, she had been kissing Molly passionately. Molly had pulled back from the force of her mouth the last time. Jackson's passion was consuming, overwhelming her.

Trying to dilute some of Jackson's intensity, Molly suggested, "Jack, what do you say we go skinny-dipping? No one's out here. The water will feel great against our bodies, don't you think?"

She waggled her eyebrows at an intoxicated Jackson.

"Naked, water, and you? Hell, yeah. Let's go!" Jackson jumped up and climbed down the ladder, swinging her body into the loft. Molly was on her heels and soon in the loft with her. Jackson pulled her close and kissed her again. "I can't wait to feel you naked against me," she panted.

"Me too," Molly replied.

They climbed down the second ladder and started removing their clothes. Jackson watched as Molly slowly removed her sleeveless top, reached around and unclasped her bra and let it fall to the floor. Jackson drank in the sight of the bare breasts. Molly pushed off the rest of her clothing, presenting herself to Jackson's appreciative eyes.

Jackson unceremoniously took her clothes off in half a second. Her tall, lean frame was illuminated by the moonlight. Extending her hand to Jackson, Molly walked closer to the naked loveliness that was her girlfriend. "God, you are gorgeous, Jack," she said. "Come on, let's get in the water."

Jackson took her hand and they walked to the edge of the boat docks. She knew the water was very shallow so she stepped in. Molly followed, gasping as the cool water touched her skin.

"Come on, this feels fantastic." Jackson trotted out into the water and when it was deep enough, she dove under. She swam a few strokes then broke the plane of the water. Molly swam after her, giggling all the while. They splashed and laughed and were soon chasing each other. Jackson knew she probably shouldn't be swimming while buzzed, but at that moment, she didn't care. At the moment, she wasn't feeling badly about the accident. Right now was about Molly, and her nakedness, and wanting to feel it against her.

She ducked under the water and sprouted up in front of a surprised Molly. "Boo!"

Molly shrieked and splashed Jackson for scaring her. Jackson grabbed her splashing hand and brought it behind her neck. "Come here."

Jackson kissed Molly, earning her a deep groan. She brought her arms around Molly and when their bodies met, she knew nothing but the sensations flowing through her core.

Erin's pencil was flying across the page. Her hands had found an incredible rhythm and her moon on the water had begun to take amazing shape. She'd been sitting out there for over an hour, but the breeze and her surroundings kept her glued to her seat. She closed her eyes and just breathed in the clean fresh air.

She watched as a few boats went under the bridge and on to their destinations. The crickets were chirping, and she'd even heard a bullfrog. Off in the distance she heard a fish jump out of the water with a big splash. Wishing her dad were next to her with his fishing pole, she smiled and continued with her nearly complete drawing.

She heard another splash, this time closer. Erin looked to her right to see if she could see the fish. She focused around the boathouse, the direction from which she'd heard the splashing. She was right about the direction of the sound, though it wasn't a fish. It was a very loud and a very naked woman running through the water. As she watched, the first woman was joined by another. *Oh, my, they're skinny-dipping.* She smiled, a little flushed, and tried not to watch. The smile soon left her face when she heard Jackson's voice. Her head shot up, stomach in knots, and it didn't take her long to figure out whom she was with. She ducked beside the chair next to her, trying not to be seen.

She watched as Jackson and Molly frolicked happily through the lake. *I can't believe they're naked!* She watched Jackson dive under the water. Molly was closer to the dock, but her back was turned. Jackson popped up in front of Molly with a playful "Boo!" She heard Molly scream and saw her begin to splash Jackson. As the next action played out, her mind rolled it in slow motion. Jackson grabbed Molly's splashing hand and placed it behind her neck and brought Molly's mouth to hers in a passionate kiss. Not believing her eyes, Erin rubbed them with curled fists. Blinking rapidly, she couldn't mistake the sounds of desire coming from the two naked girls. A wave of emotion struck her, confusion.

Jack's a...a lesbian? Like Jackie?

Erin didn't know what to think. Some of the pieces of Jack's omissions were starting to fall into place. Anger at the lack of truth from her best friend was resonating through her. *Why didn't she tell me? I'm her best friend. We're supposed to tell each other everything!*

She watched as Jackson took possession of Molly's mouth, cradling her face with her hands, bringing her impossibly closer. A shot of arousal flared through her body along with a jolt of jealous anger. She debated whether to leave while they were locked in their kiss, or just wait it out.

Patience won out as she tried not to watch the scene unfold. Jackson pulled away from Molly and motioned to the boathouse. With a nod, Molly followed Jackson. As they were headed to the boathouse, Erin decided to also take her leave. When she got up off the pier floor, her foot knocked into the chair, creating a slight scuffing sound. She quickly collected her things and, as quietly as she could, ran off the pier.

Hearing the scuff of the chair against the dock, Molly turned and watched Erin fleeing the pier. She smiled victoriously, knowing that Erin must have seen an eyeful.

Jackson was feeling no pain. Things were starting to blur a little, but that was fine with her. The more she wasn't reminded of things, the better. Sharing wet, passionate kisses with Molly had driven all rational thought from her mind. She just wanted to feel the glorious oblivion that came with orgasm.

The two naked women collected their discarded clothing and retreated to the loft. Jackson laid down the blanket and Molly was soon sprawled across it. Jackson instantly laid her naked body on top and positioned one of Molly's legs between her own. Groaning at the contact, Jackson began to grind against Molly's thigh. She looked down at the body that was giving her pleasure. Molly's eyes were shut as she pressed her body against Jackson's. Jackson closed her eyes and moved back and forth against Molly. When she opened her eyes, she didn't see Molly, only Erin. Her addled mind was in overdrive. Erin was giving her this pleasure; Erin was receiving the same from her. Her movements became quicker, stronger. Jackson could feel the beginnings of her orgasm. Putting her elbows on either side of Molly's head she began to thrust in earnest.

"God, you feel good." She thrust again and again until she felt the warmth begin to spread through her body. "Oh, Hawk, yes, yes…" Jackson's hips moved at a blinding speed as her climax washed over her. As her body slowed, she tried to calm her racing heart. She lifted her head to look into baby blue eyes, only to find angry brown ones staring back at her. Trying to catch her breath, Jackson rasped, "What's wrong?"

"Get off," Molly spat, pushing Jackson's limp body off of hers.

"Molly, honey, what's wrong?"

"Oh, now you remember my name?" Molly stood and started to put her clothing on.

"What are you talking about?" Jackson demanded, sitting up.

"What I'm *talking* about is that I don't appreciate hearing your little friend's name coming out of your mouth when I'm the one having sex with you!"

Jackson frantically tried to remember saying Erin's name, but had no idea if she had or hadn't. She didn't know what to say. "I—"

"You're a piece of work, Jackson Thomas," she said angrily, putting on the rest of her clothes.

"Molly, I'm sorry!" she blurted. "I had no idea."

Exasperated, Molly ran her fingers through her hair. "That's your problem, Jack, you are just *clueless*! It's so obvious that you're in love with her. Even I could see it, and I've only been around you two for a day!"

"I…" she began. *I am in love with her. Aw, crap.* Jack's head slumped in realization.

"Go to hell, Jack." Molly stormed down the ladder, leaving her erstwhile lover alone to stew in her drunken nakedness.

Lying back on the blanket, Jackson threw her arm over her eyes, grumbling a litany of curses to the wind.

Back inside her room, Erin let the tears fall. Her cheeks were soaking wet by the time she landed on her bed. The image of a naked Jackson kissing Molly was haunting her. She couldn't understand why Jackson hadn't told her about that aspect of her life. She flipped onto her stomach and the sobbing continued into her pillow. *She lied to me.*

That thought made her question almost every facet of their relationship. They had been friends since 1985, but even though Erin had shared every miniscule thing of her life with Jackson, Jackson hadn't done the same. *Was she writing me letters because she felt she had to? Does she hang out with me because she thinks she has to? Am I no more than just a guest to her? Even Jackie introduced me to Sandra as Jackson's favorite guest and not her friend. But Jack told me I was her best friend. God, I really am just the kid Molly said I was.*

The thought of Molly and Jackson making fun of her made her stomach ache. She remembered Jackson telling her that she hung out with Molly all summer, which was why she hadn't written.

Bull. She just didn't want to tell me that she and Molly were girlfriends. Jack even changed her eye color because Molly didn't like her eyes! Yuck. What does she even see in Molly?

Erin's mind was racing over every detail of the day. Jackson always seemed to make her question her decisions, just like a little kid. She'd asked if she was sure she wanted to water ski, she'd said she didn't have to drink if she didn't want to. In the same breath, Jackson had defended her whenever Molly was rude to her. *God, what do I think? Okay, Jack is a lesbian. I think I could be okay with that. She and Molly are obviously girlfriends. Uggh, damn it, Jack, why didn't you just tell me?*

Deciding she needed an outlet for her feelings, she took out her sketchbook and began to draw in earnest. Objects and figures matching the imagery in her head began to take shape on the page. Time ticked on and after some intense drawing and shading, Erin's picture was finished. She stared at her creation and marveled at its accuracy. With a final scribble at the bottom, she rolled up the drawing and fished in her pack for a rubber band to secure it.

With a glance at the clock, she was surprised how far into the early morning it was. Sleep did not come to her at all. The sun would be out in an hour, so she would wait to watch the sun come up and pray this day would go better than the day before. The niggling question was how was she going to handle seeing Jackson again after last night? Jackson had no idea that Erin saw her with Molly. Erin wondered if she could possibly pretend that nothing had happened, that everything was great and normal. She wasn't confident she could pull it off, but she had over three weeks left at Island City, so she had to make the best of the time.

Erin lay in bed until the daylight began to lighten her room. She got up and quietly left the cabin to watch the sunrise from the dock. The colors that came were incredible. She watched as life began its new day around her. It filled her with awe. The awe expanded when she saw a hawk circle in the sky above her. A sad smile formed on her lips. She wished she could see this every day, but sadly, after last night, she wasn't even sure if she wanted to be there any longer.

Sitting on the pier, she heard some cars pulling into the pebbled drive of the resort. She turned in her seat and saw two cars pull up and watched as a man got out and walked toward her cabin. Her mother answered the door and spoke with the gentleman briefly before shaking his hand. He gave her some papers then left in the second automobile.

Erin walked back to the waterfront cabin and stepped inside. She glanced with confusion at her mother's bags, packed and sitting by the door. "Mom, what's going on?"

Surprised by her daughter's arrival, she equivocated. "Where did you come from?" Her voice took on an edge. "You haven't been out all night, have you?"

Rolling her eyes, Erin answered, "No, Mom. I couldn't sleep and I watched the sunrise from the pier. I got in hours ago. I was awake from my big nap yesterday so I spent the time drawing." She gestured at the assembled luggage and repeated, "So, what's going on?"

"I'm leaving."

Eyes wide, Erin responded, "Why? Where's Dad?"

"He's still in bed." She had hoped to be gone before either Erin or her husband was up, so she had to improvise her explanation. "Your father and I had a strong discussion about some things yesterday. I wanted us to leave after the accident. I don't think this place is the best for us anymore. Your father didn't want to leave since he enjoys fishing up here so much, and I knew not to ask you since I *know* all too well how you feel about this place. Your father will bring you home." She paused. "I rented a car from a man who runs a dealership in town; that's who that man was. I'm driving home today."

God, could this be so easy? "Well, honestly, Mom, I'm not feeling that great, with the accident and all," she lied. "It...it wouldn't be a bad thing for me to go back with you, would it? I mean, I can stay if you want, um..."

Katie's eyes lit up like a brush fire across a mountaintop. She didn't believe what she was hearing, so she confirmed it. "You want to leave? I thought you loved it here."

Head down, Erin responded, "I do...but, um...yesterday was a really bad day, Mom. I don't know if I want to be here right now." That was a half-truth, but she knew her mother would be over the moon with her decision.

"Well, let's get you packed and we can be out of here before traffic starts to be an issue." It wasn't even seven o'clock yet.

Erin quickly got her things together. She wrote a brief letter to her dad explaining she wasn't feeling well and opted to go home with her mother. She wished him well and signed off. She laid it on top of the moonlight picture she had drawn on the pier the night before.

They packed the car and were just about to leave when Erin remembered her rolled drawing from last night. Looking to her mother, she asked, "Mom, I drew something for Jack, but I don't want to wake her to say goodbye. I'm just gonna run to the boathouse and leave it for her there. I know she'll get it. Okay?"

Ecstatic that her daughter was going to leave with her, at that moment she would've let her do anything. "Just hurry up, if we leave now we can be home by early afternoon."

"Thanks, Mom." Erin reached into her backpack and pulled out the rolled up drawing to take to Jack. Running to the boathouse, her heart was hammering. After last night, this place made her feel a little queasy. It could've been from her lack of sleep, but she wasn't too sure. She climbed up the ladder and saw the blanket laid out, empty beer bottles littered around. Not wanting to imagine any more than she already had, she laid the drawing on top of the blanket. With one final look through the window at the water, she descended the ladder and hurried to meet her mother.

Exhaustion hit her as soon as she took a seat inside the rental car. Her mother pulled out of the drive and made their way to the highway, heading for home. With the motion of the car, Erin felt her eyelids close. "Mom, I'm sorry, but I think I'm gonna pass out. I didn't sleep last night."

Smiling and giving her a brief glance, Katie touched her daughter's knee. "Go ahead and rest, honey. We've got six hours ahead of us; you may as well sleep through as much of it as you can."

Not wanting to really spend the time talking to her mother anyway, she agreed wholeheartedly. "Thanks," she said softly, fading into a deep, dreamless sleep.

Joe woke up to silence. Getting out of bed, he made his way into an empty family room. Opening Erin's door, he saw that her bed was made and her ever-present backpack missing. *She must have gone out to draw.*

He went to the bathroom to clean up and start his day. In the kitchen he found that Katie had left some bagels and cream cheese for him in the refrigerator. *She must have gone into town.* He grabbed the carton of orange juice and sneaked several sips out of the container then put it back on the shelf.

Grabbing the bagels and spread, he took them to the kitchen table where he found a drawing Erin had made of a large moon on the water. There was a note attached. He smiled softly until he read the note.

Dear Dad,

I'm sorry you and Mom had a fight. She didn't tell me what it was about. She just said she wanted to leave. She rented a car this morning and after my scare yesterday, I really didn't want to stay here either. I'm not feeling too great, so I think it will be best if I go back home. Mom said it was okay, so I decided to leave with her.

Have fun with your fishing buddies, I hope you catch "the big one." I'll call you when I get home. See you in a few weeks.

I love you,
Peanut
PS - Please tell Jack I left something for her in the boathouse.

"Damn you, Katie." Joe crumpled up his daughter's note and stalked into his room to get dressed.

Jackson awoke to pounding. She soon realized the pounding was inside her skull. Opening her eyes cautiously, she immediately slammed her lids shut against the brightness of the morning sun. As she slowly returned to full consciousness, the memories of the previous day hit her like a Mack truck: the almost drowning, the confrontation with Erin's mom, the drunken skinny-dipping with Molly. Then she visualized the sexual act that had brought on Molly's anger and quick departure.

"Uggh," she moaned aloud, thinking of the situation with Molly.

She remembered what Molly had said right before telling her to go to hell and storming out. *It's so obvious that you're in love with her. Even I could see it and I've only been around you two for a day!*

"Oh, God," she grunted, throwing both arms over her head. "Hawk," she whispered. "How do I tell you that I'm in love with you?"

Jackson slowly got up, showered, muttered some indecipherable words to Jackie and left her house in search of Erin. She walked down to the pier hoping she would be there drawing or something. Not finding her, she thought she'd take the chance she'd be in the cabin. Walking up to the door, she braced herself for another confrontation with Katie Hawkins.

"Here goes..." she whispered, and then knocked lightly on the cabin door.

After a few moments, Joe answered. Smiling brightly, he said, "Hey, Jackson. Good morning to you."

"Good morning to you, too, sir."

Joe stopped her with his hand. "Jackson, how many times do I need to tell you: call me Joe. I appreciate the 'sir' and everything, but I'm just Joe, okay?"

His smile was so much like Erin's, her heart melted. "All right, Joe. Please call me Jack, then. I insist." She chuckled along with him.

"Fair enough."

"I was wondering if Erin was here. I didn't see her on the docks this morning."

His face fell. "She must not have told you."

"Told me? Told me what?" Jackson's heart started to pound.

"She and her mother rented a car and drove home today. The boating scare really shook her up. She and her mother left before the birds got up."

"Oh, I see," she barely got out, her stomach in knots. Not knowing what else to say, she started to leave. "Okay, um, I'll see you around then."

"Hey, Jack?" he said, making her turn around. "I almost forgot to tell you, Erin said she left you something in the boathouse."

Her eyes lit up instantly. "She did?"

"I have no idea what it is, but she said it was up there for you."

Smiling a little wider, Jackson replied, "Thanks, Joe. See ya 'round."

"'Bye."

Jackson ran to the boathouse. She could smell the stale beer from the ground floor and it made her stomach churn. She quickly climbed the stairs and jumped into the loft. Looking past the scattered beer bottles, she spotted a rolled up sketchbook page resting on the blanket.

She reached down and picked it up with shaky fingers, slowly rolling down the rubber band. When she unrolled the page, her heart sank. It was a vivid picture of Jackson holding Molly's face in a passionate kiss. There was no mistaking who these two people were. Tears welling in her eyes, she scanned down to the bottom of the drawing to the single word in bold.

WHY?

That one word asked a million questions Jackson was nowhere near ready to answer. Her heart was pounding so fast she thought she was going to have a heart attack. She had tried to keep this a secret, only to have her best friend catch her in the act. Anger at herself for not simply telling Erin about her newfound sexuality, bubbled to the surface. Anger at Molly's games when Erin was around flamed through her.

Jackson was filled with so much anger she opened her mouth and screamed hoarsely, "Fuck!" The birds in the surrounding trees scattered at the sound. With wracking sobs, Jackson crumpled onto the blanket and cried until exhaustion took her to sleep.

When Jackson woke, it was mid-afternoon. Her eyes were swollen from crying and her head felt heavy. The emotional turmoil around her was deafening. She wanted to run away from it all, find a place where it didn't hurt so much. *God, I'm so sorry, Hawk. So, so sorry.*

Completely on autopilot, she climbed down from the loft and into the boathouse. Jackson's brain was so muddled she had no idea what she was doing. She aimlessly found her house and entered.

Seeing the lost and damaged look in her niece's eyes, Jackie immediately went to her. "Honey, what is it? You look like... I don't know what you look like, but it's not good. What happened?"

Jackson met the blue eyes of her aunt and instantly fell into her arms. "She's gone...it's my fault...now she's gone..." Her weeping came in huge wracking sobs.

Not understanding, Jackie held her niece tightly until she could figure out what she was talking about. Jackie moved them over to the couch so Jackson could lay her head in her lap. Sandra poked her head in from the kitchen to find out what was going on. Jackie shook her head and with her eyes said, *I don't know yet. Ask me later.*

Jackie continued to rock Jackson on the couch as she cried

out her heart's pain. Jackie repeatedly thanked everything holy that she didn't have to be a teenager again. There was just way too much that went on for them to handle things gracefully—new responsibility, major peer pressure, hormones raging… Throw in discovering one was a lesbian and it was a nice breakdown sandwich.

The sobs finally began to slow into whimpers, which eventually stopped altogether. Jackson's breathing slowed and her heart returned to a normal cadence. She wasn't sure how much she wanted to tell Jackie. Though, she figured wryly, collapsing on her aunt's lap might warrant a brief explanation. She held Jackie's knee as her head rested on her thigh.

Jackie let her stay on her lap, knowing whatever happened must have been bad to stir this kind of emotion in Jackson.

"Is being gay always this hard, Jackie?" she whispered.

"What do you mean, honey?" Jackie asked gently.

"When people find out, do they always leave you?" Her body began to shake and the whimpering cries began again.

"Oh, Jack, no, not always. Sometimes, but not always." She ran her fingers through Jackson's sweat-dampened hair, trying to soothe her niece's distress. "Is that what happened? Does Erin know you're gay?" A small nod of her head answered the question. She tilted her head back and leaned it against the couch cushion, breathing out a slow breath. *Damn.*

"She left today, went home."

Head moving upright, Jackie was confused. "What do you mean she left? I saw Joe down on the docks today."

Jackson shrugged. "Joe stayed here, but Hawk left with her mom and they went home." She sighed and slowly sat up with her aunt's assistance. She hung her head and put her face in her hands. Scrubbing her face, Jackson took a deep breath while her aunt rubbed her back. "I really gotta figure some stuff out." She leaned back and gave her aunt a kiss on her cheek. "Thanks for listening."

Jackson got up and walked slowly to her room, closing the door behind her. Sandra heard her leave and entered the living room. "What's going on?" she whispered.

"Erin found out about Jack. Evidently something happened, I have no idea what, but Erin left with her mother today."

Sandra's eyes went wide with surprise. "Really?" She shook her head. "I thought she'd be okay with Jack being gay, I really did. She seemed the type of friend to stay with Jack no matter what."

"I agree. I think there's more to it than that. I'm sure little Miss Molly had something to do with it."

"Bitch," Sandra whispered. "What does Jack see in her?"

Shrugging her shoulders, Jackie said, "You know how it is when you're that age. You find that one other person who's just like you and somehow you connect. I don't see them lasting long." She winked at Sandra. "At least I hope not."

"Amen, sister." She kissed her temple. "You're such a good mom to her, you know that?"

Jackie smiled warmly. "Thank you, that's probably the nicest thing you've ever said to me. I know my sister would've loved to seen her little girl grow up. I don't know how she would've dealt with the gay thing, but who knows. I'm just glad I'm here for Jack. I love her like she was my own."

"And it shows." The two women shared another small kiss. "It really does."

Jackson went to her bed and laid down, hands behind her head in deep thought. *Okay, I have to figure out a way to make this right. I owe Hawk an explanation. She wouldn't even stay long enough to say goodbye. I can't really blame her, though.*

"I know!" she sat up. "I'll call her and tell her…" She blew out an exasperated breath. "What could I possibly say to her to make this all better?" She lay back down with a thud. *Oh, I know. 'Hi, Hawk, it's your lesbo friend, Jack. I'm sorry I didn't tell you I like chicks but I do, and you're at the top of my list…' Yeah, that'll work. Not!* Rolling her eyes at her own idiocy, Jackson cleared her mind to concentrate.

When nothing came to her, she got up, grabbed her oboe case, and went to the boathouse. *Maybe playing some music will help.* Climbing up the ladder, she stopped in the loft and looked around at the mess. Shaking her head, she went up the second ladder only to find more bottles up there. "Jesus!"

She picked up all the garbage and put it in what was left of the cardboard box the beer came in. Taking it down the stairs, she walked to the big dumpster and trashed the beer carton. She climbed back to the loft and reached for her oboe, but stopped, trying hard not to look at Erin's drawing of Molly and herself. Feeling anger swell in her belly, she picked up the drawing and ripped it into shreds. Taking the torn paper and stuffing it in her shorts pocket, she grabbed her oboe and went to the roof.

She assembled her instrument, hung her legs over the side, and began to play. The tune started out slow and sad, like her mood. She began to think about Erin and all they'd shared since they'd become friends. Before she knew it, she was playing the song she'd written for her, 'Hawks in Flight.' Eyes closed, the melody washed over her like a warm blanket. Serenity almost followed. Almost.

Her thoughts began to swirl in earnest and built in intensity. She was imagining her life without Erin in it and she couldn't do it. Erin was such a large part of her life she knew she had to figure out a way to apologize and hopefully get Erin to trust her again. That would be the hardest part. Once trust was lost, it was nearly impossible to gain it back. She would just have to show Erin how far she was willing to go to get her back in her life.

"That's it." She stopped playing. "I'll show her how much she means to me. I don't care what her mother thinks. She's my best friend and I'm going to get her back."

Jackson's mind was plotting her next move. She knew her plan was extreme, but she was desperate. Jackie was going to be less than pleased with her once she realized what she was doing, but Jackson knew she had to do something drastic. She grabbed her wallet and shoved it into her pants pocket. She finished her note to Jackie and quietly walked to the kitchen table, then left it for her to read in the morning. Taking the keys off the coffee table, Jackson tucked her directions from the motor club into her pocket and left the house as quiet as a mouse.

Walking to her car, she realized Jackie was going to have a fit and would probably take her car away. At this point, she didn't care. She would find Erin, tell her everything, and hope she would understand. Inside the small gray Honda, Jackson closed her door and put on her seatbelt. Looking at her gas gauge, she knew she'd have to stop to fuel up before making serious mileage into Illinois. She turned over the engine, put the car into reverse, backed up slowly, turned the wheel toward the exit, found first gear, and left the resort.

Once she reached the small two-lane highway, she put in an Indigo Girls CD and sped down to the local Amoco. She filled up the tank, grabbed a couple of sodas for the road, and she was off. She drove down Highway 51 at eighty-seven miles an hour, hoping to God she wouldn't get a speeding ticket. Changing the CD to Melissa Etheridge, she laughed at the absurdity of music listened to by a newly identified lesbian. *Could I get any more stereotypical?* Laughing to herself, she belted out the songs as they played through her speakers.

She'd downed her first soda shortly into her third hour on the road and knew she'd have to stop to relieve herself before too long. Knowing she should be dead on her feet at four in the morning, she was strangely wide-awake. She let the music keep her going as she changed lanes on the highway. She'd been on I-90 for over a hundred miles and knew she'd be at Erin's within the hour.

As she got closer to Erin's house, she accepted the realization that she hadn't thought about how to get past Katie Hawkins to talk to Erin once she arrived. *I'll just have to get creative. I'm not turning back now. God, I hope this wasn't a mistake.*

Paldeer, Illinois – 5:02 a.m.

"One ninety-eight...two hundred...two twelve...two thirty-six...two fifty-two! There you are," Jackson spoke to herself, finding Erin's pale yellow ranch house. Pulling the car up to the curb of the house beside Erin's, she released her brake, put the car in gear, and turned off the engine. She looked slowly around the nice neighborhood. It was extremely quiet and the sun had yet to make an entrance into the day. She grabbed her keys and quietly opened and closed the car door. Walking around to the side of Erin's house, she was grateful for the bright moon. Full last night, but its rays continued to light her way.

Jackson walked around the house, looking in every window to find Erin's bedroom. A sharp noise to her right made her flip around to face a man hauling his garbage to the curb.

He noticed her walking around the Hawkins' home and, deciding she wasn't going to be much of a threat, approached. "Hey! What are you doing out here?" he asked loudly.

Heart racing, Jackson was trying to think of a reason she'd be snooping outside Erin's house at five in the morning.

"Hi, I'm sorry to scare you," she whispered. "I'm a good friend of Erin's, you know, next door?"

"Okay," he said, still wary.

"I live in Wisconsin and I don't get to see her much, but, um... her birthday is today and I wanted to surprise her by taking her out to breakfast." *Way to go, Jack!*

"Oh!" The man smiled. "That's very kind of you. You wouldn't be Jack, would you?"

Her eyes widened with fear. Perhaps Katie Hawkins had put out a neighborhood watch on her. Cautious, she replied, "Yes, I am."

"Oh, little Erin talks about you all the time! All we ever hear about is her friend Jack who lives in an island city or something."

Jackson smiled with relief. "The Island City is our resort. My aunt and I live there."

"Well, I think it's great you've come to surprise her." He pointed to the house. "But you're looking at the wrong end for her room. That's her mother's room on this side. Erin's room faces the rear of the house in the basement. Here, I'll show you." He started to usher Jackson to his backyard.

Could this be so easy? Unless this joker is going to kill me with no witnesses around. She tightened the grip on her keys, just in case the latter was true.

"Just be quiet. God knows you don't want to wake Katie up."

Well, well, well, Katie has quite a reputation, doesn't she? Smiling to herself, she followed the neighbor to his yard. Directing her through the shrubs, he pointed to a large double window in the basement. A small light was shining through the glass.

"I see it. Thank you…?"

"Richard. Richard Henderson. My boy Ricky is friends with Erin." A lightbulb went off in her head and a memory flashed before her eyes.

I told my neighbor Ricky that I was going there for vacation again and he called you a cheesehead.

"Ricky?"

"Yep. Has Erin mentioned him to you?" He had hopes that one day Erin would date his son.

"Once in a letter. Apparently he called me a cheesehead." She smiled. "Tell him that the cheesehead said hello."

He shook his head and chuckled with Jackson. "I will. Have fun, and wish Erin a happy birthday for us."

"Will do." *When it's her birthday, I'll mention I saw you.*

Jackson walked stealthily toward Erin's window. Crouching down, she looked inside and on her bedside table, saw a small reading lamp on. Erin's full-sized bed was in the center of the back wall and she was sleeping in the middle of it, a book lying next to her. Taking a deep breath, she raised her hand to knock. "Here goes…" With a light tap on the glass, she saw Erin stir but not wake. Tapping a little louder, she roused Erin from sleep.

A sleepy head rose off the pillow and slowly looked around. Looking at the window, she had to stop herself from screaming at the silhouette she saw there.

When Jackson saw Erin look her way, she immediately began to wave to try and dispel her fear.

As Erin's vision cleared, she wondered if she was dreaming or if Jackson was really outside her window. Getting up out of bed, she walked slowly toward the apparition. Turning on a light, her suspicions were confirmed; it was her friend on the other side of the glass.

Sliding open the window, she breathed in the fresh air coming through the screen. "Jack, what are you doing here?" she whispered, not sure which emotion she was feeling. Confusion, joy, anger, surprise, she just wasn't sure.

"I had to see you," Jackson whispered. "I couldn't leave things like that between us without talking to you."

"You can't come in here! My mother will kill you! I'm not kidding, Jack, I don't know what her deal is with you, but it won't be a good thing if she finds you here." Erin desperately tried to explain the severity of her mother's ire.

"Then don't let her find me. Come on, Hawk, I need to try to explain. I *know* you're hurt and angry, but I have to try." She stared into blue eyes and hoped she was right about her trip. "Please?"

Erin looked into the pleading eyes that made her heart hammer and knew she was lost. She pressed the latch on her screen and slid it open. She helped Jackson through the small opening and guided her feet to the floor. Closing the window, Erin turned to find a nervous, fidgety Jackson. *Unbelievable.*

"Can I um...use your bathroom first? I've had to pee for over two hours. I just didn't want to stop."

Still in shock, Erin nodded dumbly and pointed to the door connecting her room to the bath.

Erin sat on her bed as Jackson went to relieve herself. She unconsciously started to smooth down her sleep-tousled hair, and to her horror, knew she must have awful morning mouth. Quickly reaching into the drawer of her bedside table, she grabbed a container of breath mints and threw a couple in her mouth for good measure. Hearing the toilet flush, she knew Jackson would be emerging soon. *Oh, God...*

Oh, God... Jackson looked at her disheveled appearance in the mirror. Taking a deep breath, she realized her breath was less than stellar. Seeing the toothpaste on the vanity counter, she dabbed a small amount on her finger and lightly rubbed it on her teeth and tongue. She rinsed her mouth and spat the paste down the drain. Taking a few swallows of water, she knew this was going to be a very scary conversation and one she hoped would go her way. Grabbing the doorknob with more confidence than she felt, she pulled it open to face Erin.

Sharing a nervous smile between them, Erin motioned for Jackson to sit next to her on the bed. Jackson automatically went to that spot and sat down. Her hands were folded tightly together. She looked over to Erin, who hadn't looked over at her. She noted her jaw muscles working.

"Before I say anything else, Hawk, I want to apologize for the way you found out about me. It was wrong and I'm sorry I didn't tell you."

Erin turned. "Why didn't you?" she asked softly.

"I was terrified. I've known for so long that I was different from other girls, but only this year did I actually understand what that difference was. God, the girls in my school are so awful. If you don't have the right shoes with the right skirt with the right shirt and hang with the right people, you are just scum to them. I refuse to be scum for anyone.

"High school is a lot different than grade school. You're gonna find that out this year. It's bigger, there's more kids, and the decisions you make could change your whole life." She paused to see that Erin was paying rapt attention. "I don't know about you, but I wasn't ready to make decisions about my life this young. It's really kind of thrown me. My counselors at school all wanted to know where I wanted to go to college, and what I wanted to be when I grew up. You know what I wanted to know?"

"What?" Erin asked.

"I wanted to understand why I didn't like boys the way I should and why my heart raced when I saw certain girls. They don't really have that sort of answer in our curriculum or the advisor's office. So it was a really hard thing to deal with."

"But why didn't you tell *me*? I thought we were supposed to be best friends. That means we tell each other everything. I've told you every stupid thing I've ever done since we met, and I don't feel like you've done the same."

Nodding her head, Jackson agreed. "No, I haven't. I wish I could tell you something other than I wasn't ready, but that's the truth of it. I knew, for whatever reason, you and Molly wouldn't get along. And yeah, Molly probably wasn't the best person to be with, but she was like me and she liked me, so we just clicked, you know? I had a feeling that if you knew about us, it would be harder to deal with than just knowing about me." She paused. "Does that make any sense?"

"It does and I guess I understand, but Jack, you really hurt my feelings. I had so many thoughts going through my head—that you didn't really think of me as your friend, but as a guest you felt obligated to play with when I came up there with my parents. You made me feel insecure about our friendship."

Shaking her head rapidly, Jackson said, "No, Hawk. I *never* felt like I was obligated to hang with you." She put her hand on Erin's back, happy when Erin allowed the contact. "I chose to be with you because you *are* my best friend. I just haven't acted like it lately and for that I am so damn sorry. You have no reason to doubt what we've shared, I promise."

Letting Jackson's admission settle, Erin understood a little more of where she was coming from. She knew it couldn't have been easy for Jackson to realize she was a lesbian. A question formed in her mind that she voiced aloud. "Does Jackie know? That you're um…gay?"

"Yeah. I told her right before my last birthday. She kinda knew already, but I told her not to tell Sandra. She probably already knows too, but I wasn't ready to tell her yet."

Another question formed in Erin's mind. "Jack?"

"Hmm?" She looked into blue eyes and felt her heart speed up.

"How did you know which room was mine? I've only lived in the basement a short time."

Chuckling softly, she answered, "Mr. Henderson told me."

"What?" she cried loudly then covered her mouth repentantly.

They stopped talking and listened for a while to make sure they hadn't woken Erin's mother. When they heard nothing, they resumed their conversation.

"I was outside your house and he busted me. I made up a lie about it being your birthday and wanting to take you to breakfast. He was more than happy to help."

97

Erin smiled. "God, I would've peed if I were you."

"Trust me, I wasn't that far off, especially with the full bladder I was carrying."

"That was really quick thinking on your part," Erin complimented.

A soft blush reached Jackson's cheeks. "Thanks."

When silence enveloped the girls, Erin felt the nervous tension return. "Jack?"

Jackson turned to her. "Yeah?"

"What do we do now? I mean, where does all of this leave us?"

"Well, I hope you can forgive me for lying to you and I pray you can learn to trust me again."

Erin looked into her eyes and saw the warm, wonderful girl she'd grown to love very much. "I do forgive you. I was just so angry, and when I found out my mom was leaving, I just jumped ship."

"Yeah, what's up with that? Why did your mom leave?"

"God, it's a long story and I don't even know the half of it."

"I was upset that you left, but I understood why. That picture said a thousand words, words I really didn't want to hear you yell at me."

Erin blushed, having forgotten about the drawing. "Oh, um… sorry about that. It was the only way I could tell you how I felt without actually, um…telling you."

"It's okay. I think we both did some things we wish we hadn't last night."

"Yeah, we did."

They smiled at each other. Jackson didn't think that it would be prudent to tell Erin *everything* she'd done wrong.

"Does Jackie know you came here?" Erin asked.

"Oh, um…not really. I left her a note."

"What is it with us and notes? I left one for my dad before we left," Erin said with a chuckle.

"I dunno. Must be that pen pal thing we developed at a young age."

Nodding, Erin said, "Must be."

"I'm probably going to get in a lot of trouble when I get back, but…you are worth the risk."

"Thank you for driving so far to show me that."

"You're welcome." Jackson noticed the time on the clock was after six. The sun had come up and the day was beginning.

Erin saw the red rimming around Jackson's eyes and knew she needed to sleep. "Stand up." Jackson did as she was told and Erin pulled the bedcovers down. "Get in." Jackson's eyes went wide with surprise. "You need sleep and I need sleep. I don't know about you, but I haven't slept much in the last two days and I'm exhausted."

"You read my mind, but what about your mom?"

Erin walked over to her door and turned the lock on the handle. "This is one of the reasons I wanted to have my room down here. She doesn't have a key to this door and I'm safely tucked in here away from her."

"Won't she come down to check on you or something?"

"No. She was so excited I came home, I could ask for gold right now and she'd give it to me. I think she'll give me some space for a while." She looked at Jackson with sincere regret. "I'm so sorry she has it out for you. I just wish I knew why."

"Me, too, Hawk. Me, too."

Erin shut off both lights, leaving only the coming day's light to illuminate her room. Both girls climbed into the full-size bed and pulled up the covers. They stared at the ceiling, not really sure what to do. Jackson's sleepiness was suddenly gone as realization set in that she was in bed with Erin. Erin must have sensed the same thing as she continued to stiffly stare at the ceiling.

"Hawk?"

"Hmm?"

"Does it make you uncomfortable? You know, knowing that I'm gay?"

Erin slowly turned to face her bedmate. She reached out and took Jackson's closest hand in hers. "No, it doesn't. I promise you I will never act differently around you just because you're a lesbian. You're not just a lesbian to me; that's only a small part of who you are. You're just…my Jack, and I love you."

My Jack. The words were floating like a fluffy cloud through Jackson's mind. They warmed and soothed her more than she would have thought possible. "Thank you, Hawk. That means the world to me." Tears formed in Jackson's eyes and she didn't fight them.

Erin saw them glisten and held tightly to her hand with one hand and brushed the tears away with the other. Erin soon fell asleep on her side, holding Jackson's hand on her pillow.

When Jackson looked over and saw Erin asleep, she leaned over to kiss their entwined fingers and whispered, "I love you, too, Hawk. More than you'll ever know."

Chapter Seven

1990 – Paldeer, Illinois 11:30 a.m.

A knocking on her bedroom door jolted Erin awake. Her eyes went wide with the realization of who was on the other side of that door.

"Erin, honey, are you still asleep?" Katie called, jiggling the handle. "Why is your door locked?"

Jackson heard the voice and instantly sat up in a panic. Her focal expression matched Erin's who had placed a finger over her mouth, shushing her.

"Yeah, Mom, I was really beat." She paused. "I must have locked it by mistake last night. I don't wanna get up to open it, though. Did you need something?" Erin heard her mother sigh.

"I am going to the store. Since we emptied the house before we left for vacation, I need to shop. I was going to ask you if you wanted to come, but since you're still in bed, I'll go alone."

"Okay, Mom. Have fun."

"Did you want anything special from the grocery?"

Jackson kept mouthing, *"Go away"* while Erin tried hard not to laugh. "No, Mom, I'll be fine with whatever you pick. I'm gonna rest for a while longer."

"Okay, honey. I'll be back in a couple of hours."

Jackson pumped her fist. "'Kay, Mom. Bye."

The girls didn't make a sound until they heard the front door close. Both released a huge sigh and laughed nervously once the coast was clear.

"Man, that was a close one. I gotta pee!" Jackson exclaimed and ducked into the bathroom, closing the door behind her.

Erin leaned back in bed and laughed. She closed her eyes and opened them wide when she heard a knock on her outside window. Her mother had stopped on the way to the detached garage in the backyard.

"Honey?" she shouted through the closed glass.

Erin leapt off her bed and answered loudly, "Yes, Mom? Why are you *outside my window*?" She hoped Jackson heard her so she'd stay in the bathroom.

Motioning for Erin to open her window, Erin did, only to have her mother yell, "What's your screen doing open? Anyone could just climb in your room."

Thinking quickly, Erin said, "I locked myself out of the house before we left for Wisconsin. I guess I forgot to put it back. Don't worry, I always keep my window locked, Mom."

"You'd better. That isn't safe, honey."

"Mom, if someone wants to get in, they're gonna get in despite a screen."

Katie smiled. "You're so smart, dear. That's probably very true. I didn't mean to wake you. Go back to bed and I'll see you in a little bit."

Erin smiled, hoping the sweat she felt pouring from her body wasn't visible. "See ya later, Mom."

Erin watched her mother walk through the side garage door and waited until she saw the overhead door open. She watched her mother back out and close the door. The burgundy Nissan backed slowly down the drive and out of Erin's view. She quickly opened her door and raced upstairs to watch through the bay window in the living room as her mother drove off down the street.

"Oh, thank God!"

Jackson stealthily came up behind her and grabbed her sides. "Boo!"

"Hey!" Erin whipped around. "You've had the chance to pee, I haven't! I'd prefer not to do it on my living room floor." They laughed and Erin ran into the powder room.

Jackson took the opportunity to look at Erin's house for the first time. The house was very, very tidy. Everything was neatly arranged, from the sofas to the grandfather clock, to the large potted plants on Oriental carpets. All in all, it was a nicely decorated house.

Erin came out of the powder room with a loud sigh of relief. "Aahhhh, so much better."

Jackson laughed. "I'm sure. God, I'm so glad you spoke up when you did, I was ready to come out of the bathroom."

"Oh, my God! I thought I was going to die from fear! I forgot to slide the screen back into place and, *of course*, she saw it and had to ask me about it. I just hope she doesn't remember that you can only unlock the screen from the inside. I told her I always kept my window locked, but then how would I have gotten inside? Uggh! I think she bought it, though."

"I think so too or she wouldn't have left until she had you under the lights." She changed her voice and raised her hands up like she was holding lamps. "Where were you the night the screen was opened? What are you hiding?"

Erin laughed and slapped her hands away. "She's been so crazy this year. I just don't get it. She has this ridiculous idea of what she wants me to be and it's not even close to what I want."

Sighing, Jackson said, "I know, Hawk. She has this picture in her head of you going to school, graduating from the best college, finding the perfect man and settling down to have grandchildren... for her." She shook her head. "This is what *she* wants. Just stick to your guns and live the life you want."

"I'll do my best. It's so hard around her. I don't think I've ever felt like I wasn't a disappointment. My dad, on the other hand, just wants what you want and that's for me to be happy. He's really a great dad."

Jackson smiled. "I can see that. I see the way his eyes light up when you're around. That's one thing I missed, not having a dad that I knew."

"You've never told me about that."

"There's nothing to tell, Hawk. My mom got pregnant when

she wasn't married. I was the oops and the guy that did it was nowhere to be found."

Softening her voice, Erin asked, "Does that bother you at all?"

"Mmm, some, but Jackie has been a great mom and I don't think I could ask for a better life."

"True." Erin smiled. "You do seem very happy."

"I am, for the most part."

"Okay, enough of this. I need some breakfast or something. I am so hungry!" Erin exclaimed.

"Come back with me," Jackson blurted suddenly.

"What?" Erin wasn't sure she'd heard right.

"Come back to Wisconsin with me."

"Jack…"

"Hawk, your dad is up there so it's not like you don't have a place to stay or a ride home. The only obstacle would be…"

"My mother." "Your mother," they said in unison.

"That's a pretty big obstacle, Jack."

"Yeah, but she won't be home for a couple hours. We could be a third of the way back by then."

Thoughts raced through Erin's mind. *God, she'd kill me. Although, Daddy is still up there. God, she'd kill me… Still, I only get a month a year with Jack… She'll get over it.*

"Let's do it!" She knew she would be grounded until next year, but she didn't really care. "I get one month out of the year to see you and we've only had a few days."

"Are you sure, Hawk? I'm being selfish and want to spend more time with you, but I don't want you to deal with the wrath of your mom."

"I haven't even unpacked my suitcase. I just need to shower, change my clothes, and grab my art stuff. We can eat on the road."

"You're serious?" Jack could hardly contain her excitement. "You'll really come back with me?"

"Yeah. Let's get going before my mom decides to come home sooner." She ran to the kitchen and opened drawers, looking for paper.

Jackson watched, amused, happy, and really excited.

"I just need to write her..."

"A note!" they both yelled, and then laughed.

Erin wrote her mom a note with an apology and a promise to call when she got back to the resort. "She's gonna have a major cow, but I won't be here for it and I *know* she won't drive back to get me with my dad already there."

"Rock and roll! Get going, girl!"

Erin shot a toothy smile at Jackson and ran downstairs to shower and get her stuff together.

Jackson chuckled at her friend's excitement and hoped that Jackie would allow her a few last moments with Erin before she killed her.

The music was blaring from the car windows as the two teenagers sped their way up I-90. They were getting close to Madison and Jackson knew she'd soon have to be watching for her turn off. Erin was bopping to Madonna's 'Like A Prayer' CD in the player. She was singing loudly and badly, much to the amusement of her riding buddy. 'Keep it Together' was playing and the two girls began to sing it together.

"Keep people together! Yeah, Mom!" Erin shouted, making Jackson laugh.

They were having a great time in the car, both relieved that the tension between them was gone and they could simply enjoy the company and closeness that was unique in their lives. Both knew that their maternal figures were going to be less than pleased, but somehow the punishment for their crime didn't seem as bad as it would've been to not committ the offense.

For Jackson, having Erin around was like having a new supply of oxygen. Everything seemed clearer, more vivid, and her heart couldn't have been more full. With Erin coming back with her, Jackson was truly a happy girl.

Erin's head was bopping as the last track on the CD was coming to an end. She saw that Jackson got in the far right lane to get onto Route 39. Jackson had only been driving a little less than a year, but Erin thought she was doing a fantastic job.

"Hey, Jack, how'd you find out how to get to my house?"

Jackson pulled the trip ticket out of her pocket and held it out for Erin to see. "Jackie's a member of the motor club and they tell you exactly how to get to places. I looked you up a long time ago and just kept the directions in case I ever wanted to pop in and surprise you." She gave Erin a grin, making Erin giggle.

"I'm sure my mom would've loved that."

Thinking about her mother, Erin was certain she would be home by now. She knew that she would be beyond angry at her decision to get in the car with Jackson and drive all the way back to the Island City. As she thought about what punishment her mother might devise, she quickly thought about spending three more weeks with just her dad. They'd never had a vacation alone before and Erin knew she'd have a great time with him. *He is always so much more relaxed when Mom's not around.*

"We're halfway there, Hawk. God, the ride down to you seemed so much longer. Time is just flying!"

"This is so awesome! Woohoo!" she screamed out the car window. Jackson laughed at her antics. Settling back against the seat, Erin put her arm out the window and let the wind take her hand up and down, depending on the angle she held it. With Jackson by her side driving to their favorite place, this was by far one of the best days of her life and she was going to enjoy every minute of it.

1990 - Paldeer, Illinois

Katie Hawkins pulled her car up the drive and hit the button on her garage door opener. The door opened and she drove the car inside. Hitting her trunk opener, she slowly exited the vehicle and walked around to the back of the car. She pulled out a couple of bags of groceries and carried them to the back door of her home. Opening the door, she walked into the kitchen and put the bags down on the counter.

"Erin!" she shouted. "I'm back! Give me a hand with the rest of the bags, will you?" Emptying a bag, she realized Erin had not answered her. She shouted again, "Erin! Come up here and help me!"

She walked to the edge of the stairs. "Erin? Are you home?" Sighing indignantly, she descended the stairs and looked into Erin's empty room. Her bed was made, her sleep clothes were on the floor, but nothing else seemed amiss. "Erin?" She looked in the bathroom, but no one was there.

Where the hell has she gone now?

Angry, Katie made her way up the stairs and went outside to retrieve the rest of her groceries. She began her meticulous task of putting away the groceries. Martha Stewart had nothing on Katie Hawkins when it came to order. Every shelf had a label, shelf paper, and cans facing forward. Once all the groceries were put away, she grabbed all the plastic bags and wadded them up to recycle later. She opened the door to the pantry to put the bags away and noticed the garbage can was empty without a new bag inside of it. Realizing it was garbage day, she was happy that Erin had at least remembered to do that. Opening the cabinet under the sink, she grabbed a new trash liner and put it in the garbage can then closed the door.

Feeling a little hungry after leaving the house without lunch, Katie began to make herself an open-faced sandwich. She fluffed her lunchmeat just so, added a dollop of mustard, put it on a plate, and poured a glass of water. She sat down at the kitchen table. Noticing a piece of paper with Erin's handwriting on it, she picked it up and began to read as she took a drink of water. Water flew out of her mouth and she began to cough.

Dear Mom,

Don't be mad! Jackson came down from Wisconsin and paid me a visit. We had a bit of a misunderstanding, which is the truth of why I left there in the first place. We talked and made up and she offered to take me back up to the resort to spend the rest of the time with Dad. I figured since you were already leaving there without me, this wouldn't be too big of a deal.

I'm sorry we won't have any "our time" but I'll make it up to you when we get back. I'll give you a call when I arrive so you don't worry too much.

Love,
Erin

Katie slapped the kitchen table so hard and thoughtlessly that she hit the side of the plate with her hand and her sandwich flew into her lap. She screamed in uncontrolled anger as she grabbed a towel from the kitchen sink to wipe up the mess she'd made.

"Damn you, Jackson Thomas! Damn you straight to hell!"

Running to her address book, she flipped the pages until she got to the tab with "N" and found the number for Northwoods Island City resort. She picked up her receiver and dialed.

"Hello, Northwoods Island City, how can I help you?" Jackie answered.

"Miss Thomas, this is Katie Hawkins."

Jackie swallowed hard, knowing this was about Jackson and her jaunt to Illinois. "Yes, Katie?"

"Do you have any idea where Jackson is?"

"Well, she told me—"

"Let me answer that for you. Jackson is in the car right now with *my daughter*, heading back to Wisconsin!"

"Really? Well, at least they're all right."

"All right? How is two teenagers driving six hours in a car by themselves considered all right?"

"Katie, I think you're overreacting. Jackson is a responsible driver."

"There's that word again. Tell me, Jacqueline, do you always use the word *responsible* when your niece is caught doing something wrong? Or is it just when she's caught doing something to endanger my daughter?"

"Now, look here, Katie. That boating accident was *not* Jackson's fault. As you know, my niece *saved* Erin's life. I find that extremely responsible. As far as this impulsive drive to Illinois, well it was definitely not one of her better ideas, but that's for me to deal with when she gets back home."

Katie was pacing her kitchen. "Well, I suggest you put a leash on her if you expect her to listen to what she's told."

"That was uncalled for! Jackson has done nothing to warrant such hateful remarks from you."

"Your niece is unnatural and I don't want her anywhere near my daughter!"

Jackie became angry. "Excuse me?"

"Your sweet, *responsible* Jackson is unnatural and a queer. I can see it when she looks at Erin, touches her. Those are not natural thoughts from one girl to another!"

"So, what you are telling me is that not only are you overreacting about all of this, but you are a bigoted fool as well?"

"How dare you!" Katie screamed.

"How dare I? You're the one accusing my niece of...of God knows what, when all she's done to Erin is be a friend to her since they've met. I think you are the one who is a little unnatural if that's the only aspect of their friendship you have been focusing on. Tell me, Katie, how much time, really, do you spend on how Jackson touches Erin? Doesn't that sound a little unnatural to you?"

"You're no better than she is—a charmer spewing poison, like a viper. Snakes, that's what you all are."

Jackie couldn't help but laugh at the ridiculous woman. "You know what, Katie? You're right; we are snakes. But you know what? We really like to eat rats so you'd better be careful, because you'll be what's next on the menu." Jackie abruptly disconnected the call.

Katie hung up and threw the telephone, screaming out her rage.

1990 – Northwoods Island City

Jackie paced endlessly, trying to get rid of the residual anger she felt toward Katie Hawkins.

Sandra watched her walk around the house for a short while before feeling a little dizzy. "Jackie, calm down. You know that woman isn't balanced."

"I know, but damn, I wanted to reach through that phone line and strangle her! She's got a lot of nerve, that one." She mumbled a few choice words.

Sandra was a little uncomfortable with the topic since she knew her family felt the same about gays. "I'm sorry to say that my mom isn't really much better. You know she would freak out about us if she knew."

Jackie stopped and stared at her. "So, what exactly does she think of our *friendship?" I can't believe you haven't told her, yet.*

Uh-oh, bad timing, Sandra. You know this is a sore subject. "She knows we're really close friends," she said evasively.

"What does she think of us living together?" Jackie's ire was starting to turn toward Sandra.

Head suddenly falling in shame, Sandra answered, "She thinks I'm helping you with the resort this summer."

"Are you serious?" Jackie asked, disbelieving the words being spoken. "So, she still has no idea about us?"

"No, she doesn't. Honey, she would make it so hard for us. I don't want to tell her."

"Are you ashamed of who you are?"

Jackie's stare was intense and making Sandra thoroughly uncomfortable. "No, I'm not. I just don't want to hurt her and *this* would hurt her." She paused. "Jackie, you know she's from an older generation and wouldn't understand."

"*I* don't understand how you can let this *not* bother you. You are supposed to be my partner, my lover. I mean, do you have any idea how this makes me feel?"

"Jackie, I'm sorry. Believe me, I *am* bothered by this. I hate that I can't muster up the courage to tell her about us. Don't make this so hard for me. I don't want to have to choose between you and my mom."

Jackie's anger turned to disappointment in Sandra. Her last statement said far too much about their future. "I can't believe you just said that. It should not have to be a choice! You either love me for keeps or you don't. I'm too old to play games, Sandra." She took deep breaths to keep the tears at bay.

Jackie looked out the window and saw Jackson and Erin getting out of Jackson's Honda. "We'll talk more about this later. Jackson just got back and we are going to have a nice long talk."

"Okay. I'm gonna make myself scarce for a while." She walked up to Jackie, lightly kissing her cheek. "I'll give you some time alone."

Jackie gave her a wan smile and nodded. "Thanks."

Jackson and Erin walked up the path to the main house with big smiles on their faces. When the house was in sight, Jackie came out of the door with her arms crossed. *Uh-oh. Good feeling's gone.*

"Jackson Emma Thomas, you get your ass in this house immediately."

"I'll see you later, Erin." Jackson gave her an apologetic look, which was returned.

"I'm gonna go look for my dad."

"'Kay, see you later," Jackson said.

"Jackson!" Jackie shouted.

"Maybe," Jackson added with a whisper and large round eyes.

Erin hustled away in search of her dad to tell him she was back.

When Jackson reached her, Jackie grabbed an earlobe and dragged her into the house. "Ow! Jackie, come on, you haven't done that to me since I was nine!"

"Well, you behaved like a child last night. What the hell were you thinking? Driving to Illinois in the middle of the night. Did you even think once, what would happen to you if something went wrong with your car? What would have happened if you ran out of gas or had a flat tire? Just who do you think would help a young girl on the side of the road in the middle of the night? Some knight in shining armor or some sicko with teenaged girls on his mind?"

"Jackie…"

"No! You put yourself in extreme danger with this stunt, Jackson, and I'm very disappointed in you."

Those words cut deeply. Jackson absolutely hated disappointing her aunt. "I'm sorry, Jackie."

"Yeah, me too." She held out her hand. "You know this drill all too well these days. Give me your keys."

"Wha…? Aw, come on, Jackie, nothing happened!"

"Keys!"

Shaking her head in disbelief, she handed over the keys to her car.

"You'll get these back after I think of something else to do to you. You have *no* idea what you've done, do you?"

"What are you talking about?"

"I got a nasty phone call from Erin's mother." Jackson's eyes went wide. "Yeah, it was *not* pretty. Seems as though she thinks you are an unnatural snake with eyes for her daughter."

"You've got to be kidding me!" Jackson couldn't believe Katie Hawkins had the nerve to call her aunt. *On second thought, who are we talking about here?* "Erin knew she'd be mad, but God, I can't believe she called you."

"Why wouldn't she call me? You're *my* responsibility, Jack. Erin got in the car with you and you two drove four hundred miles to Wisconsin, all by yourselves! Why does this surprise you at all?"

"I dunno." Jackson sat heavily on the couch. After several long minutes of silence, Jackson whispered, "I had to go."

Slowly calming down, Jackie sat next to her niece and tried to understand what had happened that made her niece jump in the car in the middle of the night. "Tell me why."

Jackson looked up into her aunt's eyes and told her the whole sordid story about Molly. She didn't gloss over anything, just so Jackie would understand the full impact that all had had on her.

"So, you went to Paldeer to get your friend to forgive you?"

"Well, when you say it like that, it certainly doesn't sound as desperate as it felt. Jackie, I was dying inside!" she cried, tears starting to form.

"Shh, okay, okay, don't cry. Because nothing happened to you or to Erin, I'm not going to chop your head off. Just realize that it wasn't a very smart thing to do, especially at that hour. Had you told me all of that, I would've let you go during the day. Of course, I would've made you stop and call me every hour, but I would've let you go." She started to rub Jackson's back. "Don't ever do anything like that again."

"I won't, I promise. I just couldn't lose her, Jackie. She means too much to me."

"I know, honey, I know." After a few moments, she asked, "Does she know how you feel about her?"

Jackson shook her head. "No, she doesn't, but that's okay. She doesn't need to know. She's not gay, so it isn't important. What is important is that she knows I am and she still wants to be around me and be my best friend."

Smiling at her niece, she said, "You know, Jack, sometimes you are wise beyond your years. I think it's great that Erin knows about you and still loves you for who you are. Do me a favor? Next time just pick up the damn phone and call her!"

Chuckling softly, Jackson replied, "I will, but I was so afraid her mom would answer and not let me talk to her."

"Mmm, true. She's a pip, that one. I really hope the *discussion* we had today doesn't affect Erin visiting."

Jackson frowned. "Crap, I didn't think about that."

"I'll go find Joe later on and tell him the situation. He could probably use the information to gear up for the call I'm sure he's going to get from her."

"Uggh, why does he stay with that woman?"

Laughing, Jackie said, "You know...it wasn't too long ago that Sandra and I were saying the same thing about Molly."

"Ha, ha, very funny." They bumped shoulders and leaned their heads together. "So, am I grounded?" Jackson asked, not really wanting to hear the answer.

"Yes, until Christmas."

Jackson whipped around to face Jackie. "What?"

"You can't possibly think you'd get off the hook by just forking over your keys, did you?"

"No, but Jackie...Christmas?"

"You'll have a nice New Year's resolution, now won't you?" Jackson let out a sigh. "But you aren't grounded until Erin goes home."

Her face lit up immediately and she hugged her aunt. "Thank you, Jackie. Christmas is just fine."

Erin walked down to cabin six, hauling her suitcase and backpack. Pulling open the screen door, she pushed the big door open and walked inside. "Dad?"

Erin walked into her bedroom and put her stuff down, then went into her parents' room but found it empty. *Hmm...he must be out fishing.* She turned around...and ran smack dab into her father.

"Daddy!" she screamed. She threw her arms around him.

"Hey, Peanut. What are you doing here? When you called me yesterday I thought you were home." They separated and looked at each other with smiles.

"I was, Daddy, but Jack came and got me."

Joe's eyes widened at the revelation. "Jack went down to Paldeer?"

"Yep."

"And what did your mother say about all of this?" he asked, knowing full well she had come without her mother's blessing.

Erin blushed a deep red. "Um...I kind of didn't ask her."

"Uh-huh. So what did you do?"

"I, ah...wrote her a note and then we left while she was out grocery shopping."

Joe shook his head, not looking forward to the next phone call he would be receiving from his wife. "You do realize your mother is going to have a cow."

Erin nodded. "I kinda thought the same thing. But Daddy, she was leaving without me anyway! Why is it a big deal?"

"Peanut, it's a big deal because you left without asking her and you left with Jack. You know how she feels about her." Erin started to pace. "Honey, whether or not you realize it, you put yourself in danger."

She turned to regard him with a shocked expression. "Daddy, not you too! Jack is not trying to hurt me!"

"No, no, I didn't mean it like that. Come here and sit down." They walked over and sat on the couch. "What I meant was, were you prepared to handle an emergency situation on the road?" When Erin's face blanked, he continued. "What would've happened if you got a flat, or the car broke down in the middle of nowhere?

There are so many patches of dead highway on the way up here. Anyone could've found you and Jack stranded and I don't want to think about what would've happened if the wrong person had found you."

Understanding what her dad was explaining finally hit home. Erin's head hung a little. "I didn't think about that part. I just wanted to come back here." She paused and decided to tell her dad some of the truth. "Jack and I had a fight the night before I left. I didn't want to face her the next day and when I saw that Mom was leaving, I decided to take the easy way out."

"I see." Joe nodded. "You do realize that there are consequences for things like this, don't you?"

Erin's eyes welled. "Don't take me back home, Daddy, please."

"Oh, I'm gonna take you back home, all right," Erin's eyes widened, "but not for another three weeks." He shook his head. "Your mother is going to be furious and I think I'd rather keep four hundred miles between us for a while, thank you very much." He coughed and laughed.

Erin regarded him seriously. "Are you guys okay, Daddy?"

Joe hugged his daughter. "Don't you worry about us, Peanut. Your mom and I are just having a disagreement about something. We'll get past it. We love each other very much."

"Hmm...she said the same thing." She pulled back from the hug. "I guess that means to mind my own beeswax then?"

Joe laughed at his little girl. "Something like that." He ruffled her hair. "Let's see if Jack wants to go to Bosaki's with us for dinner."

"Oh, um...I don't know about that. I think she's in trouble with Jackie." He gave her a look that said, *See, this wasn't such a great idea for either of you.* "But I'll go and ask."

The phone rang. Joe looked at it and back to Erin. "Three guesses who that is and the first two don't count."

"I'm sorry, Daddy."

"It's okay, Peanut. We'll get through this." He patted her knee and got up to answer the phone on the fourth ring.

"Hello?"

"Hello, Joe."

"Katie, we were just talking about you."

"So, I guess that Erin has arrived. Let me speak to her."

"Katie, if you're not going to be calm about this, I'm not putting her on the phone. I had a long talk with her about the dangerous trip she took and she understands that it was wrong."

Katie snarled. "Oh, well, doesn't that make you Father of the Year. She left without even asking permission!"

"Is that what you're so upset about, or is it who she left with?" Joe rubbed the back of his neck with his free hand. Erin sat very still on the couch, watching him.

"Joe, she could've been killed!" Katie snapped, "Jackson is only sixteen. There could've been an accident."

Joe tried to placate his wife. "Yes, but there wasn't. Erin is fine, Jackson is fine."

"I don't give a damn about Jackson. She could've hurt Erin."

"All right, that's what I'm talking about. You need to calm down. Nothing happened. If you keep obsessing about things that *might happen*, you're going to go insane and drive all of us there with you!"

"Joseph, I am not obsessing."

"Yes, you are, *Katherine*. You've got to stop this before it tears this family apart. You were already out the door before Erin even asked to go with you, so what has you so angry about her being here with me? Am I going to harm our daughter now?" Joe turned the conversation around.

Katie was completely flustered. "What? Now you're just talking crazy."

"Then I guess I'm starting to talk like you." Joe scrunched up his face, knowing that wasn't the smartest thing to have said.

"I think you've said quite enough." Katie put her foot down. "Tell Erin she's grounded until I say differently. I will not back down from that."

"I think a grounding is very fair for this escapade. I think she's quite aware that she will be punished when we return home."

"She'd better, because she is not getting off scot free this time."

"I'll let her know."

"You do that." Katie hung up the phone loudly in Joe's ear.

He hung up the receiver and exhaled deeply. "That went well."

Erin got up and went to her father. "Daddy, I'm really sorry about this. I'll call Mom later and take the heat. I deserve it."

Not wanting to comment to his daughter about what he thought about her mother's reasoning, Joe just took her in his arms. "It'll be okay. I think after she's had some time to calm down, she'd appreciate that call."

"I'll call her after dinner."

Joe pulled back from the hug. "Go see if Jack can come with us and I'll grab a shower and a shave."

"I wasn't gonna say anything, but you stink like fish."

"See what happens when I'm left on my own for a day?"

Erin laughed. "Well, I'm here now, so you'd better wash up."

"Go on, I'll meet you back here."

"'Kay" Erin dashed out the door in search of Jackson, feeling lighter than she had in days. The summer was going to end much better than it had started and for that, she was very grateful.

Chapter Eight

1990 – Paldeer, IL - Letter to Erin from Jackson

September 12, 1990

Dear Hawk,
See, I told you I'd write. It just takes me a little longer than you. How's the grounding going? I'm sure Jackie's been a lot easier on me than your mom has been on you. I'm just glad she didn't come up and get you. That would've been a really awful scene. Your dad is a really cool guy. I'm so glad I got to spend some time with him. It was really cool to go fishing with someone who actually knew what he was doing! ☺ I'm sorry again about that bluegill smacking you in the face. I really tried to get the net down.
How is high school? Are you totally freaking out? You know you can call me anytime if you need to talk. I know how scary it was for me to be a freshman in a new school. Just remember to breathe! I don't want to hear about you passing out in the halls! ☺ School is chugging along for me. I'm taking some pretty cool classes this semester. My music teacher hooked me up with a fantastic instructor. She is really making me work. I've gotten really good with my flute and piccolo in just a couple of weeks

with her. I can't wait to see how I sound at the end of the year!

Hawk, I was asked to the Homecoming Dance! It's not until October! Can you believe it? This poor guy just doesn't get it. Oh well, I told him if he wanted to go as friends, I'd go with him, but not to expect any fireworks from me. I think Jerry is going to think about it before he commits! HA, HA.

*I hope things with your mom are going okay. I really hate the way she treats you sometimes, Hawk. I don't mean any disrespect against your mother, but damn she can be mean! *insert hug here**

Jackie and Sandra have been at each other's throats lately. I have no idea what's going on, but I don't think it's good. I'll let you know more, I know you liked Sandra. Well, except when she accidentally knocked you off the dock and into the water. That really was a mistake, Hawk. She didn't mean it.

Anyway, I have a huge test in biology and I have to study. I hate this class the most out of all of them so I really have to dig in.

Let me know if there are any jerks I gotta drive down to defend your honor from. I know how to get there now, so tell them to watch out! ☺

Friends 4 Ever.

Love,
Jack

1990 – Island City – Letter to Jackson from Erin

October 14, 1990

Dear Jack,
I am so sorry I haven't written all month. I don't think I could have any more homework. High school is going okay so far, but man, it's been a lot of work. My art classes, as I'm sure you can guess, are my favorite classes. I have two really fantastic teachers

and they seem really available to us. My friend Tom and I spend a lot of extra time in the art room after school. He's really talented, Jack, you'd like him. He can draw the most incredible cartoons! He made this one about dead people that your sick sense of humor would appreciate. It was like all the dead people had their own community and would initiate the "new" people. It's so damn funny. I'll see if he'll give me a copy of one so I can send it to you.

Uggh, don't get me started about my mom. She has been a bear to be around. I know she means well and just wants what's best for me, but sometimes she wants too much. I tried to tell her I don't want to be a cheerleader, but she made me feel bad so I'm going to tryouts. I guess a couple girls left the squad, and they need to fill the spots, so I'm gonna try out tomorrow afternoon. My dad said not to worry about it and if I didn't make it, I could just tell her that I tried. Sometimes I think she wants me to do all the things she never did.

I'm really excited to hear about your new flute instructor. Is she cute? Ha, ha, I'm kidding. I'm glad she's working your butt off. You have so much talent, you better not waste it or I'll come up to the Northwoods and kick your butt myself!

I'm sorry to hear about Jackie and Sandra. I hope they stay together, Jack. I can tell how much Jackie loves her. Give her a hug for me. Your aunt is the best and I'm so glad she's the one who raised you. She done good with you. ☺

My birthday was cool. Thanks so much for calling me, it was a HUGE surprise! It was better than any card, so don't feel badly about not sending one. I preferred to hear you sing me the happy birthday song to any Hallmark version. You're the best.

Okay, that's all the time I can spare. I have so much homework tonight I'm going to drown in textbooks! AHHH!

I miss you, Jack. Take care of yourself.

Friends 4 Ever.
Hawk

1991 – Paldeer, IL – Letter from Jackson to Erin

March 23, 1991

Dear Hawk,

How's it going? Things are getting crazy with spring break coming soon. I have one major test before we are let out. Yep, you guessed it, biology, so wish me luck. I'm at least keeping a B-minus average, so Jackie isn't riding me too hard.

I have some news that is really great, but it makes me really sad to tell you. My flute instructor told me about a great music camp in Michigan. It's a really hard-core music camp, not like the kind when we were kids. The camp provides you with some of the best teachers from across the country to help you with your craft. Everything about it is great, except for when it is. It meets for the entire summer, Hawk, which would mean we wouldn't see each other this year. I can feel your disappointment from here, believe me, I feel it too. But you've always told me to keep going with my music and Jackie said I could go, so I'm gonna do it.

Please tell me what's going on in your head. I know you, Hawk, you're a thinker (but not a stinker) ☺ *Seriously, it was a really hard decision for me to make, but I guess I do have to start thinking about my future sometime.*

Please write me back as soon as you can. Or call me if you want, if your mom will let you. I wanna hear from you soon, okay?

Friends 4 Ever – I mean it!
Love,
Jack

1991 – Island City – Letter to Jackson from Erin

April 5, 1991

Dear Jack,

Wow, that was some letter. As you can see it took me a little while to digest everything. Even though I'm incredibly sad I won't see you, I'm that much more excited that you're going to be working on your music this summer. Just like you support my artwork, I always want you to work at your music. You've been given a great opportunity and you have to take it. I'll always be here, but something like this won't be. I'm really glad you decided to go.

I told my parents that you wouldn't be up there this summer, but my dad still wants to come up. I'll have to see if I want to go with you not being there. I think it'll be too weird. But maybe I'll go just to see Jackie and she can tell me all the dirt you've been holding out on me. ☺ We'll see. I have a few months to decide.

I can't believe I have about a month and a half left of my first year of high school. It hasn't been too bad, actually. I've made some friends, but we are the "art nerds" and people always look at us funny. We just look at them and cross our eyes or something and they totally look away. Tom and I have gotten really good at making faces at the girls in the "Barbie" crowd. They are just so lame. Tom is really a cool guy. He's so gifted, Jack. Sometimes his creations make me just go…WOW, look at what you've done! He has a couple of tattoos, one he even gave to himself. They're really cool and colorful. He's gonna show me how to use the needle with inks. Who knows, it might be a skill I can fall back on. Maybe I'll tattoo a donkey on my mom's face while she's asleep so everyone can see what a pain in the ASS she is. ☺ Seriously, though, I think I might like Tom. Do you think I should ask him out on a date? Girls do that, right? I'm not really good at the dating thing, so help me out, Romeo. ☺

Don't worry about me, Jack. I'll keep my fingers crossed for you that something good will come of this camp. Who knows, maybe you're meant to run it one day. ☺ I've enclosed a self-pic I had to draw for class so you can see what I look like now. My hair is totally red now and way past my shoulders. I think I like it, though. We'll see.

Anyway, I'm so proud of you, Jack. Knock 'em dead in Michigan. You'd better write me while you're there.

Friends 4 Ever – I know you mean it!
Love,
Hawk

1992 – Island City – Letter to Jackson from Erin

May 31, 1992

Dear Jack,
I know you won't get this on the right day, but I wanted to tell you how proud I am of you. A high school graduate on her way to Indiana University. I read up on them, Jack, and they have one of the best music programs in the country. Good for you! I can't believe you got a scholarship too! I told you your music would take you far. I have missed you so much, but I know how busy you've been. School is ending in a couple weeks here as well, so I understand. I appreciate the calls when you don't have time to write. It's always so great to hear your voice.
Tom and I are still dating, but something is just off between us. I think maybe we should just stay friends. I think my mother would have a heart attack if I broke up with him. I swear she wants me to marry him. I'm not even seventeen yet! She's been nagging me about him nonstop since the first night he picked me up to go to the movies. Only time will tell, right?
I didn't want this to be a super long letter, I just wanted to drop you a note to tell you how proud I am of you. You've accomplished so much in your eighteen years. I hope I can say the same thing when I'm done with high school. I'm sorry you couldn't get a ticket for me for your graduation. My mom probably wouldn't have let me go anyway. Just know I was with you in spirit. I love you, Jack and I'm so glad you're my best friend. You're just the best.
I'll miss you, but it's a huge honor to have been asked back to the Interlochen camp. You've obviously made an impression with them. But who can blame them, you've always made a huge impression on me. I'm going up to the Northwoods with my parents

this year. It wasn't the same last year. When I sit on the boathouse roof and draw my sunsets over Lake Tomahawk, I'll think of you.

Friends 4 Ever,
Hawk

1994 – Paldeer, IL – Letter to Erin from Jackson

June 4, 1994

Dear Hawk,
I can't tell you how long I've been waiting to write this letter. HAPPY HIGH SCHOOL GRADUATION! You did it! I'm sure it seemed like the longest journey of your life, but you did it and did it well! You didn't have to call to apologize, Hawk. I know your mom wouldn't let me step foot in that auditorium. Just know that at 2:30 I was cheering for you from the Northwoods. I think the trees shook!

We have been best friends for almost ten years and, Hawk, they've been the best years I could imagine. You've given me so much to be thankful for. Your incredible gift has made me appreciate art in a way I never would've on my own. Your perspective on certain things has made me pause when I encounter situations I'm not familiar with. I usually ask myself how you'd handle a situation and I can actually hear your answer. It's usually the right one, too. You have such love of life even though your mother has made that nearly impossible for you. I can't tell you how angry I was with that whole Tom situation. That poor guy didn't even see it coming, did he? Hell, if I were him and my girlfriend's mother told me to give her a ring, I don't know if I would've had the guts to actually give it to her. It would've made me think that she was a nut job and wonder whether I really wanted her as a mother-in-law. I think you handled it the best, though, as usual. He'll find a girlfriend in school next year. I know you said you didn't feel that kind of love for him, so I think you're both better off.

I only have one more summer up in Interlochen. It really makes me kind of sad. I've grown to love everyone so much. Every year there are new kids with such dreams in their eyes. I love being able to teach to them and watch them develop their talents. You're going to see some amazing music coming from these kids in a few years. You mark my words. ☺This place has really given me an amazing feeling of accomplishment I don't know that I would've had if I hadn't come here. I'm literally feeling high all the time. It's so incredible. Maybe you were right. Maybe teaching is the way to go for me. Time will tell, right?

We need to make sure that we see each other next summer. It's been far too long since we've gotten to hang out. I really miss you, Hawk. Everyone is sick of hearing me talk about you. I kept your self-pic up in my room at school and at camp. Everyone always asks who it was. When I told them the model was my best friend, they all said I was full of it. Everyone's full of something, though, right? ☺

I am so incredibly proud of you, Hawk. You're going to knock them dead at the Art Institute. I know it! I know you wanted to get away from your mom, but hell, it's still in the city away from her and you don't have to stay at home. That's good, right? Your dad seemed pretty jazzed for you when I called. I'm so glad he's been such a positive person in your life. He really is the best dad around.

Okay, Hawk, I gotta get to my next session, but know that I love you and I'm always thinking about you.

You are my friend 4 life.
Love,
Jack

Chapter Nine

2002 – Chicago

Erin was bustling around, gathering her artwork for the show in the gallery the following week. Kim was meticulous about setting up for Erin's artwork. Erin knew that hers was the most successful work in the gallery and Kim would spare no expense to make opening night sparkle. Several canvases were taken from her studio and down to the main level of her house. Erin lined them up in her study to make her final decision.

Hearing the phone ring, she put the last of the pictures down and answered it. *It's probably Kim freaking out again.*

"Hello?" she answered.

"Hello, dear," Katie greeted in a sweet tone, much to Erin's disgust.

"Hello, Mother. What can I do for you?"

"Is that any way to treat your mother? My gosh, I'm the only parent you have."

Erin's anger flared. "Yes, I know. I was there when Daddy died, remember?" She breathed deeply to try and calm herself. "I have an event at the gallery. I have a lot to do before then."

"You didn't mention it to me." Katie pretended to sound hurt.

There is a reason for that. "No, I didn't, Mother, because you rarely want to go to these things. Except, of course, when the mayor is expected. Then you're there with bells on."

"Oh, honey, it's not like that and you know it." *Whatever.* "So how's Jeremy? When am I going to hear some good news?"

"Mother, you know damn well Jeremy and I are getting divorced. The only good news that will come from this will be for me, after the judge pronounces me a single woman."

Katie's voice became condescending. "You know that goes against the teachings of the Church, Erin. I can't believe you aren't fighting for your marriage."

"Fight for a marriage with a man who has fathered a baby with another woman? Gee, Mother, you're right. I should stand and fight with both fists. I should go the full ten rounds!" Erin paced, rubbing her forehead to ward off the inevitable migraine that came with talking to her mother.

"Don't you talk to me like that, young lady."

Katie's haughty voice was making Erin nauseous and she knew she needed to get off the phone. "Was there a real reason you called, or did you just want to push some of my buttons? I really have a lot to do, Mother, so if you don't mind, I need to go."

"I wish you'd reconsider about Jeremy. All's not lost. I'm sure he still loves you. I'm sure if you—"

"Mother, I don't love him, don't you get that? Never mind. This is like talking to a damn brick wall." She exhaled sharply. "I'm getting off the phone now. Goodbye, Mother." Erin hung up the phone without waiting for her mother's goodbye.

"God! What is wrong with me? Why don't I move to Guam? She'd never call me there."

She began to arrange her work and once again the phone rang and broke her concentration. Angrily, Erin picked up the phone. "Mother, you need to stop calling me, I'm really busy right now."

"Well, it's good to see that some things never change. Your mom still giving you a hard time, Hawk?"

Hearing Jack's voice melted Erin's soul. Flopping down onto her couch, Erin sighed. "Jack? Is…is that really you?"

Tears formed in both women's eyes. "Yeah, it's me. How…

um…God, I don't even know what to say."

They shared a nervous laugh. "I know. I'm…I'm just stunned to hear your voice. How did you get my number?" Erin gripped the phone tightly.

"Dearest Katie gave it to me."

A lightbulb went off in Erin's head. *No wonder she was pushing the Jeremy envelope so hard tonight. God, she's something else.* "I'm just gonna apologize now for anything she might have said to you. Nothing's changed with her. She's always gotta say something negative about someone, sorry to say," Erin said with a sad smile. She wiped her eyes.

"How've you been, Hawk? Your mom told me about your dad. God, I'm so sorry. I know how much he meant to you. I really wish I could've been there for you."

So do I, Jack. You have no idea. "Thanks, Jack. That means so much. It was a really horrible time for all of us. He got sick and went so fast. Less than eighteen months and he was gone."

Tears rolled down Jack's cheeks. She knew all too well how that felt. She cleared her throat. "Well, I'm really sorry. He was a wonderful man. I feel very privileged to have known him."

"He loved you like crazy, Jack. You made him laugh all the time with your fishing quote unquote tips." They shared more laughter. "Even he noticed a difference in the resort when you were in Michigan at camp."

"Yeah, it was hard knowing you all were there and I wasn't."

"I'm sure." Erin stopped the conversation before it went in a direction she wasn't ready to go. "So how are things with you? Are you happy and healthy? Did you get your teaching certificate?"

Jackson smiled, knowing Erin's thoughts always went from her well-being to her music. "I'm doing pretty well. Yes, I'm a music teacher for the gifted kids in the area. It's a really great program and I'm truly loving what I'm doing." She smiled. "Not many people can say that about their jobs."

"You're right about that. I think we both got lucky in that respect."

"Oh, Hawk, I haven't even asked you about your work. How is life as a well-known painter treating you? I've seen your work in some shops up here. I…um…" She blushed into the phone. "I even bought one."

"Shut up! You did not!" They laughed.

"Yes, I'm afraid I did. It was a sunset that I *know* was taken off of Lake Tomahawk. Made me think it came from a memory of yours from on top of the boathouse roof."

"It probably did. Thank you for supporting my work, Jack. You've always been…"

"Your biggest fan/my biggest fan," they said together and laughed again.

"God knows Jackie was tired of coming to get us off that damn roof when it was too dark to see anything."

"Yeah, she did." Jackson swallowed back the tide of emotion that was creeping up her throat.

"How is Jackie? Is she doing well?"

Silence came through the line. "Um…that's why I'm calling, Hawk. Jackie's sick. Really sick, actually," she amended.

"Oh, no!" Erin's voice dripped with sadness. "What's wrong?"

"Cancer, believe it or not. What are the odds, huh?"

Erin shook her head as more tears came. "I'm so sorry, honey." The endearment slipped out so naturally. "Is there anything I can do?"

A sad smile came to Jack's face. *Aw, Hawk, you've always had such a big heart.* "Actually, yes. Tonight Jackie asked me to find you because she'd really like to see you…um…before…" The final words weren't necessary. Both women knew the awful result of this illness.

"When should I come? I'll come tomorrow if I have to. I have a show coming up, but I don't need to be there." She immediately started making plans in her head. "Hell, I'll come tonight!"

"Whoa, whoa, Hawk, slow down. Tonight isn't necessary. I'm sure you have to do some things before you can leave town. The sooner the better, obviously, with this type of thing."

Erin's heart dropped. "How long does she have?"

"According to her team, she has about two weeks. Maybe." Voicing Jackie's prognosis aloud made her stomach clench.

Erin's head fell back on the couch cushion and she closed her eyes. "God, this is awful. Just awful…"

"I know."

"Okay, I think I can wrap things up here by tomorrow afternoon, so I could be there by late evening. Would that be okay? I'm sure I can find a hotel or something."

"Don't be ridiculous, you can stay here." Silence was Erin's response, so Jackson elaborated. "It's still off-season. We have some open cabins. You have a place to stay. We actually have a new condo we can set you up in, if you'd like to try it."

Erin's heart was racing. She couldn't imagine staying under the same roof with Jackson after everything that had happened between them and how much time had passed. She was relieved when Jackson clarified what she'd meant. "A cabin would be great. I'll bring my sketchpads and supplies, like old times. Well, kinda."

Jackson understood what she meant. "I'll tell Jackie that you're coming. She is really going to be happy to see you, Hawk."

What about you, Jack? Will you be?

"Just be warned, I don't want you to expect too much when you see her, okay? She's hooked up to a lot of machines and wires. It'll probably bring back some bad memories for you, too. But I'll be right there if you need me." *Like always.*

Like always. "Thank you, Jack. I'm so glad you called. I'm sorry I didn't do the same when my dad died. I've felt bad about that for a while," she confessed.

"Hawk, don't, okay? I know how hard it was for you not to, believe me I do. I'm glad he had you looking after him during his last days."

Christ, I can't stop crying! "Thanks, Jack." They paused, not really wanting to hang up, having so much more to say, but knowing they ought to. "Well, I should get going. I have a lot to do before tomorrow."

"Thank you for coming, Hawk."

"I'll see you tomorrow."

"Can't wait. Drive safely, okay?" Jackson cautioned.

"I will. Talk to you soon."

"Bye."

Erin hung up and held the phone reverently, not really believing she'd not dreamt that call. *Poor Jackie. Jack was right. What are the odds of both of the people we loved most getting cancer? Life just isn't very fair.*

Knowing Kim was going to be a little miffed at her departure before the art show, she needed to call and sort things out. Once she explained the situation, Erin knew she'd understand. Kim knew the entire drama revolving around Erin and Jackson. She wouldn't dream of standing in the way of Erin answering the request of someone so precious to Jackson.

With the phone hung up, Jackson leaned back on her bed and sighed a huge, relieved breath. *Hawk is coming tomorrow.* She closed her eyes and smiled. Realization washed over her and she shot out of bed. "Oh, my God! Hawk is coming tomorrow!" *I'm gonna be sick.*

Jackson hurried to tell Jackie about her successful phone call. Cindy was in with her, changing an IV bag.

Jackie saw Jackson enter and read the change in her niece's face. "She's coming, isn't she?"

Jackson's brow furrowed. "How did you know that's what I was going to tell you?"

"Jack, you've been living with me your whole life. How could I not see the difference in your eyes? I could tell as soon as you walked in here that you'd talked to her."

Cindy snickered. "She's got you pegged, doesn't she?"

"Enough out of you, Nurse Ratchet," Jackson teased.

"Hey! I resemble that remark."

The two women laughed. Jackson sat down next to Jackie and took her hand. "She'll be here tomorrow. She's really excited to see you."

"Does she know?" Jackie asked.

"Well, yeah. Why else would I have called her?"

Nodding, Jackie said, "You're right. How are you feeling about seeing her again?"

"Nervous, sick, excited, sick, terrified, sick—" Jackson's

litany was interrupted when Jackie put a hand on her arm.

"I get the picture. How did she sound?"

Jackson looked into concerned eyes. "She sounded good. According to our favorite mother, Katie says she's happily married and ready to pop out some puppies."

Jackie's eyes widened. "Really?"

"Does that surprise you? Especially with her mother?"

A dark sadness washed over Jackie. "No, I guess it doesn't." She looked up into Jackson's unique eyes. "How is dear Katie anyway?"

"Oh, her normal, crotchety old self. Man, I could feel the tides shift when she realized it was me calling to get Erin's phone number."

Jackie chuckled. "I bet. She's had it in for you since before you were born."

"I guess I can't blame her," Jackson said in a self-deprecating manner.

"Yes, you can, Jackson!" Jackie spoke harshly which induced a coughing fit. Luckily, it didn't last long. She took a deep breath. "You cannot believe that. She judged you because of what was in your heart. What kind of person would do that to you? Anyone who knows you can tell there's nothing but love in there."

"You're right, Jackie, and that's all in the past. I don't want to bring any of that up again. I don't think my heart could take it."

"Do you have a lot to do before she gets here?"

"Mm, I just have to prepare a cabin for her, make sure all the linens and stuff are clean. I'm gonna give her cabin two; it's right on the lake. It's still a little cool at night, but there's a fireplace in that one. I'll make sure there's plenty of wood."

"You're a good person, filled with kindness, Jack."

"I just learned what I was taught." She leaned down and kissed the top of Jackie's head.

"Sweet talker."

"That's me." Jackson smiled down at her aunt. "I'm gonna get to bed, I think. Tomorrow is going to be a huge day and I really need to be rested."

"Okay, honey. Sleep well."

"You too, Jackie."

Erin paced back and forth, listening to the disappointment coming through the telephone line.

"Erin, you know how much better these shows are when the artist is *actually* there."

"Kim, I do realize that, but this is an emergency. Would you rather I cancel the show? You've put so much work into it that it wouldn't seem right. This is Jackie. You know how much Jack and Jackie meant to me when I was growing up. I have to go," she insisted.

Kim could empathize, but it still didn't sit well. She knew more paintings sold when Erin attended her showings. Still, it wasn't her first show, and she understood the circumstances surrounding her departure, so she would let her go with her blessing. "Erin, honey, just be careful. I know all too well what Jackson meant to you. I don't want you getting hurt while you're up there saying your goodbyes."

"It's going to be painful, regardless of what either of us wants. I know I don't want to be hurt, but Jackie's dying. It's going to hurt to see her that way."

Kim shook her head. "You know that's not what I'm talking about."

"I know," Erin said softly. "It'll be okay. We were best friends for ten years, we have a connection, and I felt it just being on the phone with her for ten minutes. I'll be around Jackie and doing what I can for her. The last thing I'm going to do is dredge up the past." She shook her head. She couldn't go down that road again.

"So, can I help with anything else?"

"Can you come over and feed Gracie and maybe pet her a little every day?" she asked hopefully.

"Uggh. I knew you were gonna ask for cat duty." She exhaled. "Fine, just know you *really* owe me for this."

"I love you, Kimba. Thank you."

"Yeah, yeah, good luck and drive safely."

"Okay, I'll call you when I get there." She smiled. "Thank

you for everything. All the pieces will be in my study. Have a good show."

Erin hung up and finished the last of the sorting for her art show. She was certain that Kim would be pleased with the work she was including. There were a variety of pieces with different drawing and painting techniques. With a final nod, Erin placed the pieces of her work around her study in the order in which they should be displayed. She wrote notes about each piece for Kim so she'd have information in case people inquired. She reviewed the prices she'd set, knowing that Kim would change them to a higher figure. She didn't mind, as it allowed her to live a very comfortable life, a life Jeremy would no longer have the privilege of sharing with her. *Jerk.*

Erin went upstairs, hauled her suitcase from her closet and threw it on the bed. She started going through clothes in her closet—pants, jeans, sweaters, blouses, T-shirts, and sweatshirts. None of which were jumping at her to be packed. Her brain started to swirl, making her a little dizzy and a lot frantic.

"What am I going to wear!" she screamed in a panic.

After a long night of packing, a short night of sleeping, and a small plate of brunch, Erin was on the road and halfway to The Northwoods Island City. Knowing the way by heart, she traveled the highways without event and knew if she wanted, she could get there blindfolded. So many thoughts whirred around in her head regarding seeing Jackson again. *What will she look like after so long? What will she think of me? Is she harboring bitter feelings? Will she ever forgive me for my cowardice?*

Erin knew none of those answers, but would find out soon enough. As terrified as she was of seeing Jackson again, a part of her heart that had been dormant for so long had awakened with that one phone call. Yes, she was frightened of all the feelings she knew would come back to haunt her. Yes, she knew there was a chance that Jackson held some resentment toward her. Yes, Jackie probably knew the situation and wouldn't be too happy with her, but her mother no longer dictated her life and wouldn't be able to interfere with her choices this time. She was going to do what she could to help Jackie, and to help Jackson with the heaviness that would come with losing someone she loved.

She pulled out her cell phone and dialed the resort. After a few rings, she recognized Jackson's voice on the machine. *Hello, you've reached the Northwoods Island City Resort. We're unable to take your call but it is important to us, so please leave us a detailed message and we'll call you back. If this is an emergency, please page Jackson Thomas at 715-555-1968. Have a great day. Beep.* Erin got lost in the sound of Jackson's voice, almost forgetting to leave a message.

"Hi, Jack, it's Erin, err Hawk..." She shook her head. "Um, I left Chicago sooner than I expected, so I'll be getting into the resort in the late afternoon or maybe around sixish. I just wanted to give you a heads up. Um...I'm really looking forward to seeing the old place again. Talk to you soon. If you want, you can call me in the car, 773-555-5225. Bye."

Erin closed her phone and exhaled slowly then wiped her palms on her jeans. "God, even just talking to her machine gets me all crazy. I really have to settle down." She threw the phone onto the passenger seat of her Audi. She tried to do some breathing exercises to control herself before she hyperventilated. When that didn't work, she grabbed a CD from her glove box. Soon the soothing sounds of Loreena McKennitt's *The Mask & The Mirror* were coming through her speakers.

"That's better."

The music eased Erin's frazzled mind and let her relax and enjoy the picturesque drive. Halfway through the CD, her phone chirped. Not taking her eyes off the road, she pawed at the seat in search of the phone. Grabbing the antenna with her teeth, she opened the phone. "Erin Hawkins."

"My, my, my, we're so professional now."

Jackson's throaty amusement crept through the phone line and into Erin's ear. Erin laughed. "I never know who's calling me. I gotta be prepared."

"Just like the Girl Scout you never were," Jackson teased.

"It was your brilliant idea that I even joined. I told you I wasn't scout material."

"I could throw in a really bad line about lesbians eating brownies, but I won't." Jackson laughed at the untold joke.

Hearing Jackson laugh, after so many years without that sound, was a salve to her soul. "Yeah, you're such a comic, Jack. And a pig."

"Guilty." The two realized how easy it was for them to fall back into synch after so many years apart. It was as if no time had passed at all. "So you're invading a little early?"

"Invading? I do believe I was invited," Erin bantered back.

"Invade, invite…what's a couple of letters between friends?" Jackson laughed, thinking of the irony in that statement.

"Ha, ha. But yes, I'll be there around five thirty, I'm gonna guess. I'm making really good time."

"Good to hear. We'll have dinner ready for you." Jackson hoped she wasn't presuming too much.

"You guys were always so hospitable. I'll be glad to join you for dinner."

"Fantastic!" she exclaimed. "I hope fish is okay, that's all there is," she whispered jokingly.

"As long as it's breaded and fried and really bad for me, I'm in."

"Got it. Bad food while you're here. Check." They shared a chuckle. "Well, I'll let you get back to it. I'll see you in…" she checked her watch, "wow, in about two hours."

"Yep. Told you I was cruising. I'll be there before you know it."

Yes, you will. "All right, Hawk, be careful. I know how you like to daydream."

"Ha, ha. See you soon."

When the connection was broken, Erin could still feel the warmth brought on by the voice that had haunted her heart for years.

Erin pulled onto the pebbled drive of the Island City resort. As the buildings came into view, her heart sped up to a dangerous pace. Her hands were already shaking and she'd not even turned the car off yet. She took several deep calming breaths, turned her engine off and popped her trunk. Walking around to the back of the car, she pulled her suitcase from the trunk. Reaching in the still open car, she grabbed her purse and closed the door. With a press of her keychain, the beep confirmed that her alarm was set.

Jackson saw her pull up and her stomach did an incredible number of flip-flops. She knew it would be hard to see Erin, but she was nowhere near ready to face all the emotions that went along with it.

"My God, she's beautiful," Jackson whispered, watching from the window as Erin exited her car. "Damn, Hawk, how can you be even more beautiful than you already were?" *I'm gonna be sick.* Jackson put on her best smile, smoothed down her beige Henley and blue jeans, and went outside to greet her guest.

Erin watched as Jackson came out of the main house and her breath hitched. *Oh, my God...she is just...wow...* Jackson's long, dark hair was blowing in the breeze; a lovely smile was etched on her face. Erin couldn't see them yet, but she was sure those eyes would be the warmest mismatched eyes she'd ever seen. Her lips tilted up into a huge smile the closer Jackson came. She couldn't help the tears that welled in her eyes.

"Hey," she forced out.

"Hey, back." Jackson saw the tears in Erin's blue eyes and her heart simply melted at seeing her again.

Erin was not conscious of her next move. She unceremoniously dropped her suitcase and purse and rushed to embrace Jackson in a warm hug that took them both by surprise.

Jackson wrapped her arms around Erin as tightly as she could without robbing the air from her lungs. Holding her Hawk again was better than any dream she'd had since their separation. She could feel Erin's tremors as she let her tears come.

"Sshhh, don't cry, Hawk. It's okay. I'm right here." Jackson held her close. She pulled Erin even closer so Erin's head was pressed firmly against her wildly beating heart. She could feel her own tears well up and was helpless to fight them. She bent her head and smelled the fragrance that was so uniquely Erin. Her hair smelled the same to Jackson as she kissed the top of her head. She threaded her fingers through Erin's hair so they rested at the base of her neck. She stroked the skin lightly, trying to calm her friend.

After several moments, Erin pulled back and wiped her eyes. "I'm sorry, Jack. I...I had no idea I'd have..." she breathed deeply, "such a strong reaction to seeing you again."

Jackson reached out and wiped an errant tear from Erin's cheek. "It's okay. I'm sure you heard my heart ready to hammer its way out of my chest. We're even."

We're hardly even and you know it, Jack. "You look wonderful, Jack. You are even more beautiful than I remembered." Erin graced her with a watery smile.

"So are you, Hawk. So are you." They stood and reveled in the bond that they'd missed more than they knew. "Do you want to settle in, or would you like to see Jackie first? Or..."

Shaking her head, Erin replied, "It doesn't matter to me. Let's dump my bags, then you can take me to see Jackie." She looked up at Jackson. "I'm very nervous to see her." *For so many reasons.*

"You'll be fine, Hawk. I promise. If it gets too hard, you can take a breather. Jackie knows how hard it is going to be for you to see her this way after so long."

"I'm sure. Especially after you told her about my dad and his cancer."

Jackson looked down and shuffled a loose rock with her foot. "I, um...didn't tell her about your dad."

"Why not?"

"I don't know if it was me being afraid of reminding her about her inevitable death from the cancer, or what, but I just didn't want to say anything."

Erin touched her arm. "You always think of everyone else, Jack. I've never met anyone quite like you in my entire life."

"I think that's probably a good thing."

She was kidding, but Erin took her seriously. "Yes, it is. It allows me to appreciate you even more. Reminds me just how special you are."

Jackson swallowed a large lump in her throat and quickly changed the subject before she said something she'd regret later. "Let's get over to your cabin. I put you in cabin two on the water because it has a fireplace and it still gets a little chilly here at night."

Erin smiled. "That sounds great. Lead on."

As they walked, Jackson and Erin both snuck small glances at each other. The link between them was still so strong. Jackson led her up the small steps to her new home for the time being. As she opened the door, a little musty smell welcomed them. Jackson went to the window and opened it to let some fresh air in.

"Damn, I knew there was something I forgot to do. Sorry about that. The air should smell better in a little while." She pointed toward Erin's bedroom. "Your bedroom is in there so feel free to dump your bags or unpack or whatever you'd like to do. I'm gonna head back home to make sure I don't burn dinner."

"What are we having?" Erin asked with a bright smile.

"Like I said, fish. But as requested, it's breaded, battered, and fried. Just the way you like your walleye."

"Oh, wow, walleye." Erin's mouth started to water. "It's been ages since I've had Tomahawk walleye. Thank you, Jack. I can't believe you remembered that."

I remember everything about you, Hawk, but don't get me started. "Yeah, well, this brain is good for something other than musical notes."

"It's good for many things, Jack. You're one of the smartest people I know."

"You need to get out more, Hawk." She winked. "But I really do have to run. Come up to the house when you're ready."

"It really is great to see you, Jack."

"You, too."

They shared another moment smiling at each other before Jackson ran out to save their dinner.

Erin took the time to unpack, call Kim, and sit down in the recliner in the front room. She breathed heavily, trying to sort out the scattered emotions that were bubbling within her core. She needed to prepare herself to see Jackie in the state she'd seen her father in several years ago. The memories were still raw and she knew she'd have to try to keep her tears in check. Jackie didn't need her to cry for her. Jackie would want her to make sure

Jackson would be okay once she was gone. Erin knew she'd do anything for Jackson when that time came.

Erin knocked lightly on the main house door. Jackson let her in with a smile. "You don't have to knock, silly. Get in here." Erin instantly smelled the mingling odors of fried fish and the sterile smell of a hospital. All in all, not the best she could imagine. Cindy stood up from the couch and approached with a smile as Jackson introduced them. "Cindy, this is my longtime friend, Erin Hawkins. Erin, this is Cindy Appleton, Jackie's nurse."

Erin shook her hand. "It is very nice to meet you."

"You too, Erin. The way these two talk about you, I feel like I already know you," she said with a wink to Jackson, causing a blush to color her face and throat.

"And she was just leaving."

Jackson playfully nudged her with her shoulder. Erin caught the familiarity between them and wondered if there was anything more to their relationship. *Jack didn't mention a girlfriend. Oh, this could be awkward.* "Can I go see Jackie or…"

Cindy chimed in, "Actually she's resting right now. I'd let her sleep a little bit before we get her all excited. She's been coughing pretty badly today."

Erin nodded in sympathy. "Okay, I'll eat Jackson's poison and go in after dinner."

"Hey, I'll have you know I'm a great cook. I can fry anything with fins," she stated proudly.

"I just bet you can, Jacques Cousteau," Cindy ribbed.

"Enough out of you, Nurse Ratchet."

"That line's getting old, Jack. You need to find some new material."

Erin followed them like a tennis match in play. She enjoyed the banter. She looked at Jackson who'd started to go back into the kitchen. "Can I help with anything?"

"Yeah. Find something to gag that one with, will ya?" Jackson joked, pointing her cooking tongs at Cindy.

"I meant with dinner." Erin sent a smirk to Cindy, which made her shake her head.

"Oh, that—nah, I got it. Take a seat at the table. Food'll be done shortly."

Erin did as she was told and sat down at the perfectly set, small round wooden table. Each plate had a red placemat beneath it and silverware neatly placed next to it. A fluffed cloth napkin was next to the forks. Finishing off the setting, a fresh glass of water was at the top.

"This is great, Jack. You've turned into quite the hostess."

"Only the best for friends, Hawk." She winked and pulled the last of the fish out of the fryer.

Jackson grabbed their plates and began filling them with fish, steamed fresh broccoli, and wild rice. When the plates were returned to the table, Erin took a deep breath, inhaling the wonderful aromas. "This looks fantastic. Thank you so much for cooking me dinner."

Jackson smiled. "Don't thank me yet, you haven't tasted it."

"True." Erin cut a piece of fish and blew at it when the steam poured out. "Here goes nothing." She put it in her mouth and chewed.

Her eyes suddenly closed and she made a sound that hit Jackson right in her southern parts. *God, please don't do that again. You're a married woman, you're a married woman...*

Erin's eyes opened and she swallowed. "This is better than Bosaki's, Jack. Damn, that's really fantastic!" She held up her water glass and toasted, "To the chef."

"To me!" Jackson said happily, clinking their glasses together.

They ate their dinner quietly, sharing some small talk about their professions. When the plates were empty, Erin offered to clean the kitchen. Jackson immediately declined. "No way, Hawk. I haven't seen you in ages and I'm certainly not gonna let you spend the time here cleaning my kitchen. You're my guest. I'll get it before I go to bed." At Erin's doubtful glance, she reassured her. "Really, it's not a big deal." Erin acquiesced gracefully and went to sit in the front room.

Cindy came in from Jackie's room. "She's awake, and she'd like to see you, Erin."

Erin swallowed hard and smiled at Cindy. "Great." She looked to Jackson. "Are you coming?"

Jackson shook her head. "I'll let you have a moment of privacy with her, if you'd like."

Erin was grateful. "Thank you."

Cindy and Erin walked into Jackie's room. With a barely audible gasp, Erin took in the machines scattered around the room and the tubes that were in most of Jackie's orifices. A small, clear mask rested over her face, but her eyes were shining and looking right at her. With a beckoning hand, she called Erin over to her.

Erin smiled when she heard a soft, "Hey, stranger." She took Jackie's hand and sat down next to her. "Hi, Jackie." Erin tried to push the memories of her father out of her mind. It was difficult. "How are you feeling?"

Jackie whispered, "I'm feeling pretty good today. I'm so glad you could come, honey. It's so good to see you again."

Tears started to well up in her eyes. "I wish…" Erin swallowed and had to take a deep breath. "I wish…"

Jackie stopped her by squeezing her hand. "I know, Erin. You were going through a hard time with your mother. Believe me, we all were." They shared a chuckle, which broke the tension.

"She's a peach, that one. If I could turn back the hands of time, Jackie…"

"Don't do that to yourself, kid. You'll make yourself crazy. Trust me. I used those same words with Jack the other day."

Erin shook her head. "I'm so sorry you're sick, Jackie. If I could fix it, God, I'd die trying."

Jackie looked sternly at her. "No. Jack needs you more than me right now."

"Jackie, you are her, well, basically, her mother. How can you say that?"

"Because I've watched her live the last several years and without you in her life, her eyes don't sparkle anymore. … When she came in last night after talking to you, that sparkle was back. … I wouldn't have her lose that for anything in the world." Jackie smiled at Erin, but frowned when a small coughing fit began.

Cindy came in at the sound of the coughing and Erin let her

take over. Erin watched as Cindy gently maneuvered the bed so it was upright then double-checked Jackie's oxygen flow. When everything checked out and Jackie was settled again, Erin went back to her seat. "Are you okay? I can come back tomorrow after you've rested," she offered.

"God, I don't want to sleep anymore. That's all I've been doing. I just wish my body listened to me more. I can nod off in the middle of a sentence these days."

"I understand." Erin gave her a small smile, thinking about her father.

"So tell me about things. … How's your dad?"

A look of sadness washed over Erin before she could censor it. When Jackie saw it she knew she had to fill her in. "My dad died several years ago. Lung cancer."

Jackie's eyes filled with tears. "I wondered why Joe had stopped coming up here. Erin, I'm so sorry. I know how much you two loved each other."

"Thanks. He was one of the good ones." *Like you.* "So, I guess Billy Joel was right after all, the good do die young."

Jackie nodded, understanding the reference. "So seeing me like this can't be too easy for you, can it? … You didn't have to come, honey."

"Yes, I did. God, for so many reasons." She sniffed back more tears. "I know I hurt Jack and I've tried to think of a way to call her to apologize for things that happened so long ago. I was the one who asked her not to call me, so how could I possibly just call her? I wanted to believe she'd moved on with her life and was happy. I had to believe that." Tears streamed down her face. "I knew she'd tell you about us and the thought of disappointing you both has been killing me, Jackie. You were my family away from home. I've loved you forever and you have to know how sorry I am…for everything…" Erin began to cry uncontrollably.

"Come here." Jackie pulled Erin's head down to her chest and she rested her hand on top of it, stroking the auburn hair gently while she let her cry. "It's okay, I forgive you. But most of all, you have to know that Jack will too. Just make sure you explain everything to her. I know your mother must have put some serious curse on you for you to walk away like you did. Just tell her."

Erin nodded against the cloth of Jackie's nightgown. "I will, I promise I will."

They stayed that way until Erin heard the deep breathing that comes with sleep. When she looked up, she saw Jackie's eyes were closed. She gently lifted the hand from her head and sat up. She placed a soft kiss on Jackie's bruises, put her hand under the covers, took one last look at the frail, pallid woman in the bed, then got up and quietly left the room.

When Erin entered the family room, she was met by two sets of compassionate eyes. Cindy stood up and Erin said, "She's gone back to sleep. She seems to be comfortable."

Cindy went into Jackie's room to check on her and Jackson stood up from her recliner. When their eyes met, Jackson saw how red and puffy Erin's were and she immediately opened her arms. Erin practically ran to her and fell easily into the widespread invitation. She wept for the pain she knew Jackson was feeling, for Jackie being so sick. She wept for all the wrongs that she could've prevented—if she'd just been strong enough. The tears were endless, but Jackson kept her in a warm, comforting embrace and gently kissed the top of her head. When Erin pulled back, Jackson cupped her face and gently wiped her tears with her thumbs.

"Are you okay? I know that must have been so hard for you."

Erin's head bobbed up and down. "It was, but I'm so, so glad I came." She grasped Jackson's hands. "Thank you so much for calling me."

"You're welcome."

"Do you think you're up for a walk outside? I haven't been here in so long, I just want to visit it again." Erin's eyes were filled with hope.

"Sure. It's kinda chilly out, do you want a sweatshirt?" Jackson offered.

"Thanks. That would be great."

When Jackson returned with a sweatshirt, Erin pulled it over her head and breathed in Jackson's scent. The delicate balance of Jackson's lotion, laundry soap and Jackson herself was overwhelming. She took a deep breath and smiled. "Thanks."

Jackson poked her head into Jackie's room. "Cindy, we're gonna take a walk, but we'll be back later, okay?" Cindy nodded.

Walking back to the front door, Jackson held open the screen door for Erin.

Since Erin had last been there, they had added more outdoor lights to the grounds. She also noticed several of the cabins had been upgraded or rebuilt completely. "You guys must be doing well. I don't remember that big cabin over there." She pointed to the lakefront, which sported a large duplex.

"Things have been pretty good. Word is starting to spread about this place. I guess that huge ad you took out in that national paper is finally paying off. Thanks, by the way; you shouldn't have." She nudged Erin's shoulder, surprised when the smaller woman didn't nudge back. The ease between them was unmistakable even though so much was still left unsaid. Jackson would be patient. She knew her friend wouldn't be able to keep it in forever. That's not the person she was. Especially not with her.

Erin turned abruptly to face Jackson. "Why are you being so nice to me?"

Taken aback, Jackson asked her to repeat herself. "Excuse me?"

"I said, why are you being so nice to me? You should be throwing me into the lake, Jack, not coddling me." Erin's emotions were running high.

"Hawk, honey, look…" Jackson, not really knowing how far she wanted this to go, took a deep breath and gently held Erin's shoulders. "I know there's a lot we need to talk about, but I also know that you're hurting inside. Until we're ready to hash all of that out, let's just focus on Jackie, okay? If you let me care for you and try to help you through this, it'll help me as well, I swear." When Erin looked at her dumbly, she added, "Please?"

Erin exhaled, exasperated at Jack's never-ending compassion. "You really are one in a million, Jack." She gazed into the warm eyes of her best friend. "I promise you, before I leave here, I'll tell you everything."

"I can live with that."

The two walked around for nearly an hour with Jackson telling Erin all about Jackie's infirmity—from when they discovered the cancer down to the present. Erin cried now and then, throwing in a few memories of her father and his suffering. Jackson was deeply saddened by Erin's recounting of Joe's illness, knowing his last years had been extremely hard on her.

Chapter Ten

1995 – The Northwoods Island City

Jackson sat on top of the boathouse roof playing her recorder. Eyes closed, she let the music of her instrument carry her into a zone of complete peace. It had been a wonderful summer for her being back at the resort. Jackson missed Michigan, but this was her home and she'd rather spend her time here. She'd gotten letters from the kids she'd taught and those who she'd just bonded with. The connection they shared through their talents would always be there. Of that she was certain.

Lilting melodies were flowing through the polished wood, and her fingers moved gracefully into different positions creating her own special magic. As she played, she heard the footsteps of her dearest friend, whom she'd not seen for five years, which brought a smile to her lips. The footfalls got louder and soon the top of a red head could be seen.

"That wouldn't be the famous painter, Erin Hawkins, coming up my ladder, would it?" Jackson stood to greet her friend.

As Erin climbed over the top rung of the ladder, her breath caught at the sight of the woman before her. Jackson, the skinny teenaged girl, was nowhere to be seen. Erin saw a beautiful woman who had filled into her body perfectly.

Jackson was having similar thoughts as she took in the beautiful woman Erin had become.

Both girls realized they were staring and started to talk at the same time.

"Look at you!" Erin exclaimed.

"You look fantastic!" Jackson cried out.

Finally, they just did what came naturally for them and went to each other for a warm embrace. They both sighed softly at the renewal of the connection that had been missing for several summers.

Pulling back, Erin looked up into different colored eyes and smiled widely. "Heterochromia."

"Gesundheit," Jackson joked.

Erin eyed her accusingly. "Do you know how long it took me to figure out that the story you told me about your eyes was a tall tale?" she said, pointing at Jackson's eyes. "Until I took biology, I was telling everyone about the magical eyes of my best friend, Jackson Thomas. All she did was go to sleep and they magically changed colors. They'd read about it one day, she'd be so famous."

Jackson laughed heartily.

"Then all of my dreams were shattered when I learned that it can happen from a trauma in the womb or just genetics. Man…I was played. And at such an impressionable age, too! You should be ashamed of yourself."

Jackson put out her wrists. "Dear lady, I am ready when you are for my punishment."

"Bend over, this one will cost you."

Jackson did as she was told and gladly accepted the smack on her ass. "Thank you, Mistress, can I have another?"

"Oh, you!" Erin cried out goodnaturedly.

Jackson rose from her bent position and pouted. "I get one? That's it?"

"When you rate another one, I'll let you know."

Jackson bounced and clapped. "I'll be on pins and needles waiting."

Erin changed the subject quickly. "I heard you playing. You have gotten incredibly good, Jack. I'm so proud of you."

Jackson blushed under the praise. "Thanks, Hawk. It really

means a lot coming from you." She motioned to the blanket. "Have a seat. Tell me how you've been, since I know you look amazing." Jack bumped her shoulder into Erin's.

"Things are really great. I'm looking forward to my second year at the Art Institute. I have to leave a week early, though, to move into my dorm room. I'm kinda sad about that, but I promised myself that we'd just have to make three weeks feel like forever."

Jackson agreed. "I can definitely help with that. I'll make sure to fill your days with witty repartee and exciting adventures that will make you want to run back to Chicago by the time I'm all finished."

Erin laughed. "The best part is, I get to live away from home for most of the year. I knew I'd like being away from home, I didn't realize I'd love it so much. I didn't want to come home, not even for the holidays! My mother is close to driving me to drink. She is so crazy, Jack. I wonder where she gets some of the things she says. She tried everything to get Dad not to come up this summer because you'd be back."

Jackson grimaced. "I know she hasn't been the best mother for you, Hawk. At least your dad can balance it out for you some." She put her arm around Erin's shoulder and Erin rested her head against the strong body for a few moments.

"Yeah, he's really wonderful. After Mom has one of her tirades, he always calls and we talk about it. He's a great listener. I'm just so glad I haven't disappointed him, too."

"Oh, Hawk, the only reason your mom makes you feel like you've disappointed her is because you're not living the life she wants you to. You're being who *you* want. And that's what's important. Your dad can see that, she just can't. She's blind to everything around her except what she wants to see."

Erin looked up at Jackson in wonder. "You have really grown up, Jack. Sometimes I listen to you speak and I'm in awe at how much you've changed over the years. For the better, mind you. Not that anything was *wrong* with you per se…"

"Oh, well that makes me feel better," Jackson said, seeing Erin get flustered. "I'm teasing. I appreciate what you've said. I know I've matured a lot over the last few years. I guess a change of environment and mindset will do that to you. Catching fish and water skiing in the summer aren't the end all anymore."

"Uggh, I'll never water ski again."

Jackson's arm tightened around her. "I bet not. That was really scary. For all of us. God. Sometimes I still have nightmares about that."

"You do? I thought it was just me. I guess when you have a near-death experience, it tends to stay with you for a while." Erin grinned mirthlessly.

"Well, yeah. When you have to do just the right thing to make sure your best friend doesn't die in front of your eyes, it also kinda sticks with you for some time. That day scared the living shit out of me, Hawk. I was scared witless about telling your mom I'd killed you."

Erin laughed. "Oh sure! You were more worried about my mother, not that I'd be dead."

"Well, there was that, too."

"Oh, thanks for that consolation," she said sarcastically.

"My pleasure." She gave Erin her most endearing smile.

The two stayed up there for a couple of hours, catching up on life stories, the bond between them crackling with energy and alive once more.

As the days progressed, Erin and Jackson found their groove and were once again running and playing all over the grounds. Erin's mother tried time and time again to get Erin to stay in a night or two, but much to her chagrin, her husband would remind her that they were on vacation and urged her to lighten up.

With a grudging attitude, Katie continued to try to get Erin to go shopping with her, or walk the trails with her and Joe, anything to get her away from Jackson. *I will not lose this fight, Erin. That woman is not good for you to be around.*

Katie had not crossed paths with Jackie since she'd called to berate and insult her niece on that fateful day almost exactly five years ago. Katie felt that Jackie owed *her* the apology for her rude comments and, much to Joe's disappointment, wouldn't back down.

Joe had continued his amiable relationship with Jackie and Jackson. He found them to be lovely people and was pleased to be able to spend time with them. Jackson was a wonderful girl who made him smile with her wit and appealing charm. It was so clear that Erin adored her friend and Joe was glad they shared such a close bond.

Joe and Katie spent the afternoons on the bear trails simply enjoying each other's company. They laughed and talked while he picked flowers for her hair, and reconnected with the woman he loved. As they approached the end of the trail, he could feel the air around them shift. When they were alone, Katie could be the fun-loving woman he married, but once her focus turned toward Jackson, she changed completely. He hoped it wouldn't always be like that. Erin was going to graduate from the Art Institute and continue her artistry and then would most likely marry. Katie would calm down once Erin was an adult. He mentally crossed his fingers, hoping his predictions came to fruition.

Joe left their cabin after another round with his wife. He was growing tired of the constant nagging and complaining she was doing regarding their daughter. He had suggested she stay in Paldeer while Erin and he vacationed together, but she adamantly refused to sit back while that "snake" sank her fangs into her daughter.

"You have really lost it, you know that, right?" he said.

"And you are blind as to what's right in front of your eyes." The same old argument went back and forth, neither of a mind to change their opinion.

He went in search of Erin and Jackson to see if they wanted to fish with him. That was always a good time for them. When he found them, Jackson was swinging out over the water on a rope tied to a tree and then falling into the lake. When her head popped up out of the water, she motioned and shouted for Erin to grab the rope while it was coming her way. Erin grabbed on with both hands.

"I'm coming in, so watch out!" she yelled back at Jackson.

Diane S. Bauden

Backing up as far as she could, holding the rope tightly, she ran toward the edge of the bank and jumped with a piercing shriek. The rope swung her out over a deeper part of the lake. When she was at the furthest stretch of the rope, she let go and noisily fell into the water. "Whoa!"

Jackson watched as Erin broke through the surface of the water with a face-splitting smile. "That was awesome! How come we never did that when we were kids?"

Jackson laughed as she treaded water. "Probably because we would've killed ourselves doing that as kids!"

Spitting water that had gone in her mouth, she agreed. "You're right. Let's go again! I'll grab the rope and hand it to you."

"Cool."

They swam back to shore and Jackson got out, accepting the rope from Erin. When Joe appeared, Jackson smiled at him. "You want to try this, old man? Think your ticker could take it?"

"Who you callin' old?" Joe loved the easy teasing between them. He put down his fishing poles and walked over to Jackson.

Erin saw her father approaching the rope. "Dad, you can't be serious! You don't even have your..." Joe had already begun to run with the rope in hand and was quickly approaching the water. "...suit on," Erin finished.

When Joe's semi-bald head popped up, Erin howled in laughter. "I cannot believe you did that! Mom is going to kill you!"

"That was really fun!" He laughed with his daughter as he swam back to shore. "Nah, by the time I come in from the boat, I'll be dry." He slowly made his way out of the water and smirked at Jackson, who was standing there with her hands on her hips and an I-can't-believe-you-actually-did-that, good-for-you look about her.

"Nicely done. I think I liked the girly scream at the end the best." Jackson ran as Joe came after her like a tiger.

Erin laughed as she watched her father chase after Jackson with no chance of catching the faster woman. She tied the rope around the tree trunk and gathered her dad's poles then put them in his boat. Jackson ran toward her with Joe walking behind, coughing and catching his breath. When he reached them, he gave Jackson a full body hug from behind, chilling her already wet body with his soaked clothing.

"Thanks," she drawled.

"You girls want to go fishing? Your mother seems to want to do nothing but read today, so I'm on my own."

"Sure, Dad, let me just get my shorts and top. Jack, you wanna come?" Erin asked.

"Sounds good to me. I'll go grab some sodas from the fridge and tell Jackie we'll be out on the boat."

When Jackson left, Erin looked at her dad with such love in her eyes. "I'm so glad you and Jack get along so well."

"She's a wonderful person, Peanut. I enjoy people who enjoy life so much. It's really addictive."

Erin smiled at this declaration. "I agree. I just wish Mom did, too."

He shook his head in sympathy. "Peanut, sometimes you just can't change someone's point of view, as twisted and crazy as it may seem to you. Your mother has a problem with Jack and, evidently, her aunt as well. I don't want anything to do with all of that, so I just continue to live like I want, whether or not she approves."

"I wish I could do that. She's just so relentless, Dad." Erin's expression was one of defeat. "It's always something with her, but God, when it's regarding Jack, I can't do anything!"

"One day, Peanut, one day you're gonna live without your mother's constant disapproval. I fear it'll be an ugly day in our house, but you'll feel better. Just be happy, Peanut. That's all I'll ever want for you."

Erin hugged her father. "Thanks, Dad. I love you." They pulled apart and shared a grin. "Lemme get my stuff and I'll be right back."

He watched her dash to the edge of the water to grab her belongings. Anger welled inside of him but soon dissipated as he acknowledged there was nothing he could do that would change the way his wife reacted to Jackson. He knew something was going to have to change or Katie and their marriage would be in trouble.

With only a couple of days left of vacation, Erin was beginning to feel some sadness. The time she'd spent with Jackson had been fantastic. They'd had great adventure-filled days and spent a lot of nights just sitting on the boathouse roof talking about anything and everything. The nights that it rained, they would stay in the loft with a candle or two shining low and illuminating shadows of all shapes and sizes throughout the boathouse. This was Erin's Wonderland and now that Jackson was back, she didn't want to leave. Knowing Jackson still had a year left of school and would also be leaving shortly had helped ease her heart. Erin would be back next summer, and the next, until her parents didn't want to return. By then, she would just drive herself up and vacation alone.

Erin had taken her art supplies up to the loft while Jackson did some errands for Jackie. The sun had almost set, so she lit the few candles they kept in the loft. Her teenage years would be over next month and she wanted to do something to commemorate the time she had spent with Jackson. Pulling a small box from her knapsack, Erin placed it on the blanket. She had only done this a few times with some friends at school, and never to herself. She took off her shirt and bikini top. Taking some rubbing alcohol from her bag, she cleansed a patch of skin. Pulling open the box, she grabbed the needle and opened the bottle of black ink. She flicked the lighter on with her thumb and ran the needle through the flame. Now sterilized, she dipped it into the ink. Taking a deep breath, Erin began to rapidly and rhythmically press the needle into her skin. The initial sting was intense, but she was determined. On occasion she would wipe the bloodied surface with a cloth and admire her work. When the blade took shape, a smile as wide as the Grand Canyon appeared on her face.

Jackson saw the faint light in the loft from the ground floor of the boathouse. When she climbed into the loft, her eyes nearly bugged out of her head, freaked not only at the sight of Erin's bare breasts, but at what she was doing to one of them. "Hawk, what are you doing to yourself!"

Erin looked up and smiled. "Hang on, I'm almost done." She dipped the needle one last time and began the rapid stabbing until she was satisfied.

Jackson sat down in front of her and paid rapt attention. When she spoke again, her voice was filled with amazement. "Where did you learn to do that?"

"Remember my friend Tom, from high school?" Jackson nodded. "He taught me how to tattoo using just inks and needles. I did it to some of my floormates last year, but..." she paused to wipe the blood away. She looked at her work with approval. "I never did it to myself until now." She placed a sterile gauze pad over the fresh ink and looked at Jackson. "I've known you throughout my entire teenage years. And they've been the best years I could ever imagine. I wanted to commemorate that and always remember this place and the time we spent as kids." She removed the gauze and revealed her creation. On her left breast was a small black tomahawk.

Jackson's eyes went wide and then a delighted smile lit up her face. "Hawk, that is probably the coolest thing I've ever seen you do."

"What? You've seen me draw plenty of art that was far better than this little thing," she objected.

"No, Hawk. God, this small representation on your skin has so much meaning wrapped up in it." Erin smiled warmly. "Obviously to anyone who sees it, it may just appear that you have a thing for Indians, but for me, I see our lives."

"That's exactly it, it's our lives, and even though I do have a huge respect for Indians, I wouldn't call it 'a thing'."

"I was kidding."

"Man, my endorphins kicked in, my body is just...wow. Alive!" Erin laughed.

"Did it hurt?" Jackson asked, eyeing the small weapon.

"Oh yeah, initially it hurts a lot. It's piercing your skin, Jack," she explained. "It'll probably be sensitive for a day or so, too." She reached down for some alcohol and rubbed some on her skin, hissing as the cloth made contact. Jackson winced in sympathy.

The two just stared at the image now forever branded on

Erin's skin. Erin was so pleased with her work she couldn't stop looking at it.

Jackson suddenly announced, "I want one too."

Erin looked up, her eyes wide. "Seriously?"

"Yeah, sign me up. What do I have to do?"

Erin's heart began to beat wildly with excitement. It would be fitting for Jackson to have the same tattoo. *Yeah, this is a really great idea.*

"Well, with most of my friends, they usually got high or took a shot or three of alcohol. It just depends on how well you do with needles. You're not gonna pass out on me, are you? It's okay if you do, we just need to lay you down first. Then I can really drill you." She smiled evilly, causing Jackson to momentarily reconsider her decision.

"I don't like needles and I'm a real wuss when it comes to pain, so I should probably do something before I let you stick me." A thought came to her mind. "I, um…smoke a little pot now and again and keep some up here. Do you mind if I do that?"

"Jack, I had no idea you smoked dope!" she cried, amazed she didn't know about that part of Jackson's life. "Why didn't you tell me?"

"Eh, it's no big deal, I don't do it very often, just when I want to really get into my music or I can't sleep. Stuff like that. You're an artist; you can't tell me you haven't dabbled in the ganja."

Erin smiled guiltily. "I've done it several times, actually. I'm just always paranoid my mother will find things to persecute me with, so I never keep any at the house. She'd turn me over to the cops without hesitation."

"Well, you can have some if you want. I have enough." She smiled. "God, we could've done this before tonight, had I known. This will be so fun!"

"Sure, I'm game, but I'll do your tat before I do, otherwise you might get something like my mother's face with an axe through it." She giggled.

Jackson perked up. "Really, you could do that? I want two of those!" She got up, retrieved her stash, and sat back down.

"Jack!" Erin laughed.

"Fine, I'll just stick with the tomahawk…party pooper."

She pretended to pout as she opened a small wooden box she kept in a corner of the loft. She fingered the clear baggy, pulled out an unused joint, then pointed to Erin's lighter. "May I?" Erin handed over the lighter and watched as Jackson lit the marijuana cigarette. Jackson inhaled and held it in her lungs for a few moments then exhaled the sweet-smelling smoke.

"That smells good," Erin commented, watching Jackson inhale. Jackson took a few more hits then stubbed it out.

Erin suddenly realized that she was still without her shirt but didn't want to put it on because her skin was tender, so she asked, "Jack, do you mind if I leave my shirt off? I'm still really sore."

"Sure, they're already out there and all." She winked at Erin. The joking answer seemed to put her friend at ease. After a few moments, she looked at Erin with hooded eyelids and a goofy smile. "I'm feeling no pain. Let's do this."

Erin smiled at her willing participant. "One thing left." Jackson looked confused. "What?"

"You gotta take your shirt off so I can work on your skin."

"Oh." Jackson blushed a little as she lifted her shirt off. Her bra still covered the skin Erin was going to work on. *Screw it.* She unhooked her bra and let it fall into her lap, baring her breasts to Erin for the first time.

A small burn started in Erin's groin. She was familiar with these feelings. The ones regarding Jackson were fairly new this summer, but not unwelcome. Erin looked Jackson in the eye. "Are you okay? You sure you want to do this? Once it's on, it's on."

Jackson bobbed her head in the affirmative. "Yeah, let's do it."

Erin smiled at how many ways she could play on those words, but decided in Jackson's condition she probably shouldn't. She inched closer to Jackson, but couldn't get a comfortable spot with their knees in the way.

"Jack, I can't get a good position. Um…do you think you could stretch your legs out so I could bring my legs over yours?" she asked warily, not wanting to breach any barriers.

"You mean, like, straddle my legs?" Jackson asked, looking

down at her legs.

You're so malleable in this state, aren't you? "Yeah, that way I can get a better angle and I won't stab you worse than I have to."

"Sure, climb aboard."

Erin scooted back and let Jackson extend her legs and move them apart, forming a V. Erin moved closer to Jackson's body and hooked her legs over Jackson's. Both women realized what an intimate position they were in, but knew it was the best way to proceed with the tattooing. Jackson could feel Erin's breath on her exposed skin and couldn't help the goose bumps that started.

Erin noticed right away as Jackson's nipples hardened. "If you want to wrap your shirt around you, that's fine."

"No, I'm good. Let's do this before I lose my nerve." The effects of the marijuana were helping that nerve along nicely.

Erin wiped some rubbing alcohol on Jackson's chest, then picked up the needle and dipped it in ink. "All right, try not to move too much, okay?"

"'Kay." Jackson bit her lip and tensed up.

"Jack, I haven't even touched you yet. Relax, okay? Once your endorphins kick in, you'll feel a rush like you won't believe."

"Okay, on three. One...two...Ow!" Jackson winced at the first pricking of the needle in her skin, but didn't move. Erin's warm hands on her chest were almost worse for her than the needle that was moving impossibly faster into her flesh.

"You're doing great, Jack. Just breathe and relax."

Jackson did as she was told and just kept her eyes locked on Erin's, which were in deep concentration. She noticed the dark outline of blue around the lighter shade coloring her eyes. She fought the temptation to brush her knuckles down Erin's cheek. She did, however, sweep some hair out of her eyes, that had coincidentally fallen as she was watching her. She reached up and lightly tucked the strands behind Erin's ear.

"Thanks," Erin said, without looking up from her canvas. When she did look up, she did a double take at the love she saw in Jackson's eyes, love that went beyond simple friendship. Something was being said with that glance. Her heart raced and she had to try to calm her shaking hands. *Okay, that was intense. What's going on with me?*

Jackson's voice fell to a whisper. "You're welcome."

Erin continued to pierce Jackson's skin and wipe away the dots of blood that appeared. Pressing against Jackson's chest, she could feel her heart thudding rapidly. She cast another glance into the mesmerizing eyes boring into her own. She swallowed nervously, disbelieving the tide swirling in her belly. Trying to break the tension, she said, "Stop looking at me like that, you're making me nervous." She chuckled to hide the tremor in her voice.

"Sorry. I think those endorphins kicked in and I'm feeling really good right now. I mean, *really* good."

"Keep still, I'm just about finished." Erin worked for a while longer until, with one final swipe of the cloth, her masterpiece was finished. She put down the needle and dabbed some alcohol on the cloth to wipe on Jackson's chest. "This is going to sting, so hold onto something."

As Erin placed the alcohol-soaked cloth on Jackson's skin, Jackson reached up and grasped Erin's face in her hands, pulled her head down, and kissed her. The kiss initially left Erin feeling shocked, but she soon found herself lost in the sensations of Jackson's lips against her own. When she responded to the kiss, Jackson let out a whimper that traveled down Erin's stomach and into her groin. She reached out and put her arms around Jackson, pulling their half-naked torsos together. They both moaned at the contact, which intensified their kiss.

Erin wrapped her legs around Jackson tightly, until her core met Jackson's solid stomach. Jackson's tongue gently probed Erin's mouth and her eyes rolled into her head when Erin's tongue met hers with just as much eagerness. Erin's hands were wrapped in Jackson's hair, gently massaging her already invigorated scalp. As their bodies crushed closer together, Erin grimaced at the tenderness of her newly punctured skin. Slowly their bodies pulled apart, lips separating reluctantly. She noticed a little blood on both of their bodies and wiped it with the cloth.

After a few heartbeats, Erin looked up into hungry eyes and

felt Jackson's stare down to her toes. She had to look away. She took a breath. "Why did you do that?"

"You said to hold on to something. Your face was the nearest thing I could reach."

"I'm serious, Jack."

Erin's voice brought a solemn look to Jackson's face. "Because I've been wanting to do that for a long time and I just couldn't stop myself anymore."

"How long?"

Jackson's smile was warm and genuine. "My whole life."

"Wow! Well it definitely felt like that."

Erin still wasn't looking at Jackson so Jackson gently reached under Erin's chin and tilted her face up to look her in the eye. "What are you thinking?"

"I'm thinking that was some good weed!" She laughed, trying to break the tension. She didn't know what to do with all the emotions running amok inside her.

"Hawk, come on. Talk to me. If I just damaged something between us, I need to know, but I've felt something shift between us over the last few weeks, especially tonight, and I don't think I'm wrong." Erin tried to look away, but Jackson wouldn't let her.

"You're not wrong." Erin swallowed. "I just don't know what to do about it. You've had much longer to handle being attracted to girls. I didn't know I was until I saw you eighteen days ago," she said in a whisper. "I'm really confused."

Jackson caressed her face with the back of her knuckles. "It's okay, we can go at your pace. Fast, slow, it doesn't matter to me. I don't want you doing something you don't want to do."

"Thank you, Jack. I mean that." She reached up tentatively and stopped. "Can I hug...?"

"Come here."

Erin reached up and held Jackson tightly, feeling more connected to her than she'd felt with anyone before in her life. They stayed that way for a long time, relishing their closeness. Their breathing slowed and the intense grip they had on each other changed into the gentle warm embrace with which they both were very familiar.

They pulled out of their hug and realized they were still naked above the waist. Erin's blush was matched by Jackson's and soon they were covering up their chests as much as they could without it being painful.

"I'll take a hit off that now, if you don't mind." Erin pointed to the stubbed-out joint on the box.

"Sure. I may help you with that."

They finished the joint together and soon were giggling at each other. Erin put away her supplies and Jackson put away her stash. Sitting with their backs against the wall, underneath the window, they leaned against each other and tried to piece together in their addled minds what had just happened. Every now and again, they'd each look down at their new tattoos and smile at its meaning. They would have that forever, just like they'd always have each other.

After a time of soft words and gentle touches, the girls realized they'd better head back. Erin chewed on some gum from her pack, just in case there was any lingering smell of marijuana. They made their way through the dock area and out onto the grounds. As they walked over to the pier, the moon glistened brightly over the water, catching their attention. They sat in the chairs on the dock and silently watched the water ripple with tiny waves coming into shore. The night was as peaceful as either of them had ever known.

When Erin looked at her watch, she saw that it was approaching midnight. If she wasn't home before twelve, her mother would come out looking for her. "Jack, I gotta get going. It's getting late and I really don't want my mom coming out here."

"You're right. We still have a couple of days together before you go, so tomorrow let's do something just for us, okay?"

"I have no idea what that could be, but yes, let's do that."

They got up and walked hand in hand down the pier. Jackson walked Erin to her cabin. "Sleep well, Hawk. And thank you for my tomahawk. I absolutely love it. Every time I touch it or look at it, I'll think of you."

Erin was seeing Jackson in a much different light since their kiss. The attraction she felt was growing with each minute they were together. As much as she didn't want their evening to end, she knew it must. She turned to walk up the steps to the cottage, then stopped. She turned and walked back to Jackson, leading her around the corner out of sight of the door. She reached up and slowly pulled the dark head down so their lips could meet one more time. The kiss was passionate and filled with so much love, Erin was loath to break the contact. She pulled away softly, adding several kisses, each more chaste than the last, until they parted.

Jackson leaned her forehead against Erin's. "Wow," she breathed.

"Yeah, me too," Erin agreed. "Goodnight, Jack." Erin backed up, not sure if her legs would support her. With a final touch to Jackson's hand, Erin rounded the corner and went up the stairs of the cottage.

"Goodnight, Hawk," Jackson said into the air, and on shaky legs made them work to take her home.

Inside the cabin, Erin's mother was on the couch waiting for her. "Where in God's name were you? It's almost midnight, Erin!"

"Mother, calm down. I was just in the boathouse with Jack."

"Of course you were. I should've figured you'd be with…" She stopped as she noticed a spot of blood on Erin's blouse. "What the hell happened?" She pointed at the red blot.

"Oh, that, it's nothing."

"The hell it isn't. Pull your shirt up, now."

"Mother…" she objected futilely.

"Now!"

Erin gingerly pulled up her shirt and her mother saw the tattoo above her bikini top. "That had better not be what I think it is. Now you're desecrating your body? What the hell is wrong with you, Erin? Did *she* make you do this? Was this *her* idea?" She nearly spat her words at Erin making her cringe and blink wildly.

"No, Mother. I did this myself."

"Why would you do something like this to your body? You can't get those things off!"

"I don't want it off, Mother. I put it there because I wanted it there."

"Erin, why must you continually and intentionally do things that make me uncomfortable? I am sick of your attitude, young lady! You are just doing this to make me angry and upset, and you know what? It's working!"

Awakened by the shouting, Joe walked into the family room. "What is going on out here? I don't think they've heard us in Chicago, yet, but let's keep trying!" he yelled at his wife. "What could she possibly have done to warrant this, Katie?"

"Show him." She pointed at Erin's chest. "She's branded herself with a...tomahawk!"

"You're about to bust a blood vessel because she got a tattoo?"

Shaking her head wildly, she sputtered, "No, Joe. She did this *herself!*"

Joe looked at Erin and shook his head like, *why do you do this to yourself, you know she's going to yell at you?* "Peanut, why did you give yourself a tattoo?"

Erin's tears began. "I did it so I could remember all of my childhood up here. You both know how special this place is to me. It always will be. So when I thought about it, it seemed perfect, and then Jack saw it and wanted one too."

"Jackson saw your naked breasts? What else aren't you telling me?" Katie snarled.

"Nothing, Mother," she lied. "We just wanted to honor our time on Lake Tomahawk. It's not a damn crime!" she shouted, beyond upset at the way the night had shifted.

"I don't believe you!" she yelled.

"Katie! That is enough!" Joe lowered his voice. "This conversation is over. There is nothing that can be done about it now. It's midnight and I don't want to spend the rest of this night screaming at you." He turned to Erin. "Peanut, I know you wanted to do something for you guys, but it might have been a little excessive. Perhaps if you'd asked, it would've been less of a shock to your mother and me."

Erin's tears fell harder, knowing she'd disappointed her

father.

"Now, I want you to go to bed, and Katie, I want you to as well. I'm going to sleep on the couch because I am far too angry to share a close proximity with you right now."

Erin ran into her bedroom and closed the door. Katie stormed off and slammed the door to their room. Joe sat down heavily on the couch, head in his hands and sighed. "Something's gotta give here." He lay down and pulled the afghan from the top of the couch down across his body. With a final sigh, he closed his eyes and fell into a restless sleep.

Chapter Eleven

2002 – The Northwoods Island City

Erin stood on the dock in the morning sun, rubbing the tattoo she'd created years ago. Thinking back to that day was bittersweet. Her mother stating it was a desecration of her body had countered all the love and symbolism that had gone into the tattoo. Erin wished she could take back that summer and do things over again. This time, she'd have the strength to stand up to her mother and her bigotry.

Feeling Jackson approach before she saw her, Erin turned to greet her. "Good morning. It's so beautiful here, Jack. God, I can't believe how much I've missed this."

Jackson was very pleased that Erin's love of the place hadn't changed. "Morning. Yeah, I don't think I'll ever get tired of this view, either. It's so much a part of me, I can't imagine living without it." She looked right at Erin and the two didn't miss the double entendre she'd snuck in there.

"That would be like a fish out of water, Jack. If that happened, you'd be miserable, and I'd be miserable for you." The metaphor game was one Erin didn't want to play, but they weren't ready to talk yet. "So, how's Jackie this morning?"

Jackson's face fell. "She's not doing too well, Hawk. Her doctor is in with her now. She isn't at all optimistic." Jackson's eyes began to well with tears and Erin instantly put her arms around her.

"I'm so sorry, Jack." Erin could feel the tremors in Jackson's body.

The tears were falling freely down Jackson's face. She finally had someone to lean on that she trusted. Even after all this time, Erin would be the one to get her through this terrible time.

"Shh, you just let it out, honey. I'm right here." *Finally.*

Jackson cried for a while, unwilling before now to completely unleash her sadness. She sat heavily on the metal chair and stared out over the water.

Erin wanted to do something to make her friend feel better, but wasn't sure what she could do. She knew times like these made your body want to shut down, and the only thing you had energy for was to make more tears. Sometimes there was no consolation. *But I can try.* An idea came into her head and she went with it.

"Are the keys to the boat still in the boathouse?" she asked, trying to mask her excitement.

"Yeah, why?"

"I'll be right back."

"Wait, grab the keys off the far right hook. You can take the Formula."

"You mean we." Erin smiled secretively. "I'll be right back."

Erin ran to the boathouse, but once inside, her mind reminded her what had happened when she was there last. Shaking away the memories, she went to the key rack and grabbed the last set of keys. Returning quickly to Jackson, she dangled them in front of her. "Wanna go for a ride, little girl?" she asked playfully.

Jackson gave her a tiny grin. "Sure. You gonna tell me where we're going?"

"Nope, but I'm sure you will guess once we get there."

"Ha, ha. You're no fun."

"Ah, but that's where you're wrong." When the boat was untied, Erin started the engine and slowly pulled away from the dock. "Hang on!" She pushed up the lever on the side of the wheel and the boat picked up speed in very little time. "Whoa!" Erin cried, not expecting such power.

Jackson was holding on to the side of the boat. "Have you ever driven one of these before?" Her voice betrayed a little panic.

"No. But how hard can it be?"

Jackson acknowledged that she was right and sat back to enjoy the ride. The boat ran effortlessly through the water of Lake Tomahawk. As they got closer to Erin's destination, Jackson's face lit up like a child in a toy store. "You're taking me to get potato salad!"

Erin's smile was electric. "Yes, ma'am!" She watched as Jackson's energy level soared. They pulled up to the docks and Jackson waved to an old friend who'd worked that dock since she'd been a child.

"Hey, Roy! How's it going today?"

"Well, if it isn't young Jackson Thomas. Where have you been, girlie girl?" He smiled brightly at her.

"I haven't been around much, sorry for that." They tied the boat up so they could go into the convenience store that sold Jackson's ambrosia. Roy gave them a hand up and both women stood on the docks. "My aunt Jackie has cancer, Roy, so I've been taking care of her."

His face fell at the news. Having known all of the Thomases for quite some time, Roy felt a wave of sadness. "I am so sorry. She's a wonderful lady. Please give her my best, won't you, Jack?"

She lightly touched his arm. "I will. It was nice to see you. We'll just be a few minutes. I don't know if you remember my friend Erin?" She drew Erin to her side.

"Of course. My, you sure grew up from that tiny towhead I used to know. It's nice to see you again, Erin."

Erin smiled at the sweet man. "Nice to see you, too. I took this one out to get some of her favorite—"

"Don't tell me. That darn potato salad?" he guessed, making the girls laugh.

"You guessed it. I figured it could do her some good since she loves that stuff almost more than air."

Jackson listened to the conversation floating between Erin and Roy and jumped in. "Hey! Hello, I'm standing right here." *I have really missed her.*

Erin smiled and looked her up and down. "Why, yes, you are." Jackson rolled her eyes.

"Okay, you girls. I'll keep watch on your vessel in the meanwhile. Enjoy your time shopping."

The girls waved. "Thanks!" they said in unison.

Jackson picked out a two-pound container and had the deli woman fill it with her favorite side dish. When it was handed to her, Jackson asked for a plastic fork. She immediately opened the container and put a huge forkful of the salad in her mouth. Eyes closing in absolute pleasure, she moaned loudly.

Erin paid the patient woman behind the counter and apologized. "Sorry, can't take her anywhere."

"Thank you," Jackson mumbled through her full mouth, and waved her fork at the amused woman as they exited.

They thanked Roy for watching the boat and he helped launch them on their way.

"I actually thought you'd wait to eat that with lunch. Silly me," Erin joked, putting the key into the ignition.

Jackson swallowed. "This is the breakfast of champions, Hawk! It has been so long since I came over here. I didn't realize until I saw Roy that it's been at least a year since I've had this stuff." She smiled happily into her plastic container.

Erin drove the boat much slower on the return trip, just enjoying the feeling of being on the water again. "You've been a little busy."

Jackson's head bobbed. "Yeah, I guess I have." She looked at Erin with gratitude. "Thank you for being here, Hawk. Not just for the potato salad, but coming to see Jackie. I know it means so much to her."

"No thanks necessary, Jack. I wanted to come. I'll do everything I can to help you through this. Whatever you need, it's yours. You know that, right?" Erin looked over at Jackson, who was staring out into the water. Her hair was blowing wildly in the wind kicked up by the boat, and Erin thought she'd never seen anything more beautiful.

Jackson turned her head and their eyes met. Even now, the love they felt for each other was evident. "I do." She reached over and touched Erin's shoulder. "I really appreciate it."

The rest of the trip was spent in silence as the two let their thoughts carry them most of the way home.

After the boat was moored safely back in its slip, Jackson carried her booty into the house with Erin right by her side. The nurse rose and extended her hand to Erin. "Hi, I'm Janet, Jackie's day nurse. I don't think we've met."

Erin smiled at the plump, black-haired woman. "I'm Erin, nice to meet you. Jack speaks the world of Jackie's team."

"Well, that goes both ways. We love these ladies." She smiled warmly at Jackson. "We'd just wished we'd met them in different circumstances."

Jackson was touched by her words. "Thank you, Janet. I couldn't imagine better people taking care of Jackie."

"She's awake right now. Her doctor just left, but I suspect you know the substance of her findings."

Jackson nodded solemnly. "I do. I just want to make sure she's not in any pain for her last days."

Janet put a reassuring hand on Jackson's forearm. "Don't worry, she will go peacefully, I promise."

Jackson looked at Erin. "Wanna go say good morning?"

"Sure."

Jackson gently touched the small of Erin's back, leading them into Jackie's room.

A light beeping noise came from a new heart monitor that had been brought in by the doctor. Jackie's pallor had worsened since Erin had seen her the night before. She knew from the looks of her, it wouldn't be long before Jackie took her leave from this world.

"Hello, sunshine," Jackson greeted cheerfully, bringing a small twinkle to Jackie's eyes. "How are you feeling today?"

Jackie shrugged, not able to bring words forth just yet.

"Jackie, look what Hawk got me!" She showed her the plastic container she hadn't put down since its purchase. This brought a slight sound from Jackie and a small smile. "Ah ha! I knew that'd getcha." Jack looked around and, not seeing Janet, pulled the mask off of Jackie to put a small liquid smear of the salad into her aunt's mouth then quickly put the mask back on.

A light smacking of Jackie's lips and a low hum of approval made Jackson laugh. Her aunt was as much of a sucker for this stuff as she was.

Erin watched as Jackson proved once again the amazing compassion she had in her heart. She knew Jackson thought of Jackie as her mother and knew all too well how awful it was to lose a parent you loved. The tenderness Jackson showed Jackie was almost painful to watch. The memories of her father's last days were tangible as she watched the two interact.

"I'm hogging all of your stage time and poor Hawk traveled so far to see you. Let me go fill up your water jug and I'll be right back."

Erin took the spot Jackson had vacated and lightly grasped one of Jackie's hands. "Hey, lady." Jackie gripped her hand a little. She saw a book on her nightstand and asked, "Do you want me to read to you a little?" Jackie blinked slowly and lightly squeezed Erin's hand. Erin picked up the book and smiled at the title. *Moby Dick.* "Jack always did want to catch the big one, didn't she?" Jackie's eyes sparkled and Erin turned to the first page. "Call me Ishmael…"

Erin began to read the classic. When Jackson reentered with the full water jug, she quietly put it down and sat in a corner chair to listen, potato salad safely stored in the refrigerator for later. She closed her eyes and let the sound of Erin's voice soothe her wounded soul. The more she listened, the more she heard Erin's voice from the past letting her go, and she realized that she needed to know the whole story. She'd thought that she wanted to wait, but she wanted all of her pain at once rather than getting through one loss only to have it followed by another. *I just want this hurt to go away.*

After an hour of reading, Erin quietly rose and put the book down. Jackie had fallen asleep. When she turned to talk to Jackson, she, too, had nodded off. She silently walked over to Jackson, grabbed a light blanket draped over the armrest and covered her. She stirred a little, but easily went back to her dreams.

When Erin entered the living room, Janet looked up from her needlepoint and asked, "How's our girl doing?"

"Well, *both* of our girls are sleeping right now. I started reading to Jackie and they both went out," she snapped her fingers, "just like that."

"That does it every time. Maybe Jack was read to as a child, but I know whenever I read to Jackie while she's in there, she goes out faster than Jackie."

"You know, I'll have to ask Jack that when she wakes up to see if there is some Pavlovian effect going on there." Janet smiled warmly at the woman. "It's a beautiful Saturday out there, so I think I'm gonna take my sketchbook and head on out to the pier."

"That sounds like a fantastic idea. I'll let them know where you've gotten to."

"I appreciate it. It was nice to meet you, Janet. Hopefully Jackie's pain will be over soon."

"I feel the same way."

Erin sat on the pier happily drawing another landscape. Her fingers were chalky from the pastels she was using. An older man was fishing on the pier with his grandson and she'd asked if they would mind being her subjects for a while.

"We'd be happy to, young lady. After all, unless we get a fish on the hook, we'd just be sitting here waiting anyway."

Chuckling at his answer, Erin completely lost herself in her work. When she was adding the final touches to her picture, a shadow fell over her paper. Jackson sat down next to her on the wood of the pier and remained quiet. Occasionally, she'd look at Erin and when she was caught, she'd look away. This happened several times before Erin finally stopped and said, "Is there something on your mind? You're like a little kid waiting for me to ask you to speak."

"I just don't know if I want the answer."

"What's the question?" she asked quietly.

"Will you tell me what happened?" She didn't have to expand. They both knew exactly what she meant.

Erin stared at her for a few moments. "Are you sure you want to do this now? I thought you wanted—"

"I know what I thought, but having you here and not knowing is about to drive me crazy."

Erin thought for a moment. "Can you wait until tonight? I need to make a call to my event host, Kim. I just want to make sure she doesn't have any questions about the pieces for the show and whatnot."

Jackson agreed. "Sure. I'll meet you after dinner. Can we talk on the roof? That's always been a good place for us to communicate."

Erin swallowed nervously then answered, "Of course we can meet there. I haven't been up there since I got here, so I hope I can still get up the ladder." She laughed, trying to diffuse the intensity from Jackson.

"Oh, please, if I can still get up there, I know you can."

"All right, then. I'll meet you later."

Jackson got up and walked away. Erin was so full of emotion she wasn't sure what to do with it all. The question had come as a surprise to her. She thought she'd have a few more days to plan what she wanted to say. If Jackson wanted to know, then she was going to get an earful.

Finished with her drawing, she signed the bottom and pulled it out of her book. She collected her things and walked to the other side of the pier where her subjects were still waiting for a bite.

The older man looked up at the friendly woman. When she gave him the drawing, his eyes became wide. "This is just beautiful! May I have it for my grandson?" he asked, excitement clearly in his voice.

"Yes, please. Enjoy it." With a wave, she left the man on the dock unaware of the price that an original Erin Hawkins picture would draw if sold in any gallery.

She went into her cottage and sat on the couch, pondering the evening ahead. "Oh, boy, here we go," she whispered, closing her eyes, not looking forward to reliving that time.

Chapter Twelve

1995 – The Northwoods Island City

When Erin awoke the next day, her eyes burned from crying and the etching on her chest burned. She slowly got out of bed, opened her bag and pulled out the rubbing alcohol. Lifting her shirt over her head, she then applied the antiseptic to the tattoo. *I wonder if Jack's is feeling like this too.* Memories sent a flood of heat through her, memories of their bared chests while she created, Jackson's eyes blazing into her own, and Jackson's mouth on hers.

"Oh, my God," she breathed. "Jack."

She could feel a slow inferno building inside her. Thinking of their half-naked torsos touching was sending all sorts of warmth throughout her body. Her next thoughts were less exhilarating as they proceded to the shouting match that ensued when she returned to the cottage. Katie had been out of control and Erin was actually a little afraid. Her mother had been irrational before, but last night was different. She was just grateful her father had walked in when he did, even if he had been disappointed in her. That was an awful feeling for Erin. He'd always been proud of her, and to have that image marred was troubling. One thing she knew, she could always talk to him and she would surely do that today.

Putting her shirt back on, she opened her door and went to use the bathroom. The couch was empty and her mother's door was still closed. *Dad must have gotten up early and gone out fishing.* She walked into the bathroom and closed the door. Looking at her image in the mirror, Erin lifted her shirt to view her design from a different perspective. When the tomahawk came into view, she couldn't help the smile that appeared on her face. She was very proud of her creation, regardless of what her mother thought.

She used the facilities and turned on the shower. Erin got into the spray and sighed as the warm water trickled down her body. As thoughts of Jackson sifted through her mind, she began to hum, smiling unconsciously as she lathered her body. The tattoo stung a little, but that subsided when she rinsed off the soap. As she grabbed the bottle of shampoo, she heard the door to the bathroom open. Her heart raced when she saw her mother's silhouette on the other side of the shower curtain.

"Mother, I'm taking a shower. Can't you wait?"

When no answer came, she began hearing the strains of the string arrangement from the movie *Psycho* in her mind. Before another second went by, the curtain was unceremoniously pulled open, baring her naked form to her mother's angry eyes.

"What else has she marked on you?" Her mother began pawing at her like a crazy person. "Show me!"

"Mother, stop it! What is the matter with you!"

"I don't want you near that girl! She is the devil's spawn!"

Not knowing how best to deal with the irrationality, Erin pushed her mother away and aimed the showerhead; the water drenched her. "Get out of here! I can't believe you would come in here and do this!" Erin screamed. "Look at yourself, Mother!" When her mother didn't move, she yelled again, "Get out!"

Her mother gave her a glance of fury, grabbed a towel and left the bathroom. Erin quickly jumped out of the shower, locked the bathroom door, and began to cry. She sat her wet body on the toilet seat and wept into her hands. "Jesus Christ."

When Erin had finished her shower, she hurried from the

bathroom to her bedroom. She closed the door and began to dress rapidly to prevent another examination by her mother. Disbelief for what her mother had done was still racing through her mind. When she was dressed, she dragged a comb through her wet hair, slipped on her thongs, grabbed her pack, and opened her door. Her mother was sitting at the kitchen table, unmoving. Anger bubbled inside of Erin. She desperately wanted to lash out at her mother for such an invasion of her privacy. The cowardice in her won and she opted not to say a word. She shouldered her backpack and turned toward the door.

"I'm serious, Erin, I don't want you around her anymore." The voice was icy.

Erin turned to face her mother. "I'm going to hang out with Jack until I leave, Mother. If she hasn't cast an evil spell on me in the last three weeks, one more day isn't going to kill me."

They stared at each other for a long time before her mother looked away. "You'd better be home before ten tonight if you know what's good for you."

"Mother, I'm going to be twenty in about three weeks. I'm a little old for a curfew. I'll be home before midnight, as usual. I'll confer with Dad when I see him on the docks."

"I'm sure you will," she snapped.

Erin turned abruptly and left her mother alone in their cottage. As her feet hit the grass, she spotted Jackson on the dock talking and laughing with her father. Her mood instantly brightened and her step became lighter. Erin's stomach did a little flip at the sight of Jackson wearing only shorts and a bikini top.

The two of them waved at Erin and her anger vanished as she smiled and waved back. Jackson ran down the pier to greet her. "Hey, you," she called, adding a discreet wink, causing a small blush to color Erin's cheeks.

"Hey, back."

Jackson noticed the red rimming around Erin's eyes. "Hawk, what's wrong?"

Erin shook her head. "Not in front of my dad, okay?" she whispered. "I'll tell you later."

Jackson nodded. "Your dad wants to take us fishing since it's your last full day here. You up for that?"

"Yeah, Peanut. Let's catch that elusive muskie today, whaddya say?"

His exuberance was addictive and she couldn't help but agree to go. "Well, what are we waiting for then? Let's go get it!"

The afternoon was spent in the warm sun and after an hour of fishing, the girls put their poles down and went to the tip of the boat to lie in the sun. Their bodies were side by side and their smiles toward each other were warm. Joe couldn't help but notice the shift in their demeanor. Their heads were closer when they spoke, the tone of their voices was softer, and as they bathed in the sun, he didn't miss the brief squeeze Erin gave Jackson's hand. He turned and continued to fish while his mind absorbed the new information. It wasn't a surprise, it was just different to be thinking something than to see it outright.

The dinner hour eventually arrived and Joe, as usual, took his family to Bosaki's for dinner. Katie absolutely refused to have Jackson sit at their table for another meal and after the shower incident, Erin was not going to go to battle with her mother, so it was just the three of them. Dinner was a quiet affair, and in Erin's eyes, it was the most peaceful time she'd shared with her mother in days.

When they returned home, Erin grabbed her sack and went toward the door. She turned to her father who was sitting on the couch. "I'll see you before midnight, Dad," she said, not addressing her mother at all.

"Okay, Peanut. Have fun."

Without sparing her mother a glance, she left the cottage.

Jackson was waiting for Erin in the boathouse loft. When she heard footsteps getting closer, her heart began to hammer. When Erin's red head appeared, a large smile spread over Jackson's face.

"Hey," Erin greeted.

"I've been waiting for you forever," Jackson said with a pout.

"What for?"

"So I could do this." Jackson pulled Erin to her and kissed her passionately. Their lips fused together and soon their tongues began to dance. A moan escaped Erin's throat, which ratcheted up Jackson's already insatiable desire for Erin. They stayed that way for several moments, reacquainting their mouths. They pulled away slowly and Erin was the one to breathe out in wonder.

"Wow. My God, you're good at that." She giggled. "Why don't you have a girlfriend, again? They don't know what they're missing."

"I've been waiting for you," she said seriously.

Erin met her eyes and knew she wasn't teasing. "Wow."

Jackson smiled. "Your vocabulary seems to be stunted when you're kissed properly. I'll take that as a compliment." Erin lightly slapped her arm and Jackson added, "Oh, hurt me, baby."

Erin's face couldn't have been any redder, but she couldn't stop laughing. "Jack, stop!"

Jackson loved to tease Erin and now she had a whole other arsenal to bring into play—sexual discovery.

Erin moved away from Jackson's grasp to sit on the blanket. Jackson plopped down across from her, lying on her side with her hand supporting her head. As Erin looked at her, her mind began to paint. Jackson had been the subject of many pictures, but this one could be her most favorite.

"Jack, will you let me draw you like that?"

Jackson's eyebrow rose. "You want to draw me like this." It was more of a statement than a question.

"Yes, with the light coming in through the window and the lighted candles, you look…simply beautiful."

Jackson blushed red-hot at the compliment. "What do you need me to do?" she whispered, heaviness in her voice.

"Just stay put as long as you can and I'll tell you what happened this morning with my mother."

Jackson took a deep breath. "All right, Picasso, let's get this show on the road before my hand falls asleep. I might need it to knock your mother's block off."

"Ha, ha." Erin's look went from playful to serious. "You won't like what she did, though."

"I'm listening."

Erin's fingers flew across the page with grace and passion. As she sketched, she told Jackson about the incident in the shower and had to verbally restrain her from going after her mother.

"Jack, it's okay, I'm fine. Lay down, so I can finish."

Jackson's anger made her cheeks flush brightly. Erin didn't comment, but it did add nice color to her picture.

"Hawk, if she ever lays a hand on you, I…I just won't be responsible for my actions. How's that?"

"Thank you for coming to my defense; it means everything to me." She shook her head. "She's really over the edge these days. I have no idea what pushed her over, but she's just…gone."

"Maybe she needs to see someone and, I dunno, get on some medication—an antipsychotic or something."

"Maybe?"

"Okay, she does." They shared a laugh.

When Erin was finished, she turned her sketchbook around so Jackson could see the finished work. What she saw made her eyes well up with tears. Erin obviously saw her in a way she'd never seen herself.

"Wow, Hawk, this is just…breathtaking. And the picture is nice too," she joked, trying to clear the tears from her eyes.

Erin had already seen her reaction and was extremely pleased. "This is how I see you, Jack. You are breathtaking to me. Sometimes when I look at you, my heart just…hurts."

Jackson looked deeply into her eyes. "I know that feeling all too well."

Erin pulled out the drawing and gave it to Jackson. "Thank you. Now I can say I knew you when," Jackson teased.

Erin smiled, put her sketchbook away, and looked at her watch. It was after ten o'clock. Her heart sank at the knowledge this was their last night together. She pulled some Wet Naps from her bag and wiped the ink from her fingers.

Jackson watched in amusement. "Such a tidy young woman you are."

After a couple of heartbeats, Erin looked squarely into Jackson's eyes. It was unnerving for the women at first, but they soon lost their shyness at the emotions they felt radiating from each another.

"Jack...I have something else I want to give you." Erin swallowed nervously.

"Oh, yay, I love presents." Jackson sat straight up. "Gimme."

"It's right here," Erin said softly.

Jackson's heart began to beat wildly. *Did she just say what I think she said?* She swallowed hard, took a tight rein on her libido, and sought crystal clarity. "Where is it?"

Erin pushed the tiny shirt strap off her left shoulder then repeated the motion on her right. Jackson moved closer and cupped Erin's face. "Are you sure you want to do this?"

Erin leaned forward and captured Jackson's lips in a tender kiss. "Very sure."

Jackson returned the kiss, the gentleness of her lips causing Erin to sigh. They both leaned forward in their seated positions, then Jackson slowly rose to her knees with Erin following suit. Jackson cupped Erin's face gently, kissing her with incredible tenderness. She reverently placed kisses on her lips, cheeks, and eyelids then moved back to her mouth.

Erin felt like she was being worshipped and her body was responding in a way that was totally unfamiliar to her. She could feel the arousal building between her legs and she was only *kissing* Jackson. She wasn't sure if she could handle much more.

Jackson used her weight to pull Erin toward her. "Come here. Let's lie down."

Jackson's hands were shaking, Erin noticed, and she looked into Jackson's eyes. "I'm so glad you're nervous too."

"I am. I'm still waiting to wake up."

Erin kissed her gently then lay down and looked up at Jackson's smoldering eyes. "I promise I'm not a dream."

"You are to me." Jackson moved to lie on top of Erin. Erin's hands found their way into Jackson's hair and grasped it gently. Jackson leaned up and stared down into her blue eyes. "I love you, Hawk...more than I can ever say."

"Then show me," Erin whispered, and Jackson soon possessed

her mouth with her lips and tongue.

Their bodies were on fire. Jackson's hands were everywhere at once, and Erin was whimpering with desire. Jack raised Erin's shirt and gently traced lines on her stomach with her fingertips. Erin's stomach shook with fevered tremors. When she felt the first tentative touch on her breast, Erin grasped Jackson tightly. Both women sighed.

Jackson lifted Erin's shirt as high as she could, until Erin offered to remove it all together. While Erin took off her watch, shirt, and bra, Jackson did the same then pressed their bodies together. The intimate contact made them both exhale sharply and press more tightly together. Jackson opened her eyes to see Erin's closed in rapture. It was a beautiful sight. Looking down, she saw that their tattoos were touching.

"Look, they touch when our bodies are together. This bonds us completely, Hawk."

Erin smiled at the sentiment and reached up to caress Jackson's soft cheek. "I love you, Jack." Putting her hand behind Jackson's neck, she pulled her down to kiss her with all the love in her heart.

The passion took Jackson by surprise and she moaned into Erin's mouth. Jackson's kisses moved down her jawline to Erin's throat. She blazed a trail of hot kisses down her throat to the swell of her left breast. She reverently kissed the tinted skin, then moved lower to pull Erin's nipple into her mouth. She moaned at the texture of the pebbled flesh against her tongue. Erin's body began to move against Jackson's, her center wet with desire.

Jackson moved her hand down to Erin's shorts then further to her thigh and back up. She left her hand at the apex of Erin's legs and added a little pressure with the heel of her palm. Erin moved against the hand, throaty moans escaping her mouth. Erin grasped Jackson's upper back and tugged her tighter against her body. Jackson ground her hips onto Erin's thigh, causing her own moan to slip from her lips.

With a flick of her hand, Jackson opened the button on Erin's shorts and deftly slid her hand inside. Her caress touched dampness, and she smiled at Erin's arousal. Reaching beneath the undergarment, she found the flesh she'd been craving for so many years, wet and waiting for her. *For me.* Jackson stroked the engorged flesh, lightly touching the area around Erin's entrance. Erin's body jerked up, encouraging the exploring fingers.

Her fingers were relentless with their teasing and Erin soon found herself begging Jackson to make contact. "Please, Jack, please…touch me."

Without pause, Jackson moved her fingers to Erin's enlarged clitoris and began to lightly stroke all around it. Jackson's eyes closed at the intense feelings. Never in her life had she imagined she'd ever make love to Erin, despite how desperately she wanted it to happen. Erin's passionate moans made her aware of just how real this was. Jackson's fingers concentrated on the inflamed flesh and soon felt the tremblings of Erin's impending orgasm. Erin's body began to writhe uncontrollably and her panting became louder. As her passion hit its zenith, Erin's body shook against Jackson and grasped her arm as it continued to dictate her every move.

Jackson moved up to kiss Erin and smooth the damp hair from her face. The touch against Erin's skin became feather-light and soon she simply palmed her hand against the wet flesh.

Jackson and Erin were so engrossed in their lovemaking that neither heard the footsteps climbing the ladder, the sharp intake of breath, and the feet of the intruder beating a quick retreat. They continued to kiss as they reveled in the aftermath of one of the most beautiful experiences of their young lives. Erin kissed Jackson passionately, but soon couldn't catch her breath.

"Wow," she breathed at a twinkle-eyed Jackson. "That was wonderful, Jack. I always knew you'd be a passionate lover to whomever was lucky enough to love you."

Jackson tried her best *Dirty Harry* impersonation. "Are you feeling lucky, punk?"

"I am *your* lucky punk." She wiped Jackson's sweaty brow.

"Yes, you are." Jackson traced Erin's eyebrows, cheekbones, anything she could get her hands on.

"I'm really sorry to do this, but what time is it?"

Jackson reached over and grabbed Erin's watch and instantly

grimaced. "Oh, shit."

Erin sat up abruptly. Jackson handed her the watch that showed fifteen minutes past midnight. "Shit, Jack, I gotta get back before my mother comes looking for me. I know she will."

"Okay, okay. Let's get dressed and I'll take you back."

"No, I gotta run." Erin looked at her harried expression and she kissed her to soften the abrupt exit. "I'm so sorry for leaving without um…you know." She blushed and looked down.

"Don't worry about me. I think I did already anyway." It was her turn to blush.

"Without me actually…" She gestured toward Jackson's body. "Wow."

"I love that you are so tongue-tied, Hawk. Come on, you gotta get out of here."

Erin dressed quickly and put her watch on, then gathered her sack and kissed Jackson goodbye. She flew down the ladder and ran out of the boathouse, Jackson close behind her. After a quick wave to Erin, she hightailed it home.

Erin ran past the pier, coming to a sudden stop when she heard, "Hey, Peanut," from the dock chairs. She looked around quickly, a flash of panic racing through her. Once she realized where the voice had come from, she breathed a sigh of semi-relief.

"Dad? What are you doing out here?"

"Looking for you. Come here for a minute."

His voice held a tone she wasn't familiar with and it worried her. She walked out on the pier and sat in the chair next to her father. He was silent for a few minutes.

"Your mother was ready to come out searching for you. She was pretty angry you'd stayed out later than you promised." He turned to face her. "I'm so glad it was me instead of her that saw you with Jackson in the loft."

Erin's cheeks flared red and her heart skipped a beat. "When were you in the loft?" Erin hoped against all hope it wasn't when she thought it was.

"At the worst time a father could ever walk in on his daughter."

Erin's eyes welled with tears. "Oh, Dad…" She buried her

face in her hands and cried. "I'm so sorry," she choked out. "Does Mom know?" she said after a few moments. "Did you tell her you saw us?"

"Some people might think I seem a little odd, but I am not suicidal. I wouldn't put it past your mother to kill the messenger."

Erin sighed in relief. "She's really going to go through the roof about Jackson after this."

"You can't tell your mother about this, Erin. As much as I like Jack, and you know I do, this would throw her over the edge and I'm not sure even I could handle her."

Erin's tears were flowing hard. "But, Daddy, I love Jack."

He wrapped his arms around his daughter in deep sympathy. "I know, honey, I know. I'm just afraid for you, Peanut, I really am. Your mother isn't balanced and I don't know what she'd do if she found out about this."

Erin squeezed her father tighter. "What do I do, Dad?" She was almost hysterical. "I can't imagine my life without her. God, she means everything to me."

Joe pulled back and cupped his daughter's face. "Sweetheart, I can't make this decision for you. I know this is huge, but so is the situation. Just think about it with all of your heart and you'll make the right decision for you and everyone around you."

He kissed the top of her head. The action, so reminiscent of Jackson, made her cry even harder. "I never meant for you to see me like that. I'm so sorry, Dad." Fresh tears ran down her face. They were wiped away by warm, callused thumbs.

"Peanut, a father never wants to see his daughter in any intimate situation, and really doesn't expect to see her with another woman, but I know you're sorry. I know this embarrassment will be tricky for both of us to get past. We will get past it, though, I promise you," he said reassuringly. "I've thought for a while that there might be something between you two, and after today in the boat, I was pretty sure I was right. That's not to say I'm used to the idea or happy with what has transpired, but it's just not surprising to me. We'll get through it," he looked into her eyes, "no matter what you decide, okay?"

"I'm sorry I disappointed you. Your opinion means so much to me. I'm sorry I didn't talk to you and Mom about my tattoo. It just came to me last night when I was looking out over the water, then I just did it."

"Sometimes impulsive decisions can be very disruptive, though. Just make sure you think things through before you act on them, okay?" He kissed the side of her face.

"Thank you, Daddy. I love you so much." She hugged him again.

"I love you, too, Peanut. Let's go in before your mother calls the forest ranger or nine-one-one."

Erin held her father's hand, grateful for his calm. He thought communication was the key to any situation. She knew he was angry, but he had a way of expressing it that made her think about things. It was a wonderful trait that had skipped her mother completely.

Father and daughter walked into the cottage together. Katie was on the couch waiting for them. "You're lucky I didn't call the authorities to come look for you, young lady. Where were you? Oh, wait." She stopped Erin before she could answer. "Don't tell me. You were with Jackson," she said snidely.

"Katie, don't start. I found Erin and Jack on the pier saying goodbye to the lake," he lied. "She was almost on her way in."

Katie looked from her husband to her daughter. "I don't know which one of you is worse."

"Mother, we're leaving tomorrow. Is it really such a big deal?"

"Yes! You said you'd be here and you weren't. That sounds like deceit to me. You've gotten really good at that. I'm sure it's just another lovely attribute you picked up from dear old Jack."

"Katie, we're done with this. I want a peaceful night's sleep before I have to drive six hours," he directed sternly. "I don't want to hear about this crap in the car, either. We are leaving tomorrow. Let it go."

Katie shook her head and stormed off to bed without a goodnight to either of them.

"Thank you, Dad," Erin whispered.

"In all my years of marriage, I have never lied to my wife before tonight."

That statement hit Erin hard.

"I don't really want to do it again."

"Dad..."

"I don't want to talk about this night again, Erin. Ever."

"Okay, Dad. I promise." He leaned over and kissed her cheek and went to bed, leaving her alone with too many thoughts to process.

She walked slowly to her room and closed the door. Flopping down on her mattress, she put her hands behind her head and stared at the ceiling. Images of Jackson floated through her mind like a warm, exotic hallucination. Their assignation felt like a dream. Images of how her mother would react to their pairing came into view, causing her stomach to churn. All the small details of her mother's verbal abuse were crashing down on her—the nasty comments, the brutal deconstruction of Jackson and her aunt, and the irrational behavior in the shower. The vivid recollections distressed her immensely. Would her mother ever accept their relationship? Would she ever accept Jackson as part of their family? Would she be able to say her name without the venom that dripped with each syllable?

Erin rolled on her side, not knowing what to do. *I finally follow my heart only to have her put up a blockade the size of the Great Wall. Do I possibly blast through to the other side, or do I just sit here afraid of what she'll do to our family?* Tears welled in her eyes and spilled over down her face. She knew that whatever she decided, the results would stay with her forever.

The morning sunshine was cruel to Erin's unrested eyes. She'd packed her bags and loaded them in the car before her parents were up. Checkout time was nine o'clock and it was coming far too fast. Her parents woke to find her sitting at the table, staring out the window in deep thought.

"Good morning, Peanut." Her father smiled at her. Seeing her eyes, he knew she'd had a very sleepless night.

"I'm gonna go find Jack and say goodbye, okay?" she said,

knowing he wouldn't understand the impact of those words.

"Okay. Your stuff all ready to go?"

"It's in the car already, so I'll be ready when you are."

He leaned to kiss her cheek as she stood. "Tell Jack goodbye for me."

"I will." She didn't even acknowledge her mother's presence.

With a heavy heart, Erin left the cottage in search of the one person in her life who made sense to her in every way. She found her giving a small child an inner tube from the boathouse.

When Jackson's eyes met Erin's, she instantly knew something was wrong. "Hawk, what is it?"

Erin shook her head. "Not here." She motioned to the loft. "Can we go up?" With a nod of her head, Jackson led the way.

Up in the loft, Jackson's stance was tense as she waited anxiously for Erin's news. Erin's back was to her but she could tell she was crying. "Hawk, honey…" She touched her shoulder, and Erin recoiled at the contact. Jackson immediately pulled back.

Erin turned around, tears falling freely down her face. "I can't…" She took a deep breath and started again. "I can't see you anymore, Jack."

Jackson's eyes went wide with confusion and hurt. "What? What are you talking about? Did I do something?"

"My mother knows about us. She came up here last night while we were making love," she lied.

Jackson's mouth shaped into an O. She realized there was no way she would've heard anyone while she was making love to Erin. She was so focused she was oblivious to anything else.

"I'm not strong enough to handle her, Jack. I'm just not," she cried. "Not even my father can control her anymore. I can't do this to him."

Jackson's face fell. As she realized Erin was trying to make peace between her parents for her father's sake, any hope she had of changing Erin's mind was gone.

"She'd never accept us as a couple. Hell, she doesn't even want me to be friends with you." Erin's voice was nasal, filled with emotion and tears.

"Hawk, you're almost twenty years old. Can't you just move out or...I don't know—get away from her somehow?" Jackson was becoming more desperate with each second that passed.

"Jack, you know I can't. She'd make my dad stop paying for school. She'd damage my relationship with him. I can't do that to him. I just can't."

She was sobbing, each tear shattering Jackson's heart into a million pieces.

Jackson opened her arms and Erin instantly fell into the offer of comfort. She wept harder than she knew possible, her sobs choking the breath from her. Erin knew she needed to leave Jackson, but it was killing her to even think about moving. With strength she didn't know she had, she kissed Jackson with everything she could possibly give to her to show her the love in her heart.

Jackson kissed her back, a kiss filled with pain and sadness. They pulled apart and Jackson's strained voice asked, "Can I call you at least?"

Erin shook her head almost violently. "No. You can't. Please don't call or write to me anymore, Jack. It'll be too hard."

With those final words, Erin fled down the ladder, out of the boathouse and out of Jackson's life. Heart shattered, Jackson blindly climbed down the rungs of the ladder. She watched as Erin reached the car. She could see her crying, but was helpless to stop her tears. Her own tears would come later.

Katie came out just as Erin flew past her, tears streaming down her face. A brief look of confusion flashed over her face, until she saw Jackson staring numbly at Erin, now seated in the car. With a sneer of victory, she walked over to Jackson.

Only just resisting the urge to slap the woman, Jackson's anger spilled into her voice. "Well, I guess you finally got what you wanted."

"Yes, I did."

"Have you asked yourself if Erin is getting what she wants?"

"She doesn't know what she wants," her mother spat maliciously.

"She is almost twenty years old, isn't it for her to decide?"

"She's too young to make decisions like that"

Jackson shoved down the swelling need to rant. "I'd have to disagree with you there."

"Well, I guess it's good that your vote doesn't count then."

"To Erin it does."

"Like I said, you don't count anymore. Do us all a favor, Jackson, and stay away from my family." The implied threat was not an empty one.

"You know this isn't over. One day Erin is gonna get tired of your bullshit and then where will that leave you?"

"We'll just have to see. Right now, I have my daughter attending a prestigious art school and soon she'll be finding a wonderful man to share her life with. I'd say that leaves me pretty happy."

"I'd say delusional, but you say tomato…"

"Goodbye, Jackson." Erin's mother turned toward the car.

"See you later, Katie."

Jackson's arms were folded over her chest, almost as if she felt she could hold the rage and hurt inside. As the car pulled out of the lot, a part of her died, and she wasn't at all sure that she would ever feel alive again.

Chapter Thirteen

2002 – The Northwoods Island City

They sat on the roof overlooking the water, their legs dangling off the side. Jackson's head was spinning with everything Erin had just told her about what had really happened that last night and the following morning. "So, it was your father who saw us and not your mom?" she said.

"Yeah."

"Why did you tell me it was your mother then? I don't get it."

"Because if I had told you it was my decision to leave you, it would've hurt you so much more, Jack," she explained sadly. "My mother was the one ultimately to blame for it, so I just said it was her. I didn't want you to think badly of my father. I knew how much you liked him. You can imagine it was quite a shock for him to see us that way."

"I had no idea your father would be against us being together." Jackson's voice conveyed the hurt she felt.

"He wasn't."

Jackson looked at Erin, confusion plain in her eyes. "Then why didn't you stay with me?" She couldn't keep the pain inside. The tears of anguish rolled down her cheeks and she swiped them away angrily.

"When I told you I wasn't strong enough to deal with my

189

mother, that was true. She was really crazy at that point and neither of us could handle her."

"I can't believe he stayed with her as long as he did. He was too good a man."

Erin's head dropped. "Yeah, he was. This wasn't his fault, Jack, I promise you. Please don't feel resentful about him."

"Erin, you're telling me that it was him who made you decide against us, so he wouldn't have to deal with Katie."

"That's partially true. I guess a part of me was crying out because I wanted my mother to love me unconditionally." She shook her head at the futility. "She was a nightmare even after we left, so that idea was quickly quashed."

Jackson was tired of the evasions. "What is the whole truth then?"

Erin's eyes sparkled with tears. "The fact of the matter was, that night my dad already knew he was sick. His doctor called after we got back from Bosaki's but he didn't tell us until we got home. He didn't even tell my mom, Jack. He knew he was dying, and he could've left her to live out his days with me at his side, but he loved her and wanted to live out his time with her!" Erin's voice rose with emotion. "When he told me that, I knew I had made the right decision. He and Mom never could've stayed together if I had continued to see you. It was already ugly; it would've gotten worse."

Jackson absorbed the information, unsure how to feel. She knew it hadn't been an easy decision for Erin. It was too far-reaching a decision for a nineteen-year-old to take on herself. Erin was impulsive, that she knew. Her trip back home when she'd found out about Jackson's sexuality and then the return trip to the Northwoods were one example. Even though her heart was in the right place, Erin tended to act on emotion, not always thinking things through.

Erin spoke quietly. "You know, even on his deathbed, Dad thought of you."

"What do you mean?"

January 1997

Joe lay on his bed, waiting for Death to take him. His body had become unrelentingly weak and he had long since accepted that the cancer would get the better of him. For seventeen months, a horrible guilt had haunted him. Erin had chosen to make his life better instead of following her heart. It was a decision he hated on her behalf. He knew he needed to talk to her about that life-altering day in the Northwoods. It couldn't be put off any longer.

When Erin came for her morning visit, he asked her to close the door. She did as he asked, then sat down in the chair next to his bed, taking his frail hand in hers. "What is it, Dad? Do you want me to read to you again?"

"No, Peanut. I need to talk to you about what happened with Jackson."

Erin's face fell and her heart began to race. "What about Jack?"

"I never should've put you in that position."

"Dad, it was my..."

"No, it wasn't, and you know it." He stared into her eyes. "Whether or not you realize it, I made that decision for you. I could've told you that I would've supported you had you chosen to stay with Jack. I could've told you that if it got bad, I would take you away from your mother. God, I could've said so much to help you..." Tears formed in his eyes.

"Dad, what are you saying?"

"I'm saying that when I found out I was going to die, all I wanted was for my family to be with me for as long as I had left. God knows your mother and I have had a few rows over the years, but I do love her. We wouldn't have stayed together if you had chosen Jack. I knew when I saw you two that day that it would break up our family. I was selfish. I wanted us together, even though I knew you were hurting, and for that I will never forgive myself. I didn't want my last days to be filled with fights with your mother, or between your mother and you." Tears streamed down his cheeks and Erin cried with him. "God help me, I didn't want my last days to be miserable." He grasped Erin's hand. "I know you felt like the one who wasn't strong, but it was me. I am so sorry, Peanut, for being such a weak man."

Erin laid her head on his chest. "Oh, Dad, please don't do this to yourself, please. I don't think you were weak at all. You always stuck up for me." She cried on his chest. "I don't blame you for wanting your family around you when you were sick. Who wouldn't want that?"

He lifted her head as best he could to look into her eyes. "Can you forgive me?"

Their watery eyes met. "There is nothing to forgive, Dad. I would've done the same thing to keep my family together." *I did do that.* She hugged him as tightly as she dared. "But if you need me to say it, I swear, I forgive you."

"Thank you, Peanut. I love you so much." They held tightly to one another.

"I love you too, Daddy."

"He died that night," Erin said, her voice filled with emotion. She looked at Jackson, who had tears streaming down her face. "He just wanted us around him until he died." She looked out over the water. "If...If I had to make that terrible decision today, I would do the same."

Jackson nodded, knowing that it must have been an awful time for them all. She knew how much Joe's family meant to him; she could see it in his amazing ability to love Katie despite everything that had transpired.

"I know I hurt you, Jack. God knows I have lived with that knowledge every damn day, and every day I was achingly sorry for breaking your heart." She breathed heavily. "But I also know that my heart died the day I left you. Hell, my own husband picked up on that and had to go off to find love in another woman's bed. Now he's gonna be a daddy." She laughed mirthlessly.

Ouch. "But your mother said you were happy with him."

"I'm sure she also told you I was having a grandchild for her, too," Erin guessed.

Jackson nodded. "I guess I should've learned my lesson with Katie long ago and automatically figured anything she said about you would be a lie."

"You must have contacted her right before she called me, because she was drilling into me about how awful I was for going against the Church and why wouldn't I fight for my marriage." She tucked an errant strand of hair behind one of Jackson's ears. "Seven years later she is still threatened by the thought of you in my life."

One thing had stuck in Jackson's mind. "Going against the Church? You're divorcing him?"

Erin nodded. "Yeah. It's almost finalized. My soon-to-be-ex-husband wouldn't agree to me keeping the house and that's all I wanted out of this divorce. When I told him that he'd have more than the house to give me if he contested, he changed his tune."

"I'm sure. I'm sorry it didn't work out for you, Hawk. Seriously, I am."

She squeezed Jackson's knee. "Thanks. There was nothing wrong with him. He was a lovely man until this, kind and giving. It was just me not being able to love him like I should have. No one should have to live in a loveless marriage. I can't say that I blame him for stepping out, I just wish he would've told me he was unhappy." She shrugged, wiping the tears from her face.

"Where did you meet him?"

"He came to one of my art shows. His name is Jeremy, if you wanted to know," Erin added unnecessarily as Jackson knew his name all too well. Jackson nodded for her to continue. "Anyway, he was gregarious and sweet, and I liked him instantly. 'Like' being the keyword there, unfortunately. I think when we were married I did love him, but it was the kind of love you have for puppies, or something like that. You know—loving their personalities and wanting to care for them." She laughed at herself. "I wasn't *in* love with him, though, but I guess I wanted to marry him before my dad died, and I'm sure you can guess that my mother was over the moon."

"I'm sure," Jackson said with a roll of her eyes.

"But five years is a long time to be with someone who doesn't return your affections. We should've split before his infidelity, that's for certain. It would've made the parting better for us both.

Well, for me for sure," she added with a wink.

Jackson put her arm around Erin. "Thank you for telling me what happened."

Erin leaned on Jackson so naturally. "I'm so sorry for breaking your heart, Jack."

Jackson held her tighter. "I know, Hawk. I forgive you," she whispered and turned to kiss the top of Erin's head.

They stayed that way for a few moments then Erin softly said, "Jack, after you and I made love that night, I...I felt alive for the first time, I mean, *really* alive."

"So did I." Jackson's voice was rough from crying.

"I've never felt that way since," she admitted softly.

"Me either."

"Jack..."

Before Erin could continue, a voice was heard in the distance calling for Jackson. Both women stood quickly and sped down the ladders to the ground. Cindy's voice was shouting from the house and Jackson began to run, knowing the desperation in Cindy's voice could only mean one thing: Jackie.

"What is it? How's Jackie?" she panted as she reached Cindy outside of the main cabin.

"She's not good, Jack. She wants to see you and Erin. Dr. Jones is on her way."

Jackson shared a worried look with Erin and they both hurried inside. In the darkened room, the small figure on the bed looked frailer than she had even just a couple of hours before. Her eyes were closed and Jackson's heart lurched.

"Jackie?" Jackson rasped, grasping her aunt's chilled hand.

Jackie's eyes opened slowly and she gave Jackson's hand the smallest of squeezes. She saw that Erin was also in the room, standing beside Jackson.

Erin gently patted Jackie's leg. "Hey, you."

Jackie's voice was almost inaudible, her breathing labored. "I love you both," she wheezed. "Thank you for giving me ... the best life possible... I was very blessed."

Tears falling at Jackie's farewell, Jackson choked out, "You are the best mother I could've hoped for. Thank you for giving me the best life possible. I will always love you."

Jackie looked at Erin. "Take care of my little girl for me, will you? She likes to get into trouble. ... You gotta watch her close."

Erin's tears trickled down her cheeks. "I will, Jackie. I promise I'll take good care of her."

"Thank you." She gave Jackson's hand a final squeeze and drew a last deep, shuddering breath. The alarm on her heart monitor sounded and Cindy rushed into the room. Checking for pulse or respiration and confirming that Jackie had passed, she turned off the machine.

Jackson and Erin wept, leaning heavily on each other. After several minutes, Jackson bent down to place a final kiss on Jackie's forehead. Erin rubbed her back comfortingly. With a final whispered "I love you," Jackson left the room.

Erin took one last look at Jackie's lifeless form and blew her a kiss from the doorway. *Godspeed, Jackie.*

When Jackson opened the door to greet her, Doctor Glenda Jones took one look and knew her patient had died. She gave Jackson a sympathetic hug. "I'm so sorry, Jack. She was such a wonderful woman."

"Thank you, Glenda. I know you did all you could for her and for that I will be forever grateful. Cindy is in with her now."

Noticing Erin, Glenda extended her hand. "I'm Dr. Glenda, or 'the good witch from the Northwoods' as Jackie called me."

Erin managed a watery smile. "I'm Erin, an old friend of the family. Thank you for giving Jackie such great care."

"You're Erin?" She looked at Jackson then back to Erin. "I've heard your name come up several times. It's nice to meet you. You are a very well-liked woman in this house."

Erin grabbed Jackson's hand. "Thank you for saying so."

Jackson put her arm around Erin and pulled her against her chest. Glenda took that as her cue to check with Cindy about the specifics of her patient's leave-taking.

Jackson buried her head in Erin's hair and wept. Erin held her close and whispered words of comfort. When Jackson at length pulled back, she caressed Erin's face. "Thank you for being here. It meant so much to her...and to me."

"Thank you for calling me." They shared one final hug before Jackson pulled away to make the necessary phone calls and arrangements.

Three days later, a small group was gathered at Lakeside Cemetery. Jackie's plot was next to her parents and shared by her twin sister, Emma, Jackson's birth mother. After sharing their mother's womb, it was only fitting for them to share this place as well. A commemorative stone was placed in the ground to give those who wanted, a place to visit her.

The service was quite moving. The children from Jackson's advanced music class came to play *Amazing Grace*, touching Jackson to the core. Erin wasn't surprised to see how much Jackson's students cared for her. She knew the compassionate and loving woman made an impression in some way on everyone she met.

Anyone who was familiar with the family or resort came out to say their goodbyes to the woman who had been so well loved by the community. The Thomases had been a part of the area for many years and most of the community knew them well. Erin had had no luck with trying to find Sandra to tell her about Jackie's passing. Jackson was actually relieved. Seeing Sandra again might have been too much for her to handle.

It was a beautiful spring day—blue sky and temperatures around seventy degrees. Everyone had a story to tell Jackson as they hugged her or shook her hand and offered condolences. Jackson had invited their close friends to her home after the funeral. A catering company was taking care of all the food and drink. Erin had made all of those arrangements so Jackson wouldn't have to worry about a thing, except mourning the loss of the woman who'd raised her. After laying a final rose on Jackie's stone, Erin and Jackson left the other mourners.

She was given Jackie's ashes, per her request. Jackson knew her aunt's remains belonged in Lake Tomahawk; it was such a part of her. It only seemed fitting that it serve as her final resting place. Jackson wanted the same when her time came.

When they got back to the house, it was bustling with many

faces Jackson had seen most of her life. Cindy, Janet, and Dr. Jones were all in attendance and were the first to greet Jackson.

"Jack, that was a beautiful ceremony. She would've been very pleased," Glenda said warmly.

"Thank you. I'm glad it was you who took care of her. You guys have known each other since high school and I know how comfortable she was with you. Again, thank you." Jackson couldn't help the tears that seemed never ending.

Glenda leaned over to hug Jackson tightly. "It's hard to lose patients, but harder when they are friends, too." She pulled away and gave Jackson a warm look. "If you need anything, you give me a call, okay?" Glenda kissed her cheek.

"I will."

Similar thanks and respect were voiced by others. Erin was touched by how close Jackie's team had become with Jackson. She felt silly for thinking that anything was going on between Jackson and Cindy. The thought now was so foreign to her. It was her warmth and compassion that made Cindy a great nurse. There was no question that Jackie had gotten the best possible care.

When the last of the guests left the house, Jackson went outside to get some fresh air. When she looked up, she noticed the flag had been lowered to half-staff.

Coming up beside her, Erin saw what had caught her attention. "They say it's a sign of respect to a wonderful person when the flag is lowered. Jackie was the best, so I thought it was necessary."

Jackson looked at her with wonder. "You really did take care of everything for me. I can't thank you enough for helping me through this, Hawk. I'll never forget it."

Erin entwined their fingers. "I did a lot to help my mom when my dad died, so I figured I'd go with what I knew. I'm glad you're pleased with the way things went."

Jackson nodded. "I am. Jackie would've loved it."

Erin tugged on her hand. "You wanna take a walk, get some fresh air in our lungs?"

"That would be great."

The two walked around the property in silence, hands clasped between them. Jackson was turning a thought around in her head and decided that it was as good a time as any to broach it with Erin. "Hawk?"

"Yeah?"

"Will you come with me when I sprinkle her ashes? It would mean so much to me if you would."

"Oh, Jack, of course I will. You didn't even need to ask." She squeezed her hand. "Just tell me when, and I'll be happy to go."

"When," she said softly, to Erin's amusement.

"Okay, honey, let's go." Erin slipped off her shoes and dangled them from her fingers as they walked toward the boat.

Jackson smiled as she, too, took off her heels before boarding. She wiggled her toes. "Oh, that feels good."

Erin boarded the boat and saw that the ashes had already been placed inside. She smiled at the typical Jacksonism: she was never one to put things off when they were painful.

Jackson untied the rope from the cleats and pushed the boat away from the dock. They drifted out slowly to get deeper before starting the engine. Jackson steered the boat to a small cove where she had fished as a child with Jackie and her grandfather. As they approached the lily pads, Jackson killed the engine and dropped the anchor.

The cove was quiet and serene. Every time she'd been there, Erin had been struck by its beauty. *It's the perfect place to sprinkle Jackie's ashes.*

Jackson lifted the brass urn and opened the lid. She motioned for Erin to stand next to her. "This is where my mother's ashes are, as well. I thought it only right to sprinkle Jackie's with hers."

"It's a beautiful gesture, Jack."

With extreme reverence, they each took a handful of Jackie's remains and held them over the side of the boat.

"This place has always been a part of you, Jackie. I hope you spend a wonderful eternity here, where you belong. I love you," Jackson said through her tears as she sprinkled the ash into the water.

"Jackie, thank you for allowing me to come back into your lives when it truly mattered the most. I promise you that I will take care of Jack for as long as she'll let me." She sprinkled her ashes and added, "And even when she won't. I love you. Rest in peace."

Jackson tipped the urn and gently poured the remaining ashes into Lake Tomahawk. They held the side of boat as they stared into the water until the last of the powder disappeared. Erin rubbed Jackson's back as her tears fell into the water. After a few more moments, Jackson lifted the anchor and turned the boat toward home.

The ride was peaceful as each was lost in her own thoughts. The day had been very emotional and taxing for Jackson and she knew she wouldn't have made it through if it weren't for the woman sitting in the boat with her.

Erin closed her eyes, allowing the breeze to soothe some of her pain. Nothing healed her soul like the Northwoods and she would be sad when the time came for her to return to Chicago.

Jackson docked the craft in the boathouse, disembarked, and hung up the keys. Erin took her hand as they walked barefoot to the pier. The sun had begun to set, creating an amazing palette of colors. The women stayed silent, just watching, until the sun slid below the horizon.

"Do you want to come in for a drink or something?" Jackson offered. "I'd really just like to decompress for a while. This day was... Whew." She blew out a deep breath. "It's taken so much out of me."

Erin squeezed her hand. "I know, honey. Yes, I would absolutely love to come in for a drink and decompress with you." She smiled. "Come on. I think I hear the Drachenstein calling my name."

"That is a really good Riesling. It's not too dry and not too sweet. It's like...the perfect wine. Where did you get it?"

"A small wine shop in Chicago. I buy it by the case since Howard, the owner, orders it special for me."

"By the case? Have you turned into an alcoholic since we last saw each other?" Jackson asked, only half joking.

Erin snorted. "With my mother you'd think that would be the obvious answer, but no, I just like to have some on hand for dinner parties and such. This is actually the most I've had to drink in months."

Jackson laughed for the first time that day. "Well, good. I'd hate to have to carry you home." *God, it's good to have her here again.*

Chapter Fourteen

The two women sat on the couch, feet tucked under them and glasses of wine in hand. Jackson's head was leaning against the back of the couch while Erin tried to decipher what was being talked about on Larry King. Initially they weren't even paying attention, but one of his guests was an art critic and was going off on a new artist's work.

"Can you believe this jackass?" Erin asked, outraged by the man's lack of actual art knowledge. "He wouldn't know the difference between fingerpainting and Paul Gauguin."

Jackson laughed at Erin's ire at the so-called art critic. "So, if he turned around and said he liked one of *your* paintings, would he still be a jackass?" she asked playfully.

"Well, yes, he'd just be a jackass with taste and simply have chosen the wrong topic to discuss on Larry's show." She winked at Jackson and took a sip of wine.

When a commercial came on, Jackson tried to stifle a yawn. The day had taken a heavy toll on her. Erin noticed the yawn right away. "Are you ready to go to sleep? You've got to be exhausted."

Nodding, Jackson said, "My body is tired, my heart aches, but my mind just won't shut off." She put down her wineglass, laid on her side, and rested her head in Erin's lap.

Wanting to take Jackson's mind off of her pain, she said, "Jack? Tell me more about your music." Erin began to stroke the long dark hair and Jackson grasped Erin's knee, lightly stroking it with her thumb. The connection between them had completely returned.

"My music?"

"Yeah. We've spoken at length about my career, and all I know about yours is that you teach music here. I mean, did you entertain the idea of being a professionial musician?"

Jackson patted her knee. "Oh, sure. I was approached to tour the country with symphonies and whatnot, but…"

"But what?"

"This is my home. I couldn't imagine being away for such long stretches of time. I know how hard professionals work. They practice all the time and rarely have time for anything else. I knew I didn't want that kind of life. My greatest satisfaction came when I was teaching during those summers in Michigan. I would watch a student go from a stumbling starter to a solid performer in only a few years because of my help."

"I bet that felt fantastic." Erin continued to stroke her hair.

"It did. I really felt at my best when I was helping them grow as musicians. They learned to appreciate not only music, but how and why they heard the notes they played. I get that same feeling being here at home. I get the best of both worlds teaching here." She took a deep comforting breath and closed her eyes. "And now with you here, I couldn't ask for anything more." She absently squeezed Erin's knee.

Jackson hadn't asked, but Erin figured she'd stay until Jackson no longer needed her. Her mother no longer got to tell her what to do, so there was actually nothing preventing her from staying just long as she wanted. When the time came, leaving Jackson again wouldn't be at all easy.

Forty-five minutes passed and Erin noticed that Jackson was sound asleep. She was reluctant to move as she didn't want her to wake, but her bladder was reminding her of all of the wine she had inbibed. She was able to slip out from under Jackson's head, but had to fight her clutching fingers. Even in deep sleep, it seemed as if Jackson needed to keep a hold on her.

Erin leaned down and whispered soothingly, "I'll be right

back, don't worry." She kissed the side of her head and went to relieve herself. When she returned, Jackson was sitting up on the couch and had turned off the television. The clock showed that it was well past midnight. She knew Jackson would be going to bed soon. She bit her lip in hesitation then asked, "Do you need me to stay with you tonight?"

Jackson looked up at her. *Yes!* her body screamed, but she answered, "No, I should be okay. I think I'm just gonna take some time to reflect a little then go to bed."

"Are you sure?"

Jackson nodded. "Yeah, I'm sure. Thanks for offering, though." She walked Erin to the door and pulled her into a warm embrace. "Thank you for everything, Hawk. You made these last few days almost bearable."

Erin returned the hug warmly. "You are most welcome, Jack. You know I would do anything for you and Jackie. I'm glad she's out of pain now and resting with her parents and your mom."

Jackson leaned down and kissed her cheek. Erin's eyes closed at the familiar contact. When she pulled away, Erin told her, "If you need me, you know where I am, okay?"

"Thank you, Hawk. It really meant the world to us that you came." They shared a smile. "Goodnight."

"G'night, Jack."

Back in her cabin, Erin stripped off her clothes, used the bathroom to brush her hair and teeth, and slipped into bed, sighing at the feel of the clean linen against her skin. She noticed her cell phone light blinking on the bedside table. She had messages. She grabbed her phone and pushed the voice mail button, then listened to the first of four messages.

"Erin, it's your mother. Why haven't you called me back? Are you home yet? Call me when you get this."

Erin rolled her eyes and deleted the message. She listened to the next, almost the exact same message from her mother, which she also deleted.

"Hey, girl, it's Kim. Just wanted to let you know we're all set for tomorrow night, so don't worry about a thing. We already have a few regulars calling to see if they can get a sneak peek at

your stuff. Don't worry. I won't let anyone see them until it's time. They are beautiful and will do very well, as usual. I hope things are going as expected up there. I'm thinking about you. Talk to you soon, bye!"

"Ah, Kim, you're such a good egg."

"Hi, Erin, this is Paul. Just wanted you to know that Jeremy finally signed the papers, so we should be done with this in no time. Just hang in there, kiddo, we're in the home stretch. Give me a call when you get back into town."

"Thank you, Jeremy," Erin whispered aloud. *I cannot wait for this to be over and done with. We just have to work out the house documents and I am free and clear. Thank God.* Her head fell back hard against her pillow and she closed her eyes. *Man, what a day.*

Jackson laid in bed, eyes wide open, tears streaming down her face. Losing Jackie was one of the worst experiences of her life. Erin's words resonated in her head. *I'm glad she's out of pain now and resting with her parents and your mom.* That thought brought a modicum of solace. Jackie was definitely in pain toward the end, but Glenda had made sure it was as minimal as possible.

Not being able to sleep, Jackson got out of bed and went into the kitchen to eat some leftovers from the wake. She looked at the clock and saw that it was almost two in the morning. She closed the refrigerator and got a glass of water instead. "It's too damn late to eat. God, I just want to sleep."

Jackson walked back into her room and got into bed. Lying on her back, she continued to stare at the ceiling.

If you need me, you know where I am.

Jackson contemplated calling Erin, just to hear her voice. Erin being with her for almost a week had brought her such comfort, a comfort her body and soul had been missing for far too long. Rolling onto her side, Jackson closed her eyes and sighed.

A noise jostled Erin from an unsound sleep. A small clicking sound made her heart race. Not hearing the sound repeated, she held tight to her bedcovers and tried to relax enough to fall back to sleep. When she opened her eyes again, she nearly screamed at the sight of a silhouette standing in her bedroom doorway. As Jackson's figure slowly registered, she knew not to be afraid.

"Jack? Are you okay?" Her calm voice belied her frantic pulse.

Jackson took a couple of steps toward Erin's bed, removing her clothing as she neared. "I need you," she whispered hoarsely.

Without thought or hesitation, Erin pulled open her covers and invited Jackson into her bed. Jackson immediately climbed into bed and moved on top of Erin.

"I need you," she whispered again, trying not to close her eyes at the sensation of Erin's naked form beneath her.

Erin looked into Jackson's eyes. She reached up and tucked Jackson's hair behind her ears with gentle fingers, fingers that slowly traveled to Jackson's lips and tenderly traced them.

Jackson's eyes closed at the light touch and she soon found her lips captured by Erin's. The weak whimper that left Jackson's mouth fired her already crazy desire for Erin. She kissed Erin with a passion she hadn't felt in years, the raw desire to consume Erin overwhelming.

Erin responded just as passionately to the hungry kisses as her repressed yearning for Jackson returned. She held locks of Jackson's hair as they melded to each other. Tongues battled for control, eliciting sighs and moans of pleasure.

Jackson's lips moved down to Erin's throat and across her collarbones and shoulders. Finding Erin's small tomahawk on her chest, Jackson reverently kissed the icon, a few tears falling on it as well.

She moved lower and kissed and licked Erin's breast before pulling the aroused, hardened flesh into her mouth. Erin moaned, sending a surge of heat through Jackson's body. Her hand began to play with Erin's other nipple as Erin massaged her head. Kissing between her breasts, Jackson moved lower to kiss her stomach and hipbones. She idly played inside Erin's belly button with her tongue and could hardly contain herself as the scent of Erin's arousal reached her. Feeling a burning need to fill Erin with all of the love she had for her, she slowly moved lower and kissed the dark, wiry hair at the apex of Erin's thighs. Erin's body moved gently as her sighs became louder. Her hands were still wrapped in Jackson's hair, urging to her to do as she pleased.

Jackson's warm hands gently parted Erin's lips as her mouth moved closer to take the first taste of her. After the initial wet contact, both women moaned and Erin's body moved more freely. Jackson relished the taste and texture that was Erin. She explored every area she could reach, teased and tasted every orifice and inch of skin. Jackson's tongue moved into Erin causing the auburn head to lift to meet Jackson's eyes. They shared a molten stare as Jackson continued to drink from her.

Jackson rearranged her body and soon her fingers replaced her tongue inside of Erin, filling her completely.

"Oh, God, Jack..." Erin gasped.

Erin writhed on the bed as Jack slowly moved her fingers within her. Jackson had never seen a more gorgeous sight. Erin's hips were frantically trying to keep up with Jackson's feverish pace. When she felt Erin begin to quiver inside, she moved her head down and brought her tongue to Erin's clitoris. With the lightest of touches, Jackson flicked her tongue rapidly and soon Erin was begging for release. With skillful fingers and lips, Erin was brought to the precipice of the purest form of ecstasy.

Jackson rode out the waves with her, holding on tightly as Erin's body convulsed, exploding with pleasure. With relentless touches and wet kisses, Jackson quickly brought Erin to a second orgasm, finally withdrawing to move up her body. Jackson kissed and tasted every inch of Erin until she reached her panting mouth. Soon they were lost in their kisses and the taste of Erin shared between them.

Badly wanting to return the love and pleasure, Erin flipped them over, surprising them both with her strength. She gently brushed the hair from Jackson's eyes. She moved her own hair to one side and lowered herself to kiss Jackson again. She kissed down her cheek and tugged lightly on her earlobe with her teeth.

"I cannot wait to taste you," Erin whispered, filled with unimaginable desire.

Jackson whimpered when Erin moved down her body to take

one of her nipples into her mouth. The feel of the nipple between her teeth and lips was extraordinary. She had teased Jeremy in this fashion before but it was never him she was thinking of. To have the real Jackson beneath her was dizzying, electric. She sucked on the nipple as her hand wandered down Jackson's body. As she passed over the taut stomach, she felt Jackson's tremors. Soon Erin was lost in the copious wetness between trembling legs.

Jackson moaned. She grasped Erin's hand and together, they went inside of her, filling and satisfying. Jackson had never shared herself like that with anyone, but she knew Erin wasn't ever *just* anyone. Jackson felt incredibly full. She watched Erin watching their hands move together.

"So beautiful," Erin whispered, meeting Jackson's eyes.

Erin drew Jackson's hand out and sucked Jackson's fingers into her mouth, her eyes closing. The dark-haired woman closed her eyes as Erin drew each digit into her mouth and cleaned it with her tongue. Once her fingers were sipped of their nectar, Erin dipped her head and drank from the source.

When Erin's tongue touched the tip of her clitoris, Jackson arched her back and hissed loudly. With her fingers moving slowly into Jackson, Erin painted very quickly with her tongue, bringing Jackson to a feverish state of arousal.

With only a few more lingual strokes, Jackson opened her mouth and gripped the sheets as her release washed through her. When it was over, she remained still, breathing rapidly. "Sweet Jesus," she rasped, closing her eyes, thoroughly satisfied.

Erin slowly kissed her way up Jackson's body until her gaze reached the mismatched eyes. Erin's eyes filled with tears, which Jackson gently brushed away.

"What's wrong, Hawk?" she asked softly.

"I'm so sorry I wasn't strong enough before." Erin forced the words out through her tears.

"Oh, sweetheart, don't worry." She brought Erin down to kiss her with all the love she had felt for years. "I'll be strong enough for both of us, I promise. I won't lose you again."

"I love you, Jack."

"I never stopped loving you."

Erin rested her head on Jackson's chest and the larger body cuddled her close. Wrapped in a cocoon of love, the comfort and warmth lulled them into a peaceful sleep.

Erin's eyes slowly opened to the morning sun streaming through the window. The first thing she noticed was that she was alone. The smell of breakfast cooking belayed her first instinct to jump out of bed to find Jackson. She took a deep breath and smiled, stretching languidly, then pushed back the covers and walked toward the delicious smells. Jackson wore her shirt from the night before but nothing else. Erin hung back and marveled at her beauty.

Sensing she was no longer alone, Jackson turned to find Erin, still naked, watching her. An appreciative smile curved her lips. "God, I could get used to that sight every morning." She waggled her eyebrows and Erin chuckled.

She walked over to Jackson and put her arms around her. Jackson rested her chin on top of her head as they held each other in front of the stove. Pulling back, Erin gave her a tender good morning kiss.

"How did you sleep?" Erin asked, hungrily eying the bacon frying in the pan.

"I slept like a baby. You?"

"The same. You really put out the heat when you sleep. I was warm and snuggled all night long."

"I'm so glad."

"Last night was beautiful, Jack. I am just… wow."

Jackson recalled Erin's lack of vocabulary the first time they had been intimate and laughed at her current description of their lovemaking. "Your vocabulary still gets stunted when you're moved, doesn't it?"

"Don't tease me. It's usually because of something you do, so take it as an indication that you're doing it really well."

Jackson scratched her fingernails lightly over Erin's buttocks and up her back, causing a wave of goose bumps to form on Erin's skin. "Don't tease, huh? I think you like to be teased."

Erin sighed as a rush of arousal burned through her. "What's for breakfast again?" Her eyes were unfocused as she attempted to look into Jackson's eyes.

Jackson could feel a hunger radiating from Erin that had nothing to do with food. "How do you like your eggs?" she whispered into Erin's ear, wreaking havoc on her by touching and teasing her body.

"I don't want eggs," she panted, pulling Jackson's head down for a passion-filled kiss.

Jackson moaned into her mouth, turned off the stove, and lifted Erin up so she straddled her body. She walked them to Erin's bed, where they fell heavily together. Jackson's fingers filled her, and Erin knew breakfast would be postponed until at least dinner.

Several hours of love making later, Jackson and Erin got out of bed. They threw out the bacon on the stove, ordered pizza, drank gallons of water, and curled up on the couch to watch television.

Regretting she still had a resort to run, Jackson said, "I gotta run to the house and check messages. If someone needs something, I'll have to take care of it. A friend of ours, Daniel, is helping us, well, me, run the place while I deal with losing Jackie."

"Daniel must be a special guy."

"He is," Jackson said. "He worked here a few summers when we needed help or wanted to take our own vacation and whatnot. I can leave it to him for a bit while I sort out everything." She sighed. "It's going to be weird living in the main cabin without her."

Erin curled up tighter around her. "I know, honey, it's going to take some time."

"I kinda want to change the place anyway. Maybe now is the time to do it."

"What do you want done?" Erin asked.

"It just needs upgrades. We've improved most of the cabins and built new condos and the duplex, I think the old house needs a makeover."

"Could you live in one of the newer places while you redo your house?"

"Oh, absolutely. Hopefully, I can find a contractor that will get the work done before winter. I know a few people who could help me out; I just have to make the call."

The vibration of Erin's cell phone on the coffee table drew their attention.

"Hang on a sec. I'm sure it's my mother. She'll be ready to call out the cavalry since I haven't returned her calls." She picked up the phone and grimaced when she saw the number of her childhood home. "Yep. I gotta take this, sorry."

"That's okay. You talk to dear old Katie. I have to run to the house to change and take care of the resort stuff. Walking home in my jammies is going to be scandalous. I haven't done the walk of shame in ages." They laughed and kissed, and with a wave, Jackson went on her way.

Erin sighed and got comfortable on the couch. "Hello, Mother."

"Erin! Dear Lord, where have you been? I've been trying to reach you for days!"

"Yes, I know. You know full well where I am and why I'm here. What is so important that it couldn't wait? Jackie died a few days ago, if you'd even care to know."

"Oh, I'm sorry. I'll make sure to say an extra prayer for her in church this week."

You do that. Say one for your own soul while you're at it. "I'm sure it'll be a comfort to Jack that you're praying for her aunt."

"I can't believe you aren't coming home tonight to attend your own art show. Isn't that a little irresponsible?"

The voice was like fingernails on a chalkboard. "Mother! Did you not hear what I just said? I told you that Jackie died," she repeated. "Jack is a mess. I'm not going anywhere until I know she'll be okay."

"You have a life here, too, Erin. Don't forget that."

With you around, how could I?

Katie ranted on for several minutes and Erin tuned her out. She saw Jackson returning, fully dressed in jeans and a sweatshirt with her hair pulled into a ponytail. A smile lit Erin's face as Jackson gave a quick knock on the door and came in. When she saw that Erin was still on the phone, she made funny faces at her to try to lighten the mood. Erin put her finger to her lips. Erin heard the tail end of her mother's speech and she bristled.

"All I wanted to do was make sure you were all right. There's no reason you should be so snippy with me."

Erin knew better. "Bull. Why have you really been calling me? To find out if Jackson has worked her wiles on me?"

"Wha…what?" her mother stuttered, not used to being called on her hidden agenda.

"You heard me. There is no other reason you would leave these alarming messages that I call you at once."

"Erin, don't you take that tone with me."

"Mother, if you have nothing more to say to me then I'm going to go take care of Jack." Jackson sat next to her and started to kiss her neck. "She needs me." Her voice was little louder than a whisper.

"I do need you," Jackson whispered in her other ear. Erin swatted her away, trying hard not to giggle.

"Fine, you go take care of *her*."

"Mother, I just hope that one day you realize how mean you've become, because at the rate you're going, when you're older and need someone to take care of you, there won't be a single person willing to take the job. Goodbye." Erin snapped her phone closed, disconnecting the call.

"God, she infuriates me!" Erin leapt off the couch. She turned to look at Jackson and recognized the unmistakable look of desire on her face. "You cannot be serious!" she said, jarring Jackson from her haze.

"What?" Though ashamed to admit it, she was getting a little turned on by Erin's anger at her mother.

"You're looking at me like you do in the bedroom. You're getting hot, aren't you?"

Jackson's face flamed. "N…no, I um…" Jackson looked at Erin's raised eyebrow and smiled. "Um…so?"

"You are adorable, Jackson Thomas. Absolutely adorable." Erin kissed her gently and giggled at her lover's embarrassment. "I'll keep your secret, I promise," she whispered conspiratorially in Jackson's ear.

Jackson pulled Erin into her lap. After a quick make out session, she pulled back. "I just love that I can kiss you whenever I want." She smiled. "I know I should be grieving, but I'm so happy you're here, Hawk."

"I am too, honey."

"I like when you call me that," Jackson admitted shyly.

"What? Honey?"

"Yeah. It's really sweet. I like it."

"Well, honey is sweet and you're just about the sweetest person I know, so it fits." Erin gave her a quick kiss and got up to get plates for the pizza, just as the doorbell rang. She looked at Jackson. "Is that timing or what?"

"You go get the plates, I got this one." Jackson pulled out her wallet and met the deliveryman at the door. "I hope this is halfway decent. I know how particular you Chicagoans are about your pizza," she teased, bringing the piping hot pie to the table.

"We'll just have to see. If it sucks, I'm outta here." She winked at Jackson.

They shared a quiet meal and evening together, reveling in their closeness. When the hour grew late and it was time for Jackson to return home, she knew she didn't want to sleep alone in her house.

"Um, do you think it would be okay…I mean, would you…" She sighed at her tied tongue. "I'd rather you be with me on my first night there without Jackie, if that's okay."

"It's absolutely okay. I don't think I could sleep without you now."

"Good. Me either; let's go."

Chapter Fifteen

Jackson was troubled. She and Erin had spent fourteen wonderful days at the Northwoods, exploring their renewed love, and now the time had come for Erin to return to Chicago. A full state away. Jackson didn't know how she could stand to be separated, nor had she been able to come up with a workable resolution.

Could I live anywhere else to be with her? Jackson looked around. *This is my home. Do I have a right to ask her to leave her whole life to be with me? Would she want to? I just don't know what to expect. I only know for sure that I can't lose her again. I can't.* The uncertainty gnawed at Jackson as she escorted Erin to her car.

The short walk was a very quiet one. Erin sensed the tension in Jackson and knew it was probably due to all of things that were worrying her, as well. What did their futures hold? Erin had been direct with Jackson for most of her life, when she wasn't running away, but she was not running away now. There were too many questions that they hadn't addressed. And she was going to get to the bottom of them before she drove four hundred miles away.

Turning to Jackson, Erin said, "I can see the cogs spinning in that head of yours. Tell me what's going on up there and please don't leave anything out, regardless of how you think I might react."

Jackson smiled at the straightforwardness. She was still

feeling raw and vulnerable, but didn't want to sound needy. "I… um…really don't want you to leave. I just got you back, Hawk. I don't want to lose you again."

Jackson looked like she might cry and Erin didn't want that. Enough tears had been shed. "Oh, honey, you will never lose me again. I promise you. You're it for me, Jack. I was going to wait for you to do this in your own time, but I think I'm just gonna have to insist that you ask me to move here."

Jackson's eyes lit up like a child's on Christmas morning opening the most wonderful gift ever. "You mean it? You'd move up here to be with me?"

Erin was saddened by Jackson's lack of belief in the strength of their connection, but considering their history, she could hardly blame her. "Yes! There is no place in the world that I'd rather be. You are my heart, my soul and my reason to wake up every morning. If you want me here as much as I want to be here, I'll start making arrangements immediately."

Jackson picked Erin up and spun her around, as happy as she had rarely been. "You have made me the happiest woman on the planet, Hawk! I love you so much I can't even breathe."

Erin eyed her pointedly. "Jack, you still haven't asked."

Blushing, Jackson took Erin's hands and kissed them gently. *I better make this good.* "Erin, Hawk, the light of my life, the fire in my loins, will you come to The Northwoods and live with me happily ever after until we breathe our last breaths together? Pretty please?"

Erin smiled and shook her head at Jackson's description. "I'm all that, huh?"

"All that and a treble clef."

"How can I turn down such a scrumptious offer?" Erin asked playfully.

Jackson smirked. "I don't think you could."

"No, I don't think I could either." Erin wrapped her arms around Jackson and squeezed.

"I guess it's settled then," she breathed into Erin's hair.

"Yes, it is." Erin gave her a light kiss as they pulled apart. "I need a little time to get my affairs in order and put my house on the market. After I'm officially divorced, mind you, I still don't want Jeremy to have it."

Jackson looked at her seriously. "What about your work, Hawk? Your work is there."

"Jack, look around us." Jackson eyes shifted around to take in the panorama. "Where do you think I get my inspiration to paint what I do? This is my source. My work will probably get even better with my muse back in my life."

"Your muse?"

"Yes, silly. You. You've always been my biggest fan, since I was nine years old. Having you around me again is going to be magical," Erin explained with a warm smile. "I can't wait," she whispered, adding a saucy wink.

Jackson was ecstatic. "Do you need any help?" A sudden thought blew into her mind. "What about your mother? She is going to blow a gasket."

Erin laughed. "Let her blow, then. I will not let her take away the greatest joy in my life. She did it once and I thought it would kill me. Never again, Jack. I will be back, I promise."

Jackson looked a little nervous, the pain of the rejected twenty-one year old showing plainly on her face. Erin took Jackson's face in her hands. "I promise you."

Seeing the uncertainty replaced by a smile, Erin kissed her again. "You could come with me, you know. You said Daniel would help you for a couple more weeks. That would give us time to get some stuff together. Actually, I can wait to sell my house until *your* house is ready. That way I wouldn't have to put so much stuff in storage." Erin saw the excitement in Jackson's eyes and knew she'd been right to ask her. "Whaddya say? Come back with *me* this time."

"I'll have a bag ready in ten minutes!" Jackson sped off to the house, leaving Erin laughing beside her car.

Jackson threw her bag into the open trunk and quickly settled into the passenger seat, to Erin's amusement. Their trip to Chicago was managed without any setbacks. Roughly six hours later, after a few stops to grab drinks and to find a rest area, the duo arrived at Erin's home.

Jackson stopped under the stone archway over the path to Erin's front door. "Hawk, this is just beautiful," she comented.

"Thanks. It is a pretty great place. It should show well." She jiggled her key and with a twist of her wrist, opened the door. Inside, Erin closed the doors and rubbed her chilled arms. "It's a little cold in here. Let me check the thermostat real quick."

Erin led them into her living room where she reset the thermostat to bring the house back up to seventy degrees. "That's better. I'll be glad when summer arrives for good. These warm then cold days really suck."

Jackson laughed. "Yes, they do. That's the beauty of the Midwest, though. If you watch carefully, you can see all four seasons in a day."

"No kidding." Erin gestured around her. "Want me to show you around?"

"Sure. Lead on."

Erin gave her the five-cent tour, which was very impressive. It was obvious that Erin was doing very well for herself. When they crossed the threshold into Erin's studio, Jackson's sharp intake of breath made Erin smile. On every wall was a representation of The Northwoods. A few easels held canvases and a large drawing table was positioned under the one large window facing the backyard.

"Hawk, this place is amazing." She moved up close to a particular picture and pointed to it with a huge smile. "I remember when you drew this one! God, I think it was right after you told your mom that Jackie was not a viper trying to charm you, or something like that."

Erin laughed at the fractured recollection. "You're right. I went right up to the roof and drew all afternoon. You were concerned because I was so angry with her. God, that woman has a mouth on her."

"Don't look at me for an argument on that."

"Don't worry, you're the *last* person I'd seek out if I needed someone to defend my mother. Well, last except for me. I'd never defend her. As far as I'm concerned, she gets what she gets."

"Right on."

Erin's cell phone vibrated in her pocket and she pulled it out to see her mother's phone number. "God, that woman has a sixth sense."

"Uh-oh, I smell trouble," Jackson joked. Erin waggled a finger at her.

"I'm gonna take this really fast to get rid of her. Two seconds." She hit the Talk button. "Hello, Mother."

"Erin, dear, it's good to see your car in your driveway. May I come in?" Erin paled and Jackson raised an eyebrow in question.

"You're out front?"

Both women's eyes went round then Jackson smirked and nodded her head, encouraging the visit from Katie. "Sure, Mother, I'll be right down."

Katie uttered a quick, "Thank you" and hung up the phone.

Erin turned to Jackson. "Are you feeling like causing trouble or something? Why would you want her to come in?"

"Aw, come on, I haven't seen Katie in a long time. I'm sure she'd like to give me a big ol' hug."

"I'm sure she'd like to give you something all right, but a hug isn't what comes to mind."

The doorbell chimed and they descended the stairs to greet Katie together. Erin grabbed the knob and looked to Jackson. "Here goes…"

Erin opened the door and her mother walked in. "Mother. How nice of you to stop by."

Katie pulled her purse strap over her shoulder. "I'm glad you're home," she started, not seeing Jackson behind the door. "I think two weeks was more than enough time for you to give to that girl. Frankly, I think you spent way too much time up there."

Katie kept talking and Erin just let her continue to hang herself in front of Jackson, whose arms were now crossed over her chest. "I'm sure she has a…I don't even know what to call one of those people…to take care of her needs."

"A girlfriend? A lover? A lezzzbian?" Jackson's low voice made Katie spin around, her face blazing red.

"J…Jackson!"

"Hello, Katie. So nice to hear you again."

Katie turned to her daughter, her eyes shooting daggers. "Why didn't you tell me she was coming back with you?"

Erin put her hands on her hips. "Frankly, because it's none of your business."

"Erin! Do not speak to me like that!"

"I'm sorry, Mother; you're right, I should show you the same amount of respect you've always shown me." She stalked into the living room, her mother and Jackson following in her wake. Jackson wiggled her eyebrows as Katie passed, causing the flustered woman to pick up her pace.

Erin pulled out her phonebook from an end table, sat on the couch and grabbed a sheet of paper. *Might as well get this out of the way now.* "Mother, what's the name of that moving company you used to ship your furniture to St. Gregory's bazaar?"

"It was Wilkens', but why do you need a moving company?" she asked, a sinking feeling washing through her.

"Because I'm going to need to move some things into storage while our house is being renovated," she explained cryptically, enjoying the play of emotions on her mother's features.

"Oh, lovely, Erin. What are you and Jeremy doing to your house?"

"Not Jeremy, Mother. And this is *certainly* not his house anymore."

Our house. "Who's the other half of the 'our'?"

"Jack, of course. Mother, I'm moving up to The Northwoods." Even though her heart was pounding in her chest, Erin continued to nonchalantly look in her book.

"You're what!" Katie cried. "Why on earth would you do something so ridiculous?"

Erin turned to face her. "It's quite simple, Mother. Because I love her."

Katie could hardly form her next words she was so flabbergasted. "Wh...what do you mean by that?"

"I. Love. Her. Does that honestly surprise you? Did you think I could ever forget about her, even after all this time?" When Katie just sat and stared at her, she continued. "I know you did your damnedest to keep us apart, Mother, but I'm not a child anymore and I'm finally going to live my life the way I choose. I choose to be with Jack."

Katie's eyes went wide. "You can't possibly be telling me you're going to live with her as a...a lesbian?"

"No, you're right, Mother, I'm not a lesbian." She looked to Jackson. "I'm a Jacksian." Jackson couldn't contain her burst of laughter. She quickly covered her mouth when Katie shot her a dirty look. "Mother, I may not consider myself a lesbian, but I am in love with Jack. I've always been in love with her. So all of your tirades were correct, after all—I did fall into her trap, just like you said. If I wasn't so angry with you for making my adolescence a living hell, I'd probably thank you for making me so aware of my feelings for her."

"Don't you dare blame me for this! All I ever did was try to protect you."

"From what, Mother? From love? Love is not wrong! It's a gift you should be thankful for if you are lucky enough to receive it. You tried to make me someone I wasn't and in the process made me resent you for many years, but you know what, Mother? I'm done feeling badly about you. You've chosen to live your life this way and that life is all yours. I want no part of it if you can't accept me for the person I am and always have been."

Jackson wanted to take her in her arms and kiss her, but stayed put.

"Jack and Dad were the loves in my life and my biggest supporters. I lost Dad to cancer, and I almost lost Jack because of you. I'd die before going through that again."

"You ungrateful girl!" her mother said. "I gave you everything a little girl could want and this is the appreciation I get?"

"You're right, Mother. Some little girl *may* have wanted all that you offered, but I didn't and you *knew* I didn't. Yet, you kept at it as if you could make me give in or change my mind. I might not have been strong enough before, Mother, but I'm not giving in this time." Erin looked directly into Jackson's eyes. "Jack is my heart and soul, and I'm going to live out the rest of my days with her." She turned back to her mother. "With or without you in my life."

Katie pulled her car keys out of her purse. "I fear for your soul, Erin. You'll be lucky if you see your father in the Afterlife." She stomped toward the front door, turned in front of Jackson then looked at Erin. "You make it so hard for me to love you."

Erin smiled at her mother. "You know, Katie, I was thinking the exact same thing."

Her mother shot her a final glare then left the house, slamming the door behind her.

Jackson looked at Erin with boundless love pouring from her eyes. "I cannot believe you just did that!"

"Yeah, well, she's had it coming for years. I figured now was just about as good a time as any to give her my new address." Erin went to Jackson and put her arms around her. "Thank you for being here. Just your presence gave me that little extra that I needed."

"I'll always be here for you. Always."

Several months later...

Erin hauled the last of her boxes into the spacious studio and sighed as the last of them was placed on the floor. She had spent the last few months at the Northwoods marveling at the change from spring to summer. Autumn would soon prove to be more beautiful than even her imagination could conjure. With more seasons added to her colorful Island City repertoire, she could barely wait to get the new pieces to Kim. Her studio would provide the perfect workspace for her creations. The newly renovated house was beginning to feel like home, though this would be their first official night spent inside.

Grace was creeping around investigating every part of her new home. The orange tabby was happy to be reunited with her owner after spending two weeks with Kim while they moved. Jackson and Grace were still battling to see who wrapped around Erin's body when it came time for bed. Unfortunately for Grace, Jackson consistently won that battle and wouldn't be giving up her title anytime soon.

Jackson walked into the studio and smiled at the look on

Erin's face. She could tell she was enormously pleased. "They did well, right?"

"Jack, this is absolutely perfect! My view is unbelievable. God, I never thought I'd be able to just look out and see the beauty of this place whenever I wanted. I'm so grateful that you're sharing that part of yourself with me."

"I'm not sharing, this place has always been a part of you, too. I knew that from the very first day we met. I could tell it was more to you than just a vacation spot and you've proven that with every picture you've painted or drawn."

Erin pulled one of her cherished drawings out of a box on the floor. "Yes, it was much more to me than a vacation spot. I found my heart here." She turned to hand Jackson the picture from her *Serenity Collection*. Jackson's eyes went wide.

"Oh, Hawk. This is…wow…" She was always amazed at how Erin had seen her. "No one else seems to think I'm this flawless goddess you keep making me out to be."

Erin smiled warmly. "They just don't know you the way I do." She leaned up and shared a kiss with Jackson. "You've always been my inspiration. I've kept these in boxes for so long; now that you're back in my life, I can't wait to put them up."

Jackson took in the number of large boxes and her eyes widened in surprise. "These all contain pictures of…me?"

Erin nodded, blushing. "Yeah. I'm going to put up the ones that mean the most to me, but I think I'm ready to sell the others. Don't worry, I won't sell any that identify you. There are some with just a profile and unless someone knows you, they won't put it together. If…if that's okay with you."

"Absolutely. They are yours to sell, Hawk. I'm honored to have been a subject you drew so often."

"I was gonna hang all of them then have you look at the walls, but I figured that might be a little too much. I think it will be a little less intimidating now that I've given you fair warning."

Jackson smiled sheepishly. "I think if I had walked in and seen my face everywhere, it would've been a little weird."

"But it's such a pretty face," she complimented, taking Jackson's hands.

Blushing, Jackson squeezed Erin's hands and said almost inaudibly, "Thanks." She looked around. "Want me to help hang?"

Erin's face lit up. "That would be great. Let me get them all arranged and we can do it together."

After a couple of hours, the *Serenity Collection* had been sorted through and some were placed on the walls while others were crated for shipping to the gallery. They walked around the room together, looking at the paintings and drawings of Jackson surrounded by the Northwoods.

"This is why I called it the *Serenity Collection*. Just look at your face, in every picture."

Jackson did as she was instructed, amazed at what she saw. "Yeah, I guess this place does have that effect on me." She turned to face Erin. "But I think it was mostly you who made me feel that way."

"Smooth talker," Erin said with a sparkle in her eye.

Jackson pulled her close and looked into her eyes for a long while. "It was you." She lowered her head and they shared a tender kiss. Erin sighed and rested her head against Jackson's strong shoulder.

As the sun was beginning to set on the first night in their newly minted home, Jackson and Erin walked hand in hand toward the pier, reflecting on the perfection surrounding them. Erin gently squeezed Jackson's hand as they spotted a hawk soaring free in the colorful sky. The reds and oranges were breathtaking. Erin was already beginning the painting in her mind.

Sitting on the chairs facing Lake Tomahawk, they realized that in many ways it was more than simply a body of water. It held more memories than any photo or scrapbook. It was the birthplace of their friendship and a nurturing environment in which their talents had grown. It was a resting place for Jackson's mothers, but most of all, it was a symbol etched into their hearts to remind them to overcome any obstacle that kept them from the love and the life they deserved.

Epilogue
A few years later…

Erin pulled her car into the parking lot of the Island City resort and turned off her engine. She grabbed her backpack and the grocery bags from the front seat of her car, bumped the door closed with her hip and walked toward the house. Inside, she placed the bags on the counter and began to sort and put away her foodstuffs.

"Jack? You here?" she called out. She walked around their home in the Northwoods searching for her partner, only to find she was alone. *She must be doing something down by the water. She always is.* Erin smiled to herself and strolled down to the main office.

As she entered the building she found, Daniel, their trusted friend and caretaker of the resort, sitting behind the front desk. She greeted him with a large, toothy grin.

"Hey, big guy!"

Daniel's face lit up. "Hey! Welcome home!" He hurried around the desk and gave Erin a hug and a kiss on the cheek.

Erin mussed Daniel's hair affectionately. "Thanks. It's good to be home. It was only a few days, but sometimes these shows can be too much. I must be getting old."

"Hardly." He smiled. "Did you have a successful one at least?"

Erin nodded. "Kim was pleased at the turnout and we did sell most of the pieces. The ones that didn't she's going to keep at the gallery and they'll go when they're meant to sell."

"That's great! Congratulations."

Erin smiled. "Thanks." She looked around. "So where is my taller half? Is she trying to entertain our guests with her newfound gift of storytelling?" Daniel laughed. "She really needs to stop telling people how we got together. Not everyone is going to be thrilled with the tale."

"It's a sweet story, Erin, no doubt about it. Jack is ridiculously happy and is simply sharing that with the world. I'm not sure there is anyone who could stop her."

Erin chuckled. "That's very true. She does get a little focused."

"The last I saw her she was giving a 'family history lesson' down by the water."

Erin closed her eyes and shook her head. "That poor girl. Jack is going to give her nightmares."

"Nah. I think she likes them."

"We'll see. Perhaps we can look for a cheap therapist, just in case. Grab the Yellow Pages, would ya?" They both laughed. "I'm gonna go down and see what kind of damage control I can do." She turned to leave, but stopped at the hand on her arm.

"Erin…"

She looked up at warm green eyes staring down at her. "What's up?"

"I just wanted to say thank you, again, for everything. It's been really special for me."

"Danny, we can't thank *you* enough. Can we talk about special? I thought for sure you'd be sick of us saying thank you by now. Not many men would do what you've done for us and then stick around to watch it unfold."

"Well, like I've said a million times, I'm not like most men. I love it here and I love you guys so much. The day may come when I want to leave and find someone for myself, but I'm just not there yet. I'm really happy about every aspect of my life and am glad I could help."

Tears in her eyes, Erin hugged Daniel again. "You've done so much more than help us, Danny. Jack and I will always be in your debt. We couldn't possibly know how to pay you back. Just know, if there is ever anything you want or need, all you have to do is ask, and it's yours."

"I know." Daniel smiled.

"Good." Erin sniffed and wiped her eyes. "I'm gonna go before I get carried away."

"Have fun!"

Walking down toward the water, Erin saw Jack on the pier with a small child in her arms. Her heart melted. As she got closer she could hear Jackson telling the little girl about her grandmothers. Jackson tickled the little girl into fits of giggles.

"Hey, what's a girl gotta do to get a welcome home hug?" Erin called out.

Twin sets of mismatched eyes turned to look at Erin. "Momma!" the little girl cried, pulling out of Jackson's embrace to run down the pier. Erin met her halfway and scooped the little girl into her arms.

"Hi, baby. Momma missed you." Erin kissed her cheek and ran a hand through the soft, fine blond hair.

"I missed Momma, too," Jackson said playfully, kissing Erin's offered lips. "We were just having a little story time."

Erin scowled. "Can you just *try* not to give Emma nightmares? She doesn't need to imagine that her grandmothers actually will come out of the water one day and scare the bejeezus out of her. She's not even two years old!"

Jackson tried to look innocent. "What? She knows her grandmothers live in Lake Tomahawk. They're mermaids!" Jackson said, grabbing Emma from Erin's arms and swirling around. Emma squealed at Jackson's antics. "Right, baby? Can you say mermaid?"

"Moomay!"

Erin couldn't help laughing. "What am I gonna do with you?"

Jackson wiggled her eyebrows. "Well, you were gone an awful long time. You could take me home and..."

Erin plunked her hand over Jackson's mouth. *"Jackson!* Don't you even go there while holding our daughter."

Jackson laughed around Erin's fingers. She put Emma on her hip and pulled Erin to her with her other arm. "I love you."

"I love you, too." The women kissed again and Emma blew a raspberry kiss on Jackson's cheek making them giggle. "So, what are your plans for the day?"

"Well, Emma and I were gonna have our first real lesson. I think it's time we see if she wants to play the recorder." She put Emma down and took her hand as they walked down the pier toward the water.

"Oh, you do, do you? Don't you think she's a little young?"

"Not at all! There are a lot of kids who start playing music at her age. If she doesn't seem interested, I certainly won't push her. I just want to see if she has my genes."

"Well, she *is* your daughter, of course she has your genes."

"Correction, she's *our* daughter. I was just technically the one who gave birth to her. Anyway, Jackie started teaching me when I was about four, so we'll see what happens. If she throws the instrument into the water, I'll know it's either too early or it's just not her thing." Jackson sat down on the edge of the pier with Emma between her legs.

Erin sat down next to them and breathed deeply of the warm summer air. She closed her eyes and let the serenity of Lake Tomahawk soothe her psyche. Even being gone just a few days had her missing the peace and tranquility she always felt here. Jackson played a few bars of 'Hawks in Flight' and Erin smiled. She kept her eyes closed as she let the sweet melody wash over her.

"Mommy, me! Me!" Emma cried, reaching to grab the recorder from Jackson's hands.

"Gently, baby. Here, let me help." Erin watched as Jackson tried to teach her how to use the instrument.

Jackson had Emma blow into her face a few times, then Jackson blew into the baby's and then into the recorder. Emma slowly figured out that she could blow into the instrument to make noise come out. The sounds were loud and hair-raising, but nothing matched the sweet sounds of laughter that followed as Emma realized she'd done it right. She'd blow into the recorder, make a few sounds and then laugh.

Jackson was encouraged by Emma's enthusiasm, but knew it would be a while before she could tell if it was just a new toy to her daughter. She put her fingers over a few holes as Emma blew so she could change the sound. Together, they played a very rough version of 'Mary Had a Little Lamb' and laughed when it was over.

After the three had dinner, Jackson and Erin took Emma to her room to get her ready for bed. The room was decorated with images from Dr. Seuss' *Oh, the Places You'll Go*. Jackson wanted Emma to always know she could move mountains if she really wanted to.

Emma was positioned between her two moms in her big girl bed. Jackson sang a lullaby while holding the tiny girl in her arms. Once she got her song, Emma would be treated to a story read by Erin. Her choice for a bedtime story was always *The Very Hungry Caterpillar* and Erin was always willing to read it. After the furry insect ate its way through the week, Emma snored softly next to an enamored Erin. She gently stroked the sleeping child's cheek with the backs of her fingers.

"God, she's beautiful, Jack. We are so lucky to have her." Not hearing a reply, Erin looked to the other side of their child, and wasn't surprised to find Jackson was asleep. She smiled and shook her head. "I should know by now that you fall asleep when being read to. I should just tuck you both into the same bed."

Erin got up and walked around to pull the blanket up over Jackson's shoulders. Jackson stirred slightly and snuggled into Emma, who had fully situated herself against her mother's chest. Erin smiled down at her two girls, her heart swelling at the sight. She slowly lay with her front to Jackson's back and reached her arm around both mother and child, feeling a completeness she had never known would be possible. Each day their love grew stronger and their future grew brighter, and each night brought with it a new tomorrow. Erin tightened her hold and sighed with incredible hopefulness that there would be many more tomorrows to come.

About the Author

Diane lives in the Midwest with her longtime partner, and their two dogs, Matty and Bella. She has seven siblings who are the foundation of her being. In addition to writing, Diane owns and operates a pet-sitting service and the online newswire service, The Open Press, Inc. Di is also the production editor on the fabulous Chicago GLBT podcast, *Windy City Queercast*. She loves playing golf and playing in her rose garden. She can be found on MySpace in addition to her own Web site www. dsbauden.com.

Private Dancer by T.J. Vertigo   ISBN: 978-1-933113-58-6 $16.95

Revelations by Erin O'Reilly   ISBN: 978-1-933113-75-3 $16.95

Romance For Life by Lori L Lake (editor) and Tara Young (editor)

                                              ISBN: 978-1933113-59-3 $16.95

She Waits by Kate Sweeney   ISBN: 978-1-933113-40-1 $15.95

She's the One by Verda Foster and B.L. Miller   ISBN: 978-1-933113-80-7 $16.95

Southern Hearts by Katie P. Moore   ISBN: 978-1-933113-28-9 $14.95

Storm Surge by KatLyn   ISBN: 978-1-933113-06-7 $16.95

Taking of Eden, The by Robin Alexander   ISBN: 978-1-933113-53-1 $15.95

These Dreams by Verda Foster   ISBN: 978-1-933113-12-8 $15.75

Tomahawk'd by Diane S Bauden   ISBN: 978-1-933113-90-6 $16.95

Traffic Stop by Tara Wentz   ISBN: 978-1-933113-73-9 $16.95

Trouble with Murder, The by Kate Sweeney   ISBN: 978-1-933113-85-2 $16.95

Value of Valor, The by Lynn Ames   ISBN: 978-1-933113-46-3 $16.95

War Between the Hearts, The by Nann Dunne   ISBN: 978-1-933113-27-2 $16.95

With Every Breath by Alex Alexander   ISBN: 978-1-933113-39-5 $15.25

You can purchase other Intaglio
Publications books online at
www.bellabooks.com, www.scp-inc.biz, or at
your local book store.

Published by
Intaglio Publications
Walker, LA

Visit us on the web
www.intagliopub.com